The new Zebra Regency R...
cover is a photograph of...
The fashionable regency l...
with a satin or velvet riband around her wrist to carry a
fragrant nosegay. Usually made of gold or silver, tuzzy-muz-
zies varied in design from the elegantly simple to the exqui-
sitely ornate. The Zebra Regency Romance tuzzy-muzzy is
made of alabaster with a silver filigree edging.

A MOMENT OF DANGER

"He escaped." Roland spoke against her hair. "I
couldn't see who it was."

"A man?" She looked up into his face. His warm
breath fanned her cheek.

"Or a woman." His voice sounded tight.

Netta pulled closer to him. "At least you aren't
harmed. I was afraid for you."

For a moment he didn't move. His gaze rested on
her face, his expression unreadable in the moonlight,
but his eyes glowed with an intensity that set her
pulse racing. Gently, he stroked a curl back from her
forehead, his fingers lingering as if loath to break
contact.

Hesitant, as if against his will, he traced the line
of her cheek to the corner of her lips. Then with a
soft groan, he lowered his head, claiming her mouth
with his own. She clung to him, lost in an unfamiliar
whirl of sensation, knowing only that this was what
she wanted, what she had longed for, what only he
could bring her . . .

A Dangerous Intrigue

Janice Bennett

ZEBRA BOOKS
KENSINGTON PUBLISHING CORP.

ZEBRA BOOKS

are published by

Kensington Publishing Corp.
475 Park Avenue South
New York, NY 10016

First Printing: December, 1992

Printed in the United States of America

For Ida

Chapter One

Lady Henrietta Galbraith glided with practiced ease through the steps of the country dance, and longed for the speedy advent of widowhood.

Now *there* was a shocking thought for a young lady to entertain at her own betrothal ball. Her reprehensible sense of the ridiculous bubbled to the surface, and for a couple of minutes she indulged herself by mentally devising possible fates for her second cousin and soon-to-be bridegroom, Desmond Marmaduke Augustus Galbraith, seventh earl of Tavistock.

Which reminded her, she had not checked on him for over half an hour. He could—and most likely would—be up to anything. It always amazed her the quantity of champagne he could consume in so short an amount of time.

She glanced around the crowded ballroom at Tavistock House, Cavendish Square, at last spotting Desmond's stolid figure on the fringe of the dancers, in conversation with the massive Dowager Lady Rumbold. No, not in conversation, she corrected herself as that lady's turbaned head jerked back, setting her ostrich plume bouncing against her too rounded shoulder. Desmond must have insulted her again. Lady Henrietta sighed, knowing she would have to pour oil over troubled waters. Again. She was beginning to feel like an unguent pot.

"Is my dancing as bad as that, Lady Netta?" The music stopped, and her partner, Mr. Kenneth Lambert, raised her fingers to his lips before releasing her. "I must crave a thousand pardons."

"Have no fear, you have not trodden on my toes." She brushed a vivid, flame-colored tendril of hair from her eyes and directed a rueful smile at the dark-haired Corinthian before looking back to Desmond. Her cousin, his expression one of sneering amusement, now watched Lady Rumbold's outraged retreat.

Mr. Lambert followed the direction of her gaze. "Ah, the *dis*honorable earl of Tavistock. You can not really mean to go through with this madness, Lady Netta?" His fingers closed once more over hers in a warm caress. "I cannot believe you would willingly throw yourself away on a man of his reputation, despite his title and—"

"Oh, fiddle. You know perfectly well I can deal with Desmond."

"Then you have the honor of being the only person to ever exercise the least influence over him," came his tart response.

"Except for our Great-aunt Lavinia." And

thank heaven, Netta reflected, that aging eccentric had chosen not to leave their country estate to attend the betrothal ball. Then again, Great-aunt Lavinia might be just what this affair needed. For a delightful moment, she envisioned the wizened little woman hobbling about among the guests, jabbing anyone who got in her way with her cane, peering into their faces and cackling in that disconcerting way of hers as she made ominous proclamations of doom.

"I doubt he would heed even her at present." Lambert nodded toward Desmond. "I have never known him to be less than belligerent when in his cups."

"Oh, the—the devil," Netta muttered. "You are quite right. I shall have to see to him. Pray excuse me."

She would *not* have regrets, she told herself firmly as she pushed her way through the milling throng. She married Desmond for all of their sakes—his, hers, Great-aunt Lavinia's, Cousin Phemie's—and she could manage him. In the morning she would cajole him into taking them back to Ravenswood Court, then on some pretext or another keep him there in the country, where he could not get into as much trouble, for the two weeks until the wedding.

After that—She shied from contemplating the future. She had grown up under the same roof with Desmond, had spent all her life learning to manage his queer starts. And she got steadily better at it, she assured herself. The key lay in dealing with one situation at a time. Right now she would send for strong coffee, and force it down his disagreeable throat if she had to.

In less than an hour he would announce their betrothal—if she could sober him enough so he would not make a sad botch of the business. She resisted the temptation to let him drink himself into a stupor to avoid having to receive the well-wishes of their vast acquaintance. Yet it would do her no good. The papers would still puff it off in the morning, for she had sent the announcement into them already.

And she had to marry Desmond; she had never had any choice. Her father and his—his *damnable* will had seen to that.

Across the elegant ballroom, she caught a glimpse of her elderly cousin and chaperon, Miss Euphemia Wrenn, inveigling their country neighbor Sir Archibald Carncross into partnering a poor little dab of a chit. Dear Cousin Phemie, the fact she hostessed what she called "a sad crush" delighted her—though she lamented the necessity of Desmond's being the bridegroom. Well, so did Netta.

A commotion at the door caught her attention. She glanced over her shoulder and stopped in her tracks, thoughts of her difficult betrothed evaporating.

Around her, the strains of the music faded, the dancers beginning the intricate steps of the cotillion blurred, even the candlelight flickering off the myriad crystal dewdrops on the chandeliers dimmed. She saw nothing but the dynamic gentle-man who filled the doorway a scant thirty feet away.

Something stirred in her—memory?—though she would swear she never before had seen the frowning lines of his countenance. Surely she would have remembered all those intriguing angles and planes, and the thick dark brown hair, flecked with gray, that waved back from a widow's peak low on his forehead. Such a man as this would not easily be forgotten.

To her surprise, she found she walked toward him, as if drawn by a spell of enthrallment. Her gaze rested on his compelling features, then trans-ferred to the elegance of his black velvet coat that stretched to perfection across his broad shoulders. Black satin knee breeches and white stockings covered his muscled legs, and a pigeon's blood ruby nestled in the intricate folds of his neckcloth.

He moved forward with a predatory grace. Like a panther, she thought. Fascinating. Mesmerizing. Dangerous.

The second footman, arrayed in the black and gold Tavistock livery, intercepted him. They ex-changed a few low-voiced words, then the lad turned and announced in tones that just reached her over the music: "Mr. Roland Galbraith."

Roland? Netta froze only a few feet from him, numb, as a tangled jumble of emotions swept through her. It couldn't be possible, this awe-in-spiring gentleman couldn't really be her long-ab-sent distant cousin. Roland had gone. He would

11

never come back. How many times had Great-aunt Lavinia promised her that . . .

Not far from her, Desmond choked on his champagne and whirled about. For several seconds he stared bleary-eyed at the tall gentleman, then a smirk settled over his thin-lipped mouth. Excusing himself to his companions, he strolled over to join the new arrival.

"Roland." He stopped before the man, weaving only slightly as, with deliberation, he looked him over from head to toe. "So, the prodigal son returns," he pronounced with care. "Do you expect us to kill the fatted calf for you?"

"I should be very much surprised if you did, Little Cousin." Roland Galbraith's steady gaze lingered on Desmond in cynical amusement. The golden glints of his hazel eyes darkened to amber. "You do not favor your late cousin."

"Nor do you." Desmond's brow creased. "Can't think why, but I remembered you as being lighter of limb. Taller, too."

"I fail to see why you should remember me at all. You were barely breeched when I left."

Desmond bristled. "I was turned seven. And while we are on the subject," he added, enunciating each word with care, "why have you returned? It was our hope—vain, I now perceive—that you would remain in India."

Roland's satirical eyebrows rose a fraction. "Indeed, how could you think I would miss such a momentous event as your betrothal ball? Where, by the bye, is your delightful bride? Our little. . . ." His voice trailed off as his gaze came to rest on Netta.

Of course he'd recognize her. Her vivid red hair and pale complexion with its sprinkling of freckles hadn't changed one whit since her fifth birthday. Yet everything else had.

She knew the truth about him now. If even half of Great-aunt Lavinia's tales about Roland's cruelties were true, she should be terrified of him. So why didn't the sight of him or the sound of his voice send shivers of horror through her? Her fingers strayed to her right wrist where her long kid leather gloves covered the old scar, received that last day when her father had banished him from the house, from England.

"Little Hen." Roland advanced on her, only to stop a pace away. The harsh lines about his eyes softened. "What a little beauty you've become. And so elegant. I remember you all in ribands and furbelows."

"Do you? The lamentable taste of my nurse." To her pleasure, her voice sounded cool and controlled, disguising her inner confusion. "Why have you returned?"

He drew an enameled snuffbox from his pocket, then turned it over in his hand without opening it. "The climate in India. I did not find it salubrious. And having made my fortune, I thought I would return to hearth and home to pay my respects to the head of the family."

Desmond raised disbelieving eyebrows. "Have you indeed? Your—respects?"

"Naturally. And to wish my lovely cousin all felicitations, of course."

"Thank you." Even to Netta herself, her words sounded hollow.

"How did you know about our wedding?" Desmond demanded.

"My Aunt Phemie has—"

"Lord, Cousin Phemie." Desmond's lip curled. "I should have known she'd write you. Always had her wrapped about your little finger, didn't you? So you came rushing to see with your own eyes if we were really going to be leg-shackled." He rocked back on his heels, his expression a muddled gloat. "Well, Cousin, you may be very sure we shall be. Heir-presumptive is an empty title in your case. I'll have sons soon to fill the empty nursery at Ravenswood Court."

"Good God!" Roland recoiled as if struck. "Do you truly believe I'd want to inherit the title? Tavistock!" His voice held nothing but contempt. "Only my desire to assure myself that I will *not* inherit has brought me into this house again."

Desmond snorted. "Doing it too brown, Coz. But this I swear—" he swayed forward on unsteady legs to waggle a finger beneath Roland's nose, "you will never inherit either title or fortune."

"Fortune?" Roland's tone mocked the word. "Is that what you call it?"

"*You* might well," Desmond responded at once, his lip curling.

"I'm surprised you do." Roland regarded him

with cousinly disapproval. "Forever fishing your-self out of the River Tick, from what I've been hearing. I can only wonder why you did not long ago wed an heiress, instead. Little Hen's portion cannot be more than a pittance."

"It isn't, thank you," Netta snapped. "But per-haps you are not acquainted with the terms of my father's will."

Roland frowned. "My Aunt Phemie wrote something about it, but it made no sense."

Desmond chuckled. "Nothing she says does."

Netta directed a quelling glance at her inebri-ated bridegroom-to-be. "It is quite simple. If Roland and I do not marry before his twenty-fifth birthday—in two weeks—all the unentailed prop-erty—and that includes Ravenswood Court and its income—will be given to charity. Desmond would be left with nothing but the townhouse, and I would have my fifty pounds a year on which to support myself, Cousin Phemie, and Great-aunt Lavinia—unless you can see Desmond spending his meager funds on his indigent female relatives."

Roland's brow snapped down. "I cannot. Did no one think to contest such an outlandish docu-ment? What was your father thinking of?"

"Providing for me, as well as for his heir." Netta kept her tone cool, controlled. "As you have already pointed out, he could not supply me with a sufficient dowry to tempt any other gentleman. And it is not as if it came as a shock to us. Des and I have known for the better part of our lives we must marry. One grows accustomed."

"Good God. I—" Roland began.

"Netta, my love!" Miss Euphemia Wrenn fluttered up to them, her plump little figure enveloped in clouds of lavender and silver gauze. The speculative gaze of her bright brown eyes rested on Roland.

"You must remember Roland, Cousin Phemie," Netta said. "Probably far better than do Desmond and I."

"Roland!" Cousin Phemie clasped her hands together. "Can it really be you? Oh, of all things, how delightful to have you once more with us." She embraced as much of his solid figure as she could. "You never mentioned a word about coming home in your letters, dear boy, not a single word! And now here you are. How I have longed for this moment."

Roland set his effusive aunt aside and supplied her with his handkerchief.

She dabbed at the corners of her eyes and beamed at him. "Is it not wonderful?" she sighed.

"You may think so for all of us, Cousin Phemie," Desmond informed her. "I, for one, could wish him at the devil."

"Desmond!" Phemie fixed her shocked regard on him, then turned to her nephew. "Dear Roland, I am sure he did not mean—That is, you must know what he is like, though to be sure, how could you when you have been away for so very long—"

"It is quite all right. Now, if your guests can

16

spare you, come tell me how you go on." He led the little woman away.

"How she can be pleased to see him—" Desmond shook his head, somewhat sobered by the encounter. "She probably does so only to spite Great-aunt Lavinia. Lord, won't Lavinia be livid to learn he's come back."

"Thank heavens she isn't here." An irrepressible giggle escaped Netta. "Couldn't you just envision it, with her denouncing him in front of everyone with that sepulchral voice of hers?"

His eyes gleamed, and his lips twitched upward. "Lord, Netta, I'd give worlds to see it."

"You would. But only think of the agonies poor Cousin Phemie would suffer at such a scene."

Desmond's grin widened. "I am."

"Detestable," she informed him.

"Well said, Lady Henrietta. Detestable he is, not a doubt of it." Mr. Josiah Underhill joined them, his small eyes brimming with calculated amusement. The exertions of the dance had heightened the ruddiness of his complexion, making him look more than ever the picture of a stout country squire. He looked Desmond over and shook his head. "So, your gaming debts have finally driven you into parson's mousetrap, have they?"

Gaming debts? Netta cast a swift glance at Desmond's flushed countenance, and her heart sank. She'd heard rumors but hoped they'd been exaggerated. Judging from her cousin's reaction to Mr.

Underhill's jibe, though, they hadn't. She fought off the sensation of being smothered beneath a crushing pile of debts of honor.

Mr. Underhill schooled his expression into one of pious virtue. "Never could understand why a man would marry just to pay off his vowels. Like as not wind up living under the sign of the cat's paw."

"Thank you." Netta's humor resurfaced at this maladroit comment. "Am I truly such a shrew?"

Josiah Underhill chuckled. "Straight-forward gel. You don't tolerate his nonsense. Probably be the making of him."

Desmond's eyes blazed. "You just have a care to your own wife, Underhill."

"What the devil are you implying by that?"

Desmond laughed unpleasantly. "Why nothing. I merely pass along some sage advice." He turned on his heel and strolled off.

Netta stared after him. Now what—? Her heart sank. Desmond headed directly toward the raven-haired Lady Beatrix Underhill. Merciful heavens, did Desmond intend to provoke a fight with Underhill in the middle of the ball? With a murmured word of excuse, she set off in pursuit.

But not quickly enough. Lady Beatrix saw Desmond's approach, and the look she directed at him should have laid him out where he stood. For a long moment the young woman allowed her contemptuous gaze to rest on him, then her lip curled in a sneer worthy of Desmond himself, and she stalked off.

Desmond's soft chuckle reached Netta, and her exasperation swelled. He positively delighted in creating scenes, marveling that her own humor did not encompass the discomfiture of others, as did his.

She caught him before he could continue his pursuit of Underhill's wife. A malicious gleam lingered in his eye. "What are we to do about Roland?" she asked, snatching at a topic sure to divert Desmond from his current purpose.

His brow snapped down. "Insufferable man. Good God, why did he have to return? To prevent our marriage?"

"How could he—?" She broke off as possibilities, unwelcome and frightening, occurred to her. She shivered in spite of the heat of the crowded room.

"Great-aunt Lavinia says he is capable of anything," Desmond said, as if mirroring her thoughts. "Well, he'll not inherit, I promise you that."

Netta glanced over her shoulder to where their cousin now leaned against a wall, surveying the assembled company. Something stirred in her, not quite fear, more a fluttering of nerves in the pit of her stomach. She could not deny her fascination, yet she could certainly regret it. "I wish he hadn't come."

Desmond gave a short laugh devoid of mirth. "He's the devil himself, or so Great-aunt Lavinia has always said. I'm beginning to believe it."

He turned from her, but she caught his arm.

"Why did you invite the Underhills tonight?"

His lips twisted into a mirthless smile. "I have my reasons."

"You've hated the man since you were together at Eton."

"Yes," he mused. "A hatred I have quite grown to enjoy. And now, my dear, are you not neglecting your partners?"

As he started away from her, Kenneth Lambert elbowed his way through the crowd of dancers leaving the floor and bore down on him. He stopped in Desmond's path, his scowl marring the classical perfection of his features. "A word with you, Tavistock!"

"What, only one? You disappoint me, Lambert." He turned away.

Mr. Lambert caught him by the arm and pulled him around.

Desmond looked down at his hand. "You are creasing my sleeve, sir."

"The devil with your sleeve. For a man about to become a tenant-for-life willingly, your attentions to another lady might be construed as insulting to Lady Henrietta!"

Dismayed, Netta opened her mouth to protest—then prudently shut it once more. Desmond would cause less trouble if she left him alone. She wished she could melt into the floor.

"You are mistaken, my dear Lambert." Desmond shook the man off.

"You are *not* contemplating a liaison with Lady Beatrix?"

"No, I am not becoming leg-shackled willingly." He accompanied these haughty words with a wink at Netta which Lambert could not see.

Netta made a face at him. Her ramshackle cousin had absolutely no sense of decorum.

Lambert's complexion darkened. "It grates against me that she should be so coerced into marrying a loose fish. I am warning you, Tavistock, you will mend your libertine ways and make Lady Netta a good husband."

"Will I?" Desmond frowned in exaggerated contemplation. "Do you know, Lambert, you fail to convince me."

"You will." Lambert's voice softened to a hiss. "If you do not make her happy, you will answer to me, Tavistock. Is that clear? To *me*."

The color seeped from Desmond's face, and Netta intervened. "That is very sweet of you, Kenneth, but do you truly think me such a poor honey that I cannot look after my own interests?"

Kenneth Lambert directed a curt bow toward her. "I did not mean to offend you."

"Indeed, how could you? You are far too dear a friend. But should you not be with your next partner? The sets are already forming. And you," she added to her cousin as Lambert took himself off, "are behaving abominably."

He shrugged a pettish shoulder. "I want more champagne. If I'm expected to—Good, God, here comes our little counter-coxcomb."

Netta glanced up to see Sir Archibald Carncross, dazzling in a coat of puce satin, mincing his way toward them. The uncharacteristic grim line of his mouth warned her this would be no simple exchange of pleasantries between neighbors.

Desmond, a devilish glint in his eye, raised his quizzing glass, surveyed the approach through it, and gave a visible shudder. "Well, my tulip?" he asked. "How have I offended you this time?"

Sir Archibald squared his young shoulders and barged ahead. "If Netta has cause to complain of your treatment, I—I shall know what to do," he stammered.

"Will you?" Desmond regarded him as if fascinated. "And what is that? Toddle across the garden from the Dower House and land me a facer? Ah, perhaps I should say *try* to land me a facer? Or do I mean *try* to toddle across from the Dower House?"

"Desmond!" Netta hissed, and directed a telling kick to her cousin's ankle.

Sir Archy flushed to the roots of his sandy hair. With a curt nod to Netta, he stormed away.

Desmond shook his head. "Why you allow that simpering mama's boy about you is a mystery, Netta. But I'm putting an end to that moon-calf hanging about Ravenswood." Obviously pleased with himself, he headed toward the table where Fenton, the butler, poured champagne.

"Despicable." The soft voice of Cousin Phemie sounded near Netta's ear. The little woman shook her head, setting her faded blond curls, now mostly gray, fluffing about her full cheeks and rounded chin. She clutched her fan in both gloved hands. "He has quite put the staff in an uproar this night, for what must he do but countermand my every order."

"Cousin Phemie — "

The little woman rushed on, as if oblivious to the interruption. "He can be so — so supercilious, it quite drives one to distraction. That lordly manner of his puts me in mind of your late papa, my love, though *he* could never be accused of being less than meticulously polite, which though it grieves me to say it, Desmond is not." She fixed Netta with a worried gaze. "You will not let him cast me out as soon as you are married, will you?"

"Cast you out?" Startled, Netta stared at her beloved relative. "What nonsense is this?"

"He was in one of his pets, I suppose, though I fear he meant it." Tears glistened in Cousin Phemie's eyes, and she dabbed at their corners with a wisp of lace handkerchief. "He can be so dreadfully unpleasant. I do not see how you could prevent him, though. Oh, I wish you did not have to wed him." She raised her woebegone gaze to Netta's face, and her sudden look of consternation bordered on the comical. "Oh! Forgive me, my dear. I am not myself tonight. I cannot think what nonsense I have been talking. Now, do not let my troubles distress you. Everything will turn out all for the best, I make no doubt. I'll not let him harm us. Now, let me uncrush your sleeves, my love. Desmond is signaling the musicians. I fear he is about to make the announcement."

And seal her fate. Netta recognized her urge for rebellion and quelled it. She could not behave so shabbily, not with Cousin Phemie and Great-aunt Lavinia depending on her. Even Desmond. He had not the head to manage Tavistock House, let alone the Ravenswood estate. Her father had acted only in the interests of the family in creating that will and this marriage.

The music broke off and a fanfare sounded. Forcing a smile to her lips, Netta joined Desmond where he stood at the far end of the ballroom, his hand held out imperiously for her. It wavered slightly, mute testimony to his having found the champagne he sought.

He managed the announcement with only a few slurred words. Netta caught his elbow, holding him erect as people gathered about them. She paid little heed to their congratulations and well-wishes. At any moment, Des might say something outrageous, and she intended to prevent it.

"Confound it," Desmond exclaimed, "where the devil is the wedding goblet? You," he signaled the second footman. "Where is it? Could use a whole bottle," he added in a muttered aside to Netta as the flustered lad ran off.

"You've already had two, by the look of you," Netta pointed out.

"Three." Desmond beamed at her with pride.

Near the door, the footman grasped the tray on which rested the golden goblet. The last of the Tavistock treasures, Netta reflected. Somehow,

24

that seemed only fitting. A few feet away she noticed Roland leaning against the wall, arms crossed, a saturnine expression on his face. Then the footman reached them and Desmond snatched up the goblet.

"A toast to my bride," Desmond pronounced with care, "as each of the six previous earls of Tavistock have done before me." A gleam lit his eyes, and he lifted the golden vessel to his lips and swallowed, gulping down the alcoholic contents. At last he pressed it into Netta's hands.

He'd all but drained it. Knowing his proclivities, she was surprised he'd left any at all. A conciliatory gesture, perhaps?

She raised the goblet in a silent toast, not in anticipation of her marriage of convenience, but in farewell to her romantic daydreams. Yet as she brought the rim to her lips, she knew those longings would never die. She might be tied to Desmond, more as his nursemaid than as his wife, yet she would continue to yearn for a happiness he would never bring her.

She lowered the goblet, untasted. She had never thought herself such a sentimental pea-goose. In another moment, she would see the funny side of all this and be carried off in an unbecoming fit of the giggles.

Someone took the goblet from her; she didn't see whom. She gave herself a mental shake and swept forward, determined to play her role with grace. Behind her, she could hear Desmond calling for more champagne. She would have to tell the footman to provide him with punch, instead.

She looked about for the lad, but he had vanished amidst the throng. Fenton could convey her message. She started toward where the butler hovered near the refreshment table, filling glasses.

An anguished gasp from Desmond brought her up short. She spun toward him as he doubled over, clutching his stomach, pain contorting his face. His knees buckled, dropping him onto the floor where he lay moaning.

"Here." Underhill strode forward, pushing his way through the startled throng. "Drunk as a wheelbarrow," he diagnosed, sounding pleased. "Disgusting behavior. You." He gestured to the senior footman who appeared. "Get him out of here."

Desmond rolled to his side as his stomach spasmed.

Cousin Phemie, who hurried toward Netta, giggled, a nervous sound. "Oh, dear," she exclaimed with hopeless inadequacy.

Netta knelt beside Desmond as the footman grabbed his shoulders. Perspiration dotted her cousin's brow. For one moment he stared at her with wide, unseeing eyes, then with another retching spasm, he fell back.

"He's ill," she announced. "Fenton—" Desperate, she looked about for the butler.

Roland pushed through the staring throng and dropped to Desmond's other side. With surprisingly gentle hands, he looked the man over and swore under his breath. "Get everyone out of here," he commanded.

Netta stood, turning to the nearest of the guests. "It would be best—" she began, but the babble of voices drowned her out.

A frail, wiry matron pushed her way to the fore, and with relief Netta recognized her neighbor from the country, Lady Carncross, Sir Archibald's indomitable parent.

The woman stared at Desmond's now-writhing form for a moment, pursed her lips, then gave a short nod. "You won't be wanting this crowd here." She turned around and started ordering people to go home in a voice that, while neither loud nor carrying, brooked no opposition. About them, people began to fall back.

Relieved, Netta turned her attention once more to Desmond. Roland carried his shoulders, and the younger footman—Jeremy—now supported his feet. The elderly Fenton hovered over them, wringing his hands, distress in every line of his wrinkled face.

Roland shifted his grip as Desmond moaned and twisted. "Easy there, Little Cousin. We'll have you tucked up between sheets in a trice."

"It was such a sudden attack." Netta paced beside them, feeling useless. "I have never known champagne to disagree with him so."

Roland stopped. "It didn't." He sounded as if the realization had just struck him.

Netta's throat felt dry. "Then—?"

Roland's gaze traveled to Desmond's distorted face. "He's been poisoned."

Chapter Two

Netta cast Roland an exasperated glance and fought back the chill that crept up her spine. "Great-aunt Lavinia always said you had a cruel sense of humor. I do not find that in the least amusing."

"Neither do I." Roland started forward once more with Desmond, and the footman perforce accompanied him.

As they neared the ballroom door, Mr. Josiah Underhill pushed his way up to them. He gazed down at Desmond's unconscious form, and a slow, unpleasant smile twisted the corners of his lips. "Poison, did you say? Demmed clever idea of someone's. Saves the rest of us the trouble. Making a great to-do over it, isn't he? Pity it probably won't carry him off. You'd do a dashed sight better without him, Lady Henrietta." He shook his head. "Pray convey my thanks to his lordship — when he recovers — for a rare evening's entertainment." With a curt nod, he turned on his heel, calling for his hat and cape.

Netta closed her eyes. *Poison,* of all things. Roland certainly lived up to his reputation by making that ridiculous suggestion in front of everyone. It would be all over London as the latest *on dit* by morning. And if she knew Josiah Underhill, he would be dropping loud hints that Netta herself had tried to kill Desmond to avoid having to marry her troublesome cousin.

Oh, how Desmond would enjoy this — when he felt better. To make such a scandal of his betrothal ball! Her lips twitched at the thought of his delight. He would be in alt.

At the moment, though, he looked very ill, indeed. She glanced about, seeing the guests taking their leave, herded implacably by the efficient Lady Carncross. Netta need have no fears with that formidable little woman in charge. Tongues might wag, but they would be doing it elsewhere. She could concentrate on tending to poor Des.

She started toward the door to move aside an elderly couple who blocked the way and came face-to-face with Mr. Underhill's wife, Lady Beatrix. The dark-haired woman stared past her, at Desmond, her expression an odd mixture of stunned relief and dismay that made no sense. Netta started to speak, but the woman hurried away after her husband without sparing her so much as a glance.

"There, my love." Cousin Phemie bustled to her side. "Dear Lady Carncross is such a prop and a mainstay, is she not? I vow, there is nothing for me to do." She glanced at Desmond as Roland and the footman carried him through the doorway, and clucked her tongue. "If that is not a Judgment, his taking so ill. If only he will heed this as a Sign, and mend his wicked ways. Now, where did I put my vinaigrette, for I felt quite certain I should need it this evening. Why, here it is, in the top of my reticule, just where I placed it. Is that not remarkable?" She brandished a tiny glass bottle with a perforated silver lid. "It quite amazes me how things seem to move about on their own, as if they wished to *hide* from us. Now, my dear, if you will just breathe in—" She held it out toward Netta.

Netta waved it away. "I have not the least need of it. A glass of brandy would be more to the purpose. No, pray do not look shocked, Cousin Phemie. I shall do my best to be every bit as faint as you could wish later, but at the moment I have not the time. Please, will you not find Stebbing? I should have thought one of the footmen would have summoned him by now."

Even as she spoke, Desmond's haughty valet made his stately way across the hall from the servants' door and presented himself at his master's side. One glance, though, proved sufficient to wipe the superior expression from the man's face. Visibly he faltered and turned first to the footman, then to Netta.

"He has been taken ill," she explained. "If

someone has not already done so, please send for a doctor."

The man nodded mutely and staggered off.

Netta followed the procession up to the next flight where Desmond's rooms lay. After hurrying ahead to open the door for them, she threw back the covers on the bed. Roland and the footman deposited their burden.

Stebbing arrived while Roland fumbled with his cousin's neckcloth. The shaken valet protested, then set about making his master more comfortable.

Netta watched Desmond's renewed spasms of agony until she could no longer contain her distress. "Can't anyone do something for him?" she demanded, looking from Stebbing's strained features to Roland's grim countenance. "Will the doctor be long?"

Roland laid a strong hand on her shoulder. "Come, we can do no good here." With surprising gentleness, he steered her from the room. "Let his man do his work."

She halted in the hall while he closed the door behind them. "I ought to be doing something for him," she protested.

"Perhaps you may sit with him after the doctor has finished." He took her elbow and guided her firmly toward the staircase. "Where is your bed-chamber?"

"No!" She shook him off. "I do *not* want to lie down. Stop treating me like a child."

"Am I?" Amusement touched his voice, only to fade at once. "Come down to the bookroom, then. That brandy you wanted should do you no harm. I very much fear this will not be an easy night for you."

"It was hardly that to begin with." Ignoring his piercing look, she headed down the steps.

She led the way to the bookroom, where a cut-crystal decanter set stood on a small table. Roland poured, and handed a glass to Netta. She sipped it, sending burning liquid coursing down her throat, easing the chill that gripped her, soothing the tension from her muscles. She had no idea how long her temples had been throbbing.

She sank back in a comfortable chair. Something caught at her head, and with a muttered word, she dragged an ostrich plume from its lacy nest in her hair and cast it aside. Her companion paid her no heed, busying himself instead once more with the decanter.

By her fifth sip, her world steadied. Too much had happened this night, that was what plagued her. Topped by the unexpected return of Roland.

She peered at him over the rim of her glass. He didn't appear dangerous at the moment, yet she knew him too well—at least she knew too much *of* him—to be fooled. Her own memories might be sketchy, but she had the scar on her wrist as proof, and she had often heard the disturbing tales Great-aunt Lavinia loved to tell of his detestable behavior.

Still, he had been quite kind to her this night. Like the big cousin he should be. Warmth stirred in her, an unexpected longing for she knew not what. He confused her, and she didn't like that sensation.

She forced herself to study him through objective eyes — which was no easy task. He seemed taller and of a sturdier build than the general run of Galbraiths. He also had a darker cast to his countenance — though she supposed life in India could account for his tanned and weathered complexion. It might also account for the grimness of his expression. An air of repressed energy seemed to emanate from him, as if his hold on it might break at any moment. On the whole, she decided it would be safer not to trust him.

He replaced the stopper with precise, crisp movements and turned toward her. Before he could speak, a knock sounded on the door.

The distraught Fenton looked in. "The doctor has arrived, Miss Netta."

Roland returned his untasted glass to the tray. "Take him up at once. No, stay here," he directed Netta as she started to rise.

"I will not!" Strain sharpened her words.

"My dear child—"

Her frayed nerves snapped. "I am *not* a child!"

The creases in his brow deepened. "You are overwrought. Perhaps you will feel better when you have finished your brandy." He strode after the butler without sparing her another glance.

Several of Great-aunt Lavinia's more lurid accounts of Roland's conniving ways sprang to her mind. Deceitful, callous, manipulative—and now he had come back into their lives! What was his purpose in doing that, anyway? Whatever it might be, she would not allow him to succeed. She certainly would not permit him to assume control like this, as if Desmond were dead and not just ill!

Fuming, Netta set off in pursuit, catching them at the foot of the stairs. "I do not suffer high-handedness from Desmond," she informed him in an undervoice, "and I certainly shall not tolerate it from you. I shall thank you to remember you have no right to give orders in this house."

A muscle at the corner of Roland's mouth twitched, giving him a cynical, almost derisive, appearance. "I beg your pardon, Lady Henrietta."

"For heaven's sake, do try not to be detestable," she snapped, and pushed past.

At the door to her cousin's room, though, the doctor refused her admittance. To her further fury, he permitted Roland into this sanctum, leaving her to kick her heels in the hall. This she did with a vengeance, pacing the length of the corridor with seething impatience and thinking up several new names to call Roland that had escaped Great-aunt Lavinia.

Cousin Phemie bustled up the stairs, adjuring the two housemaids behind her to be quick about it and not dally all night. They reached the landing at last, each bearing a pitcher filled with steaming water. Behind them came a footman with basins appropriated from the kitchen. The procession disappeared into Desmond's bedchamber, and the door closed behind them, allowing Netta no more than the barest peek at the small group clustered about the bedside.

Minutes later the servants reemerged with Cousin Phemie still in attendance. The little woman cast Netta a speaking glance. "So dreadful, the poor boy, though to be sure . . ." The rest of her comment faded as she shook her head and hurried after the servants who disappeared toward the nether regions of the house.

When the door at last opened again, Netta once more had reached the staircase in her distraught perambulations. Roland emerged, then leaned against the wall, his head lowered. She hurried toward him, only to slow her steps as she took in the forbidding lines of his face. Even by the flickering candlelight she could see the pallor that underlay his darkened skin.

"Desmond—" she began, but could not continue. A chill started in her blood and seeped through her veins to every part of her body.

He crossed to her and laid large, work-roughened hands on her shoulders.

"Is he going to be all right?" she demanded.

He shook his head. "I am sorry."

She blinked. "What do you mean? Is there nothing the doctor can do for him?

"I mean—"

This time the doctor emerged, fatigue in every line of his withered frame. He drew his spectacles from his beaked nose and rubbed a hand over his eyes. "Terrible business," was all he said.

"*What* is?" Netta demanded. "Desmond—"

"I'm sorry, my dear. He went quickly, which is a blessing. I once saw a similar case drag on for hours. Depends on how much was taken, you know."

"I do *not* know," she protested. "Are you telling me Desmond is—dead?" She looked from one man to the other and read the confirmation in their faces. "But—*how?* He was not in the least ill until he collapsed. He has always enjoyed excellent health."

"Even the most robust of constitutions cannot but suffer from poison."

"From—I thought it was some cruel hoax!" She rounded on Roland. "When you said—"

"A dose of laudanum?" the doctor asked Roland.

"How could that have—" Netta began, then stared at the man in horror. "Do you mean for *me?* Certainly not." With an effort, she collected herself. "Desmond was poisoned," she said, proving to the men she had a clear grasp of the essential facts. "Have you any idea how? Something in our dinner that was not properly prepared, perhaps?"

Again, the men exchanged glances. "Not unless

your cook is in the habit of seasoning his dishes with oleander," the doctor said.

"Oleander? But that's a rat poison! No one would put that in food. Surely you must be mistaken."

Roland took her hands. "I greatly fear not. I have seen similar cases in India." He glanced at the doctor. "It also acts very quickly. I should imagine no more than minutes elapsed between the time he took it and the time the first convulsion took him."

Minutes. And he had just toasted her with the wedding goblet. . . .

"Little Hen?"

She became conscious of Roland's deep voice. He supported her, one arm about her waist, the other ready to scoop her up if she fainted. The wave of dizziness seeped away, leaving her trembling and clammy.

"Take her to her bedchamber," the doctor decreed. "I'll send someone for a Runner I know. Discreet fellow, as unlikely as that may seem. Efficient, too. I'll be with her in a moment."

Netta made no protest as Roland led her away. By the time they reached the stairs, though, she gathered her strength and shook him off. She paused on the next landing and faced him. "He was poisoned on purpose." It was more a statement than a question. "Someone *murdered* him?"

"That is still to be determined." Roland took her elbow and urged her upward.

After three more steps, she stopped again. "I should have drunk from that cup, too."

His grip tightened. "Why did you not?"

"There was only a sip left. And I—I didn't want to," she finished lamely. How could she explain her feelings of that moment when she hardly understood them herself?

"He drank most of it?" Roland's brow lowered, his features intent. "Is there any reason he might have taken this poison on purpose?"

Netta's lip twitched. "Do you mean as a preferable fate to wedding me? No, he is quite—was quite looking forward to at last being able to broach the capital and get himself out from under the hatches. He has talked of little else for weeks."

"And you were reconciled to this marriage, as well?"

"Of course not, but I found it preferable to entering the workhouse in St. James's Parish."

Roland stopped, staring at her.

A choke of stressed laughter escaped her at his reaction to her irreverent response. "No, pray, do not look so, or I shall go off into whoops, which would be quite shocking of me." She sobered at once, her stomach tightening at the reality of Desmond's death. "In truth, I know many females who have entered marriages that held out even less hope of contentment. Des might not be—have been—a model of all the virtues, but I have—had—quite the knack of managing him." She turned away, stumbling up the next step. She couldn't let herself think of Desmond, not yet.

"Would Ravenswood really have been turned over to a charity?" He sounded casual, as if he sought to divert her.

With an effort she commanded her voice. "Dreadful, is it not?"

"On the contrary. I should consider it the best possible thing."

She glanced at him, surprised at his vehemence. "It is a trifle gloomy, to be sure. But you must remember the Galbraiths have already lost Larkspur. I could not bear it for Papa's heirs not to have any estate. Can you imagine an earldom with no more than a townhouse to its credit?"

"Rather shabby," Roland agreed, his tone dry.

Netta stopped in her tracks and stared at Roland, knowing she beheld a newly inherited earl without a country estate.

"My love," Cousin Phemie called from below, "I vow, I have never been more shocked. Poor, poor Desmond. But at least now he will not be able to upset us anymore. Should we not go in to him?"

"Definitely not." Roland intercepted the plump little lady as she reached them. "Leave him to his man for now. You may do all that is proper in the morning."

Phemie regarded him in concern. "I would not wish to be backward in any attention."

"Then tend to Little Hen. Desmond is beyond any ministrations now."

A flicker of satisfaction flashed across Cousin Phemie's face, only to vanish at once. Or had Netta seen it at all? It had been so quick, she might have been mistaken.

Roland left her to Phemie's care, taking himself downstairs, apparently to await the arrival of the Bow Street Runner. Netta resumed the climb to her own chamber.

"What people will say." Cousin Phemie shook her head, dismayed. "Imagine, to have a murder in the family! I've never heard of such a thing. We have not even a ghost in our halls, for Ravenswood is not haunted, though there might be one at Larkspur, I suppose. Not that I ever heard of one, of course. Murder!" she repeated. "Your dear Papa would be scandalized."

"Anyone would."

Cousin Phemie clucked her tongue, apparently misinterpreting the dryness of Netta's tone. "There, now, my love. We will not quite be ostracized, I am sure. My dear godson will not desert us, of that you may be certain."

"No, I doubt he will quite cut our acquaintance," Netta agreed. That prospect must please Cousin Phemie. She had always favored Mr. Kenneth Lambert's suit for Netta, though she had known it hopeless. And while Mr. Lambert might find their present situation distasteful, his attentions to herself had been sufficiently marked in the past for her to hope he would now stand their friend.

Another thought struck her, and aghast, she faltered on the next step. Had he cared enough for her to have removed Desmond to free her from this marriage? Then a vestige of her usual humor came to her rescue. She must be shockingly set up in her own conceit if she ever thought her manifest charms might lead to murder. If she were a great heiress rather than a virtual pauper, of course, the idea might not be so absurd.

During the next hour and more, she sat before the fire in her room, trying to accept the fact of Desmond's death. It still didn't seem real to her; it would be a long while before it did, she knew.

At last, a respectful rapping sounded on her door. Netta looked up from her contemplation of the flickering flames and called: "Come in."

Fenton stood on the threshold, his gaunt face drawn with fatigue and shock. "The Runner, Miss Netta," he announced.

Netta rose. "I will come down at once."

She followed the butler to the bookroom on the ground floor. Desmond had always liked this apartment, preferring it for entertaining his friends to the salons above, where he might find one or more of his female relatives. Netta stepped inside and stiffened at sight of Roland sitting at the desk. Already, he took over Des's position.

"Lady Henrietta Galbraith?" A slightly built man of just above average height rose, fixing the regard of his wide-set blue eyes on her. Smile lines crinkled at their corners, though his expression now was as somber as one might expect for the occasion.

She inclined her head, cautious.

"Benjamin Frake." He introduced himself with an elegant bow. His close-cropped blond hair glistened with reddish highlights in the wavering light of the candelabrum. "From Bow Street," he added. "May I offer my condolences?" His sharp gaze rested on her.

"Thank you." She suffered the distinct sensation those deceptively innocent eyes missed nothing. "How may I help you?" She took the seat Roland placed for her and found herself glad he had set it before the hearth. A comforting warmth flowed over her, welcome in spite of the fact the May night held only the slightest chill.

The Runner rocked back on his heels. "Well, now, m'lady, I've learned a fair piece already." The slightest of Scottish burrs sounded in his voice. "We'll just see if we can't answer a few more questions."

"Please—tell me what you know."

Mr. Frake pursed his lips and consulted the notebook he had laid on his chair. "The poor gentleman was one Desmond Marmaduke Augustus Galbraith, seventh earl of Tavistock, residing at both Tavistock House, Cavendish Square, and Ravenswood Court, near Brighton." He glanced at her, as if checking to see if he had his facts correct.

She nodded.

"Cause of death is poison, most likely oleander, and most likely administered in the gold wedding goblet with which he toasted your betrothal."

Netta nodded again. Would this constant repetition, she wondered, hammer these facts into her mind so she might really accept them as the truth? She shivered.

The Runner's eyes narrowed. "Now, it seems highly unlikely this could have been an accident. Do you agree?"

She swallowed. "Then you think it deliberate murder?"

"Aye, m'lady. That I do. Oleander." He shook his head. "Nasty stuff. Rat poison, you know. And his lordship wasn't a rat, was he?"

He had his moments, she reflected—but not aloud.

Mr. Frake cleared his throat. "Well, well, well," he murmured, and his graphite pencil scratched across a page of the notebook. After a moment he looked up. "Now, this tangle isn't as difficult to unravel as it might be. There cannot be that many people who both came near the wedding goblet *and* would have been glad to see his lordship dead."

"I—I cannot imagine *anyone* . . ." Her voice trailed off. Something about the way the Runner regarded her made her uneasy.

"Now, m'lady." His unwavering gaze rested on her face. "This here ball was to announce your betrothal to his late lordship, was it not?"

"Yes." Netta straightened her slight frame, her chin tilting upward as if to counteract the sinking in her stomach.

The Runner drew a gnarled briarwood pipe from the depths of his pocket and tapped it with a thoughtful finger. "Now, his lordship here—" he nodded toward Roland, who leaned against the mantel, "has told me about the terms of your father's will."

"How kind of him." Netta directed a falsely sweet smile at her distant cousin. His lordship. That would take growing accustomed to, also.

The gaze of the Runner's disconcerting blue eyes rested on her, but he let her comment pass. "Now, your father was the sixth earl? Odd, wasn't it, his threatening to leave the unentailed portions of the estate to charity like that?"

Netta's jaw tightened. "It was more than a threat. The Galbraith fortunes have been considerably diminished since the time of the Pretender. My father sought to assure I would be provided for without depriving his heir of an estate."

The Runner looked up from his notes. "And this estate—Ravenswood Court—is not entailed?"

"It is not." Roland folded his arms. "Only this house is. Our illustrious ancestor supported the Pretender, you must know. Our estate—Larkspur, which is in the Lake District—was forfeit to the

Crown. The one we now hold was won by Lady Henrietta's grandfather. At cards."

The pencil scribbled on for several seconds. "I see," Mr. Frake said at last. "So it may be disposed of as the owner wishes. A most unfortunate arrangement for the heir." His discerning gaze rested on Netta. "If you did not fulfill this marital requirement, would you have been left penniless?"

"I have a small amount from my mother. Not enough on which to live," she admitted.

"And his late lordship?"

"This house, a few paintings, the wedding goblet." She spoke the last with a bitter laugh. "That is the entire entail."

"And now? Did your father allow for such a contingency as the death of one or the other of you before the marriage could take place?"

Netta swallowed. "In this event, the survivor would inherit the unentailed properties. But pray do not think I have become a great heiress." She rushed on, nettled by the gleam in his eyes. "I will have Ravenswood, but it must be brought to support itself. In truth, I fear what little capital there is will be swallowed in that attempt. I can only be grateful Desmond's gaming debts will not encumber it. Those, I believe, are inherited with the title." She cast Roland her brightest smile.

"I could wish he might have kept both," Roland said.

The Runner's sharp gaze rested on him, assessing. When he spoke, though, he said merely: "A gamester, was his late lordship?"

"He was partial to the tables," Netta admitted. "But I believe that is a common weakness of gentlemen."

A muffled snort escaped Roland. Netta glared at him. Why did he seem so annoyed? He had just inherited a title—an earldom, no less—and an elegant townhouse with a prestigious address. And if he had truly earned his fortune in India, Desmond's debts would put little burden on him.

The Runner chewed on the stem of his pipe. "Were you and his late lordship much attached to one another?"

Netta lowered her gaze. "We were accustomed to one another."

Roland's lips twitched. "She means that if our cousin had discovered an heiress of sufficient fortune and breeding to suit his purposes, he would have left Lady Henrietta to her fate without a qualm."

"And I should have done the same to him, had I 'fallen in love,' as the vulgar parlance would have it." She cast a fulminating glance at Roland. "Neither of us would have let the other's plight prevent us from seeking happiness. But although I have had several suitors," she directed this also at Roland, "I have not cared enough for any of them to deprive my father's heir of our estate and meager capital. There, have I given you sufficient cause to believe me guilty of his—" She broke off, unable to say the word.

Frake closed his Occurrence Book. "Well, now, that seems to be enough for this one night. Need time to think for a bit, I do. Why don't you get what sleep you can, and I'll call on you later in the morning, if that's all right."

And if it wasn't? But she refrained from voicing that question. The Runner would come when he wished, and she had best make it convenient for herself. As Roland escorted him out, she found herself feeling like the prime suspect.

She headed for the stairs and encountered Cousin Phemie lying in wait for her.

"What did he say to you, my love?"

A rueful smile just touched Netta's lips as she started up the first flight. "I cannot but wonder why he didn't take me into custody and be done with it."

Phemie gasped, indignant. "If only your father had not left that despicable will. But to think you guilty of such a dreadful crime is—is positively indecent!"

"Who is more likely?" Even as she voiced the question, she knew.

"Thank heavens Roland has come home." Phemie patted her hand. "He will protect us both."

Or use them for his own ends.

Netta saw Cousin Phemie to her room, then crossed the hall to her own. As she closed the door, a chill left her trembling. Roland. He might well have killed Desmond to inherit the title. Might he have meant to kill her as well? Only Desmond's greedy swallowing of the heady wine had kept her from consuming the deadly poison, too. Had his murderer anticipated that — or not?

Her cold fingers sought the key and turned it in the lock. With her death as well as Desmond's, Roland would inherit not only the title and London townhouse, but Ravenswood Court and what little fortune the family could boast. Why else did he reappear after an absence of seventeen years, at just this moment, if not for that purpose?

A long-repressed memory of fear rose to haunt her, of herself as a small child, Desmond not much older. Only impressions remained, of intense pain, of Roland's contorted face, of Lavinia as a much younger woman attacking Roland, driving him away from where Netta screamed, her wrist bleeding. . . .

Only this time there would be no vigilant great-aunt to save her from him if he desired her death.

She had to protect herself.

Chapter Three

Netta roused from a troubled sleep to the sound of someone hammering on her door. Fear welled in her, the continuation of a nightmare in which a shadowy figure pursued her through the halls of a demented version of Ravenswood Court. She gasped a steadying breath, and the fogs of terror cleared to reveal her chamber at Tavistock House filled with late morning light.

Hours must have passed, she realized as she dragged herself up in bed. When she had at last reached her chamber in the creeping dawn, she had not thought sleep possible.

The determined rapping repeated on her door, this time accompanied by her abigail's anxious voice. Why didn't the woman just come in?

Because she couldn't, Netta realized the next moment. The last vestiges of sleep fell away. Her nightmares had been well-founded. She'd locked her door because someone—Roland?—might well want her dead.

Netta threw back the covers and padded across

to turn the key. Wembly, a tray balanced on one hand, regarded her with concern. After a moment the little woman nodded to herself in apparent satisfaction and stepped inside.

"Time and past you was up and about, Lady Netta." She deposited her burden on the bedside table.

For once, the woman's sharp-featured face and severely drawn-back dark hair did not seem comforting and familiar to Netta. Even her customary gown of black bombazine took on a more funereal appearance than normal.

Funeral. Desmond was really dead.

A wave of grief washed over her, frightening in its intensity. She had tolerated her cousin more than liked him, but always he'd been there, always he'd been part of her life—and now he never would be again. Everything would seem strange and unfamiliar without him.

Everything, an inner voice whispered in her ear, would be a great deal easier and more pleasant.

She dragged her attention from that reprehensible thought. Mourning clothes. She'd have to make do somehow. She had not the wherewithal to purchase a new gown. And she hated black.

With the assistance of Wembly, she consulted her wardrobe. Her abigail clucked her tongue and shook her head, turning over one garment after another.

A rueful smile tugged at Netta's lips. "Hopeless, is it not? Well, we simply shall have to mend those two gowns I wore six years ago on my father's death. And here." She pulled out a jaconet muslin in a disagreeable shade of green that clashed with her hair. "A bath in black dye can only improve this."

Wembly endorsed this decision. After assisting Netta into a round gown of jonquil crepe, she gathered the detested jaconet along with a spencer of dark blue gros de Naples, and set off on her errand. Netta herself would spend an hour or two that morning with a needle and be more suitably attired by the afternoon.

Breakfast first, though. Hunger seemed incongruous after the horrible events of the night before, but the hot chocolate brought by Wembly merely served to whet her appetite. She set forth to see if the household staff continued to function in spite of the death of their master.

On the first landing she encountered a parlor-maid, who first gaped at her silent and wide-eyed, then squealed and scurried away. Netta stared after her, amazed. Merciful heavens, did the staff already bandy about tales — probably suspecting *her* of Desmond's murder? Netta continued down the stairs with a deep sense of foreboding.

She entered the breakfast parlor, only to stop short in the doorway, her heart skipping a beat at the sight of Roland seated at the mahogany table. Was this, she wondered, the consternation—the uncertainty—the servants experienced when they saw her? She could pity them.

Her gaze lingered on Roland's dark, brooding appearance. Was he a murderer? A shiver raced through her, and with a sense of shock, she realized it was not wholly fear. The intensity of his expression intrigued her. Strength marked every line of his face, as of one who had been tested beyond endurance, yet survived.

He looked up from his tankard of ale, and the compelling regard of his hazel eyes rested on her. Her knees seemed to be assailed by an unaccountable weakness. He mesmerized her, like one of those Indian cobra snakes of which she had heard tell.

"What are you doing here?" She rushed into speech, hoping her unsettled emotions didn't sound in her voice.

"I have given up the rooms I had taken."

"You—do you mean you have moved in *here?*"

His mouth tightened. "If I must take charge, I might as well do so at once and get it over with. My aunt suggested it after you retired to bed last night."

Cousin Phemie. Netta might have known. She crossed to the side table, picked up a plate, and lifted the lid from the first dish. "Of course, how foolish of me. Tavistock House is now yours, is it not? How soon do you wish me to remove?"

"I wish nothing of the sort." He stabbed a

piece of rare beef with his fork. "You will do as you wish—or as that blasted Runner permits."

She looked over her shoulder at him. "Pray, what do you mean by that? That you both think I am the one who murdered Desmond?"

For answer, he merely regarded her from beneath his scowling brows.

Netta spun back to the sideboard, her cheeks burning. Insufferable man! "Since you are here," she said with her back to him, "you may make the arrangements for Desmond's funeral. And there will be his man of affairs to be seen, the notice to be put in the Times—"

"You need only concern yourself with ordering your weeds. Do you indeed mourn him?"

"I will certainly need a period of adjusting to his absence. And what of you? He was your second cousin as well as mine. Surely you must show respect for the man whose title and dignities you have inherited."

"I could wish that fate on someone else."

Her lip curled. "Forgive me if I do not believe you."

"Good God, madam, why should I wish upon myself a mountain of responsibilities not of my own choosing and a title I have grown to despise? I have earned my peace, and I cannot welcome this turn of events."

"Nor could Desmond," she snapped back before she could stop herself.

An unexpected touch of self-deprecating humor flickered across his stern features. "You are quite right. I can think of nothing he would have liked less than my inheriting."

Except to be poisoned. . . .

She was spared the necessity of making any coherent response by the door opening. Miss Euphemia Wrenn fluttered in, trailing lavender and purple gauze in her wake. Her face, drawn and pale from their late night, broke into a smile at sight of the two occupants.

"Dear Roland. And Netta, my love. I thought I should sleep the day away. What a dreadful night," she added, the innate cheerfulness never wavering from her voice. "Such a tragedy. I vow, I never thought it should turn out so well. Only think, my love, we are free of Desmond at last."

"He was your cousin," Netta pointed out, reproving.

"Oh, fiddle. *He* never let that weigh with him, so why should I? When I think how he intended to cast me from his household, from beneath the only roof I have ever known, once the knot was tied between you — well, that is neither here nor there, is it? What has our good Cook prepared?"

She joined Netta in the selection of her breakfast, then carried her plate to sit across from Roland. "Are you quite settled in?" She took a sip of tea. "I asked Fenton to place you in the best guest chamber. You really should have the master's rooms, of course, but that isn't possible just yet." She sighed in regret.

"I shall do quite well." Roland returned his attention to his tankard.

Phemie looked from him to where Netta drew out a chair a little removed from them. "Is it not delightful to have him with us, my love? Just think of it, after all these years."

Netta did think, and didn't like her conclusions one bit. "Indeed," was all she said, but the cold word seemed to hover in the air between them. Netta made no move to ease the awkwardness.

"My love, you should not—" Phemie broke off under Netta's frigid gaze. "You have sustained a terrible shock, and you are all to pieces, I make no doubt. There, now what am I about? You shall have a pastille and a cup of tea and—"

"Next you will be threatening to burn feathers beneath my nose. I need no such coddling." Netta thrust back her chair, rising. "There are things I must be about this morning."

She strode from the room, but as the door closed behind her, she could hear Phemie gently begging Roland to excuse her petulance.

Netta closed her eyes. What would really make her feel better would be to march back in there and pour her unfinished cup of tea over Roland's head. Contemplation of his probable reaction brought a smile to her lips.

It faded the next moment. How could Cousin Phemie be so calm? Desmond hadn't simply died, he'd been *murdered*. The thought of someone so wantonly taking the life of another sickened her. Desmond might not have been the most amiable of souls, but no one deserved oleander's painful death.

And she might well have shared it with him.

The door knocker banged imperiously, and Netta retreated to the stairs. Had the news gotten about already? Would she shortly be inundated by the vulgarly curious come to gape at her and wonder if she had killed the man she was to wed?

Jeremy, the harassed younger footman, ran to answer it, stopped at the mirror to straighten his livery, then opened the door. The murmur of a feminine voice reached Netta, then Jeremy informed the caller the family was not at home to visitors. An admirable young man, Netta reflected. As he started to close the door, however, it swung wide, sweeping him back a pace.

An erect little figure in a flowing bishop's blue carriage dress swept in, her walking cane wielded like a weapon. "Lady Henrietta will see me," Lady Carncross announced. "We are such old friends, there is no need to stand upon ceremony with us."

"But—" The footman gave way before her.

"No, really, Mama." Sir Archibald scurried after his parent, embarrassment on every feature. "The man has his orders, you can't just—"

"It's all right, Jeremy." Netta hurried down the

flight. "Indeed, it is most kind of you to call, Lady Carncross. And Archy."

Sir Archibald cast her an uncertain smile. "Well, naturally we came," he said.

The woman surged forward to clasp Netta's hands, setting the feathers bouncing in her bonnet. "My dearest child! How is Tavistock? Is he quite recovered?"

Stealing her nerve, Netta broke the news.

For a long moment neither of her visitors said a word.

"Did he—" Sir Archibald began, then broke off and ran a finger around the dashing height of his neckcloth. "What caused it, do you know? Something he ate?"

"The doctor believes he drank oleander. From the wedding goblet."

"Ole—" The young dandy's eyes widened. "How the devil did he get that? Rat poison, ain't it?"

Lady Carncross shot her son a quelling look. "Most unpleasant, most unpleasant indeed. Not that we can call this a dreadful event. Frightful man, I always thought him. So very insulting— though I suppose I should not speak ill of the dead."

Archy cast a beseeching look at his outspoken parent. "How are you managing?" he asked Netta.

"None of it, thank heavens, falls to my lot. Desmond never thought to make a proper will, so my cousin Roland, as his heir, will be in charge."

Archy shook his head. "Dashed unpleasant business. Glad to help in any way, if I can."

"Netta, my love?" Cousin Phemie's voice drifted down from the hall above. "Netta, I—Oh, my dear Lady Carncross." She bustled down the stairs and fell on the woman, dabbing at her eyes with a wispy lace handkerchief. "Such troubles as we have had, as I am sure Netta has told you. I can only be so grateful we have my dear Roland to help us through them."

Lady Carncross disentangled herself and patted Phemie's hand. "Your sentiments do you credit, Miss Wrenn. He is your brother's nephew, is he not? So very trying for you. Archy, come make your bow."

Her son came forward dutifully and made an elegant leg. Cousin Phemie turned her vague gaze on him and beamed.

"Such a gentleman," she murmured. "I vow, he must be the greatest comfort to you, dear Lady Carncross."

His mother emitted a sound perilously near a snort.

Cousin Phemie didn't appear to notice. "So fortunate he did not take the measles like the other children. How do they go on? But you must not stay in the entry hall," she continued before Lady Carncross could answer. "Netta, my love, what can you be thinking of? Do come into the front salon."

She led the way across the tiled floor and through a door to their right, into an elegantly appointed chamber decorated in shades of gold and blue, now a trifle faded by the years. She gestured for their visitors to be seated.

Lady Carncross took an armchair near the window, and Sir Archy meandered over to the chimney piece and struck a graceful pose. With a practiced air, he drew from his pocket a snuff-box enameled with a scene from classical mythology and flicked it open. After casting a surreptitious glance at Netta, as if to make sure she observed his finesse, he took a pinch and inhaled too deeply. The subsequent fit of sneezing doubled him over.

Lady Carncross closed her eyes for a pregnant moment. When she turned back to Netta, her expression betrayed nothing but benign sympathy. "Whatever will you do now that that dangerous cousin of yours has inherited everything?" She shivered. "And how ever shall we go on once he establishes himself at Ravenswood?"

"Dangerous?" Cousin Phemie bristled.

"I shall endeavor to keep the wolf at bay," Netta promised with mock solemnity.

"But can you? Once he takes control—"

Netta took pity on her. "You may be easy on that head, ma'am. Ravenswood is mine."

"Is it?" A gleam lit Lady Carncross's gray eyes. For a long moment she stared out the windows to where a curricle rattled by on the street. She gave herself a quick shake. "My dear, I cannot tell you how glad I am. Ravenswood is such a lovely estate. I cannot think how my papa-in-law could ever have brought himself to risk it in a game of chance. But there, I must not run on on that head. Having a stranger there would be quite unthinkable. But at least it shall remain with you, and I have quite come to think of you as family."

Archy blinked, staring at his mother in surprise. Whatever comment sprang to his lips, though, he swallowed.

"Now," Lady Carncross continued, "should you need a temporary refuge, you know you have but to call upon me. I shall be only too delighted to give you and Miss Wrenn shelter. You cannot wish to remain in a house belonging to a man of whom I have heard nothing but ill."

Cousin Phemie stiffened. "Then you must have heard only the vilest of evil-natured reports."

Lady Carncross's eyebrows rose. "Indeed? I am glad to stand corrected. Still, he *is* a single gentleman, is he not? And with all the unpleasant tasks to be performed in the next few days—" She broke off and shook her head, so that one elegantly curled plume brushed her faded cheek. "You cannot wish to remain in this house once poor Tavistock has been laid out in state in the main drawing room."

Phemie colored a becoming pink. "There, I always knew you were a good friend to us."

"Indeed," Netta agreed. "I thank you for your kind offer, but there is no need. Tavistock House has always been my home. I daresay I shall not return here again, but for the present I—I find comfort here."

"Of course." Lady Carncross took her hand and patted it. "Feel free to come to me at any time, though, should you change your mind. And if the prospect of Ravenswood should prove daunting, you know you will always find a welcome at the Dower House."

"It is very kind of you." Netta smiled, masking her inner conjectures. The offer seemed a shade calculated, to her way of thinking. No, she should not be so unkind. Of what did she suspect Lady Carncross? Surely not of murder. It was just the woman's direct manner, a bit overbearing, unexpected from so tiny a woman. More likely she plotted a bit of matrimony between Netta and poor Archy to regain Ravenswood once more for the Carncross family.

Lady Carncross's eyes narrowed. "You must do as you wish, of course. Still, if there is indeed some question as to how that dreadful poison came to be in that wedding goblet, I should think you would feel safer away from here."

Once more, Phemie bristled. "And what, pray,

are you implying? That Roland murdered his cousin for the title? I assure you, he cares not a fig for being Tavistock. He told me last night he considers being the eighth earl to be the greatest drudgery."

"Hah!" Sir Archibald looked up from his examination of his neckcloth in the mirror over the mantel. "Now, that's a plumper. Not want to be Tavistock? That's trying it on too rare and thick by half. You take care, Netta. Can't have that dashed outsider running Ravenswood. Nothing but a tradesman in India, I'll wager. Before you know it—"

He broke off as the door opened and Roland himself strolled in. His coat of blue superfine seemed molded to his broad shoulders, and his firm jaw gave him a challenging, powerful air. This was a man who would get whatever he wanted, Netta realized. Especially, a little voice whispered in her mind, if it were a woman's favors. She looked away, both embarrassed and intrigued by the direction of her thoughts. Instead, she had better wonder how much he might want Ravenswood.

"Cousin Netta," he began, then stopped as his gaze came to rest on the visitors. The crease in his brow deepened as if in an effort of memory.

"Lady Carncross and Sir Archibald," Netta supplied. "I cannot remember if you were introduced to them last night."

"Reintroduced. I retain some memories of my

distant past." With a lessening of his frown that might be taken for a smile, he advanced into the room and bowed over Lady Carncross's hand, then awarded a curt nod to her son.

Sir Archy watched him through narrowed eyes. "Convenient, your returning from India just when you did."

"Yes, is it not?" Cousin Phemie beamed on Roland. "I declare, I do not know how we would go on without a gentleman in the house."

Netta kept to herself the reflection that she might like to try. This gentleman did not seem safe for her peace of mind. Or body, either, if he had tried to murder her.

Sir Archy drew out his snuffbox once more. "Been thinking it's time I bought a townhouse. Be glad of the benefit of your opinion, Netta. Something bang up to the mark, you know. In the first stare of elegance." He turned to Roland as he flicked open the enameled lid. "Care for a pinch? My own special sort, for morning use. Have it made up for me by Fribourg and Treyer. Just a hint of ambergris." He extended the box.

Roland waved it away. "Cousin Netta, might I have a word with you?"

She frowned. "Perhaps in a bit?"

"The matter is of some urgency."

Lady Carncross rose. "We must be on our way."

"But there is no need—"

The woman waved Netta's protest aside. "We

63

shall call upon you later, my dear. And do not forget my offer." With a significant glance at Roland, she took her leave, her dutiful son in tow.

After seeing them to the door, Netta turned on Roland. "You were extremely rude to Sir Archy."

He waved that aside. "If he only comes to play off the airs of an exquisite, he must come to expect such treatment."

Phemie shook her head. "She was quite right in one respect, my love. Although I cannot consider Desmond's death to be a tragedy, the consequences over the next few days must be quite unpleasant. Having the house draped in black crepe quite lowers my spirits."

"You must not say so, Cousin Phemie," Netta protested.

"Pray, and why not? Is there something wrong with disliking black?"

"Not in the least. But you must not let it be known you are glad Desmond is dead."

"Oh, fiddle. He was quite the most detestable boy. I have always thought so, even when he was a child. How Lavinia could dote upon him has always amazed me."

"Perhaps she recognized the similarities between them," Roland murmured.

Phemie nodded. "I daresay you are right."

"Do not encourage her so." Netta frowned at Roland and observed this made no effect on the exasperating man. "And do not forget we must still break the news to Great-aunt Lavinia." She regarded her two companions, both of whom her elderly relative despised, and accepted her fate. "It had best come from me, I suppose. Now," she addressed Roland, "what do you have to say to me that is of such importance?"

"Actually, I merely thought to free you of unwelcome visitors."

"Did you, indeed?" Her indignation swelled. "I am quite capable of doing that for myself, thank you. *If* I want to. There is not the least need for you to interfere."

"Now, my love, I am sure Roland knows best. So kind of him to wish to spare you any strain. Such care as he takes of us."

"Such meddling, you mean." She glared at him. "I am not a child in need of a nursemaid."

He inclined his head, but made no other response.

Her jaw tightened. "How do the funeral arrangements progress?"

He raised his eyebrows in an expression of mild surprise. "I thought you wished nothing to do with them."

"Since I was betrothed to him," she said through clenched teeth, "you should have realized the matter might be of some small interest to me."

"I beg your pardon. What are your wishes?"

She might have found the apology more acceptable had he not sounded as if he humored a child on the verge of a tantrum. She sought for suitably scathing terms in which to tell him.

Phemie patted her arm. "There, my love, Roland is quite right not to bother you with the dreary details. Let us just leave everything in his capable hands. Gentlemen always know best, do they not?"

Roland's lips twitched, softening the sternness of his expression. "I doubt very much you shall bring her to agree, Aunt. Will you not see to the ordering of the cards from the proper stationer? We must not slight his memory. He was, after all, Tavistock."

And now Roland had inherited the title. Netta stalked away, feeling his gaze piercing her back. Not for a moment could she afford to forget that only she stood between him and a country estate.

And had Desmond not drained the wedding goblet — an unforeseeable circumstance — Roland would now be making funeral arrangements for two.

Chapter Four

Mr. Benjamin Frake, elbows propped on the edge of his small table, stared moodily into the cup of coffee he held in his hands. Unpleasant business, murder, especially when it involved members of the ton. Fortunately, it wasn't that common. He could remember another case, though, and only last year, when a young marchioness had been stabbed to death in her box at the opera, of all places.

Beside him, an aging marmalade tom finished the last of its breakfast scraps and began its ablutions.

Mr. Frake shook his head. "Give me a nice, uncomplicated domestic bludgeoning any time, Sylvester. Much easier."

The cat regarded him through yellow eyes, then returned its attention to the pressing matter of one hind leg.

"Yes, sir." Frake rose and went to his window, which looked down on a narrow alley behind Covent Garden. "A nice, clear-cut act of spontaneous violence. That's what I like. None of this sneaking around slipping poison into cups. Cowardly, that seems. What do you think?"

Sylvester, intent on his paw, ignored him.

"Not venturing any guesses yet? Can't say as I blame you. What we need here is a motive. Now, who has something to gain from this earl's death, I ask you? Hmmm?" He paced to the chimney piece and picked up the briarwood pipe that rested there and absently rubbed his thumb over the gnarled grain. "On the one hand, this Lady Henrietta might have been the one to poison her betrothed. On the other, someone else altogether might have wanted to be rid of them both."

Sylvester stopped in mid-lick and fixed his unwavering regard on him.

"What, you think it most likely someone wanted the earl dead and didn't care if Lady Henrietta died right along with him?" Frake drew a deep breath and chewed on the much-mangled mouthpiece, considering. "Well, in either of the last two instances, I'd wager our most likely candidate would be this Roland Galbraith—Tavistock, now. The eighth earl. That's not something you can wave a stick at—nor a tail, neither," he added as Sylvester stood and stretched, swaying that appendage in the air. "But don't you go thinking I'm all fixed on that solution. Not by a long shot, I'm not. Never ignore other possibilities, that's my motto. Some surprising answers can turn up if you look in every nook and cranny."

He slid the unlit briarwood into the depths of one pocket, set his curly beaver on his close-cropped blond hair, and picked up the walking cane which rested in a stand by the door. "Come, Sylvester, there are people I must see this morning."

The cat rubbed against his ankles, depositing a number of orange hairs on the otherwise impeccable boots. Together they made their way along the narrow hall and down the stairs to the alley below. There they parted ways, the cat to pursue its own interests and the Runner to continue his inquiries.

When Frake reached St. Martin's Lane, he hailed a hackney which eventually set him down in Half Moon Street at the elegant townhouse occupied by Mr. Josiah and Lady Beatrix Underhill. For a long moment he stood in the street, staring up at the windows, mentally reviewing the notes he had taken the evening before during his brief but enlightening conversation with the butler at Tavistock House.

With a curt nod to himself, he mounted the steps and applied the knocker. After several minutes the door swung wide to reveal an imperious individual of commanding height and skeletal frailty. His balding head sloped down to a high forehead and a beaky nose set between a pair of dark, piercing eyes. Frake squared his shoulders. "Benjamin Frake of Bow Street to see Mr. Underhill."

The butler stepped back, permitting him to enter, then showed him into a small sitting room on the ground floor and left him to kick his heels.

Frake wandered about the apartment, appraising the contents. Not in the first style of elegance, he decided. Rented furnished for the season, he was willing to wager, and probably got for a bargain. Although the address was unimpeachable, the owners had not indulged in any great expense over the appointments.

From his breast pocket he drew out his Occurrence Book and jotted a note to himself to check on the Underhill financial position.

Perhaps ten minutes passed before Underhill erupted into the room, a scowl on his heavy features. He marched up to Frake and peered at him, his too-solid frame leaning precariously forward. "Hah!" he pronounced. "Runner, are you? Why the devil is a Runner bothering me?"

Frake stood his ground. "I regret to inform you that his lordship, the earl of Tavistock, died early this morning after consuming a dose of poisonous oleander."

Underhill blinked. "What the devil did he want to go and do that for?"

"If you mean die, I doubt he had the choice," Frake pointed out. "If you mean take the poison, I doubt he did that by choice, either. Someone poured it into the wedding goblet he drank from."

Underhill stood stock still for a very long moment. "Hah!" he declared once again. "Demmed rum business. So, who finally took all they could stomach from him?"

"That is what I am attempting to ascertain. Now, sir, if I might ask you some questions?"

Underhill blinked. "What for?"

"Just a formality, sir. I need to know where you were at the time his lordship sent for the wedding goblet—in case you might have seen anyone tamper with it."

Underhill, who had begun to thrust out his jaw in belligerence, deflated. "Oh." He frowned in an effort of thought. "Near the refreshment table, I think. Wondering how soon I could leave. Number of people about. Demmed over-crowded affair. Can't see why people get so set up about such things. Uncomfortable, if you ask me."

"I am asking you." Frake did his best to give the impression of one who hung on his every word. "Hot, was it?"

"Aye, that's the ticket. Went to get something to drink. So had everyone else, it felt like."

"Did you see the footman bring out the wedding goblet?"

"Might have. Can't say as I paid it any heed. Rubbishing business, that ridiculous toast. Can't see why Lady Henrietta went along with it. Decent gel, that. Doesn't have her head all stuffed with nonsense like others I could name."

Frake checked his list of questions. "Are you in London for the Season?"

Underhill snorted. "As little of it as I could manage. Only came up two weeks ago."

"You don't care for London?"

"Can't stand it, except for the cockpits and bear-baiting. Now, there's some real sport to be had at a good dogfight, mind, but give me a fowling piece and a brace of pheasants any day."

Frake tapped his notebook. "Why did you come up then?"

"Beatrix, of course. M'wife. Likes to waste the ready at the gaming hells. Poor sport for her in the country. Only problem is that it brings her too close to that demmed scoundrel."

"Tavistock, do you mean?"

"Aye, who else? Forever turning up at the same houses as she, with never a good word to say. Finally had to order her to leave any table he joined. That put paid to his account."

"I can imagine it did." So, for some reason, Desmond Galbraith had persecuted Lady Beatrix Underhill. Interesting. He jotted down a note to that effect, then turned back to his host. "And now, if I might have a word with her ladyship?"

A crimson hue suffused Underhill's face. "What the devil for? She had nothing to say to such a dashed here-'n'-therein."

"Now, why would you go a-calling him that?" Frake allowed only the mildest curiosity into his voice.

Underhill's fists clenched into punishing bunches of fives. "Taken to flogging his lamed hunters in Hyde Park to unwary Cits and young bucks not up to snuff. All in an attempt to out-run the constable. No wonder he'd at last agreed to go through with that wedding."

"Not eager to tie the knot, were they? Or so I hear."

Underhill snorted. "Been dragging their feet for years. Never would have done it at all if they could have found some way to get around her father's will."

No, no love lost in that quarter. Frake jotted down another note. "Now, sir. If I might speak with her ladyship? And I'd rather break the news about Tavistock to her myself, if you don't mind."

Underhill bristled, but beyond muttering "demmed impertinence," made no objection. He rang for his butler, then sent that individual to locate Lady Beatrix.

Several minutes passed in silence — except for Underhill's muttered oaths — before that lady put in an appearance. She paused on the threshold, a no-nonsense figure robed in a simple round gown of serviceable muslin. She had dragged back her thick black hair, fastening it into a becoming chignon. A pair of piercing gray eyes and a firm chin dominated her face. No air of nervousness or guilt hung about her, Frake noted — though he well knew how little that could mean.

"Mr. — Frake?" She raised inquiring eyebrows, looking first at him, then at her husband.

Frake stepped forward to bow over her hand.

Retaining it, he led her farther into the room and to a chair. She sat on the edge.

"I am afraid I am the bearer of bad news," he began, and launched into a brief explanation.

Not a trace of a reaction could he detect, except for the twitching of a muscle at the edge of her mouth. After a long moment's silence, her gaze, which had been fixed on his face, shifted sideways to seek out her husband.

"It's all right, Trixie. He knows we ain't— wasn't—on the best of terms."

She fixed Frake with her unwavering regard. "That don't mean we either of us take pleasure in his death."

"A very proper sentiment, I am sure." And not one to which she paid more than lip service, either, he reckoned.

A slight frown creased her brow, which she eased almost at once. The lady, it seemed, entertained mixed feelings concerning the murder. He must proceed with caution.

He turned to Underhill. "Thank you for your cooperation, sir. I'll not detain you any longer. Her ladyship can tell me anything else I need to know."

Underhill's lower lip jutted out in obstinacy.

"Yes, do go, Josiah," his wife said. "Think you I'm not able to answer a few simple questions on my own?"

Underhill humphed, cast an irritated glance at Frake, and took himself off.

Frake watched the door as it slammed shut behind the man, then turned to face Lady Beatrix. She perched on her chair, back straight, hands folded in her lap. A slight whiteness about the knuckles caught his attention, and he fixed his piercing regard on her face and read the falsity of her fixed smile. Defiance? Nerves? Well, well, well.

Her chin rose, her gaze meeting his. "What do you want to know?"

No beating about the bush, here, it seemed. "Did you game with Tavistock on a regular basis?"

She hesitated a moment. "Yes. Capital player at piquet. Always gave me a good game, which is more than I can say for others."

"Even after your husband forbade your sitting at his tables?"

"Yes." Again, the slight hesitation. "Can't have a man coming down all over me and dictating what I do, can I?" She shrugged. "Makes him so happy to think he rules the roost, I let him believe it. Then I go my own way."

So, a determined woman adept at deception. To what lengths might she go to prevent her husband's discovery of her little game? He scribbled a quick note in his Occurrence Book, then turned back to her. "Did your association with Tavistock extend beyond the gaming tables?"

"Beyond the—" She broke off with a laugh. Only the slightest tremor betrayed her nervousness.

She hid something, Frake decided, but what?

"What possible interest could a man of Tavistock's stamp have for me?" she asked.

Frake allowed that to pass. "Did you come near the wedding goblet last night?"

She tilted her head to one side, frowning. "No idea," she said at last. "If I did, I didn't pay it any heed."

"Would it surprise you to be told you had been seen staring at it?" One of the footmen, in fact, had recalled her in considerable detail.

"Was I? Doesn't surprise me, exactly. Could well have been seen staring at any number of things all over the ballroom, for all I know. Had a tiresome matter on my mind."

"That being?"

She shook her head. "Nothing of interest to you."

Frake jotted a question mark into his book. "Now, my lady. Would you consider your husband to have a violent temper?"

"Violent? No. Barks a great deal, and loudly, mind, but he's never been known to take so much as a nip out of anyone."

Did he believe that? Frake regarded her through narrowed eyes. She didn't quite disguise her nervousness. Had he come close to the mark? He would do well to investigate her gaming activities a bit closer. He nodded to himself. "Where did you play most often?"

"You mean with Tavistock? At a place called A Club House, in Bennet Street. One of his favorites, that one. And Mrs. Wickham's, off Jermyn Street." Her eyes shifted, as if with racing thoughts. "Gamed there most recently," she added.

"And when was that?"

She drew a deep breath. "Night before last."

Frake smiled. The night before he died. That sounded like a house he would do well to visit in the very near future.

After thanking her, he took his leave and set forth for Jermyn Street. He found the direction with little trouble and mounted the steps and knocked.

A fresh-faced maid in apron and mobcap, from beneath which a fluff of dusky curls peeked, opened the door. She clutched a feather duster in one hand and regarded him through wide brown eyes. "Yes, sir?"

"I wish to see Mrs. Wickham." He gave her an encouraging smile.

"She ain't up yet, sir. Not 'til noon, and even then she don't always leave her chamber afore two."

"I'm afraid today she will have to. Please tell her Mr. Benjamin Frake has called. From Bow Street."

The girl's mouth dropped open. "Lawks!" she breathed, and backed away. "Oh, sir, we ain't done nothin' wrong, has we?"

"Not as I'm aware of—yet."

Her mouth formed an O, and she turned on her heel and scurried up the stairs.

Frake, smiling, strolled into the entry hall and

closed the door behind himself.

Someone had decorated with a lavish hand in not quite the best of taste. Bright red paper sprigged with gold fleur-de-lis covered the walls, which were hung at intervals with gilt-framed mirrors and candle sconces. The occasional tables showed nicks in their carved wooden legs, and an elaborate flower arrangement of roses and chrysanthemums didn't quite cover the chips in the bowl.

He placed his hat on one of the tables. Strolling over the worn carpet, he tried to imagine the setting in flickering light, as its owner meant it to be seen. Impressive enough, he decided. Morning light could often be cruel to those who dazzled by night.

Heavy footsteps sounded down the hall, and a man with all the appearance of a hung-over butler hove into view. He stopped dead, gave his head a careful shake, straightened his coat, and came forward. Frake repeated his request, adding that a maid had gone to inform their mistress. The butler's lips thinned into a straight line. With little ceremony, he consigned Frake to a front salon decorated in a similar style only in green and gold, and vanished once more.

Frake hoped he hadn't gotten the maid into trouble. A taking little thing, much like his own dear Moira had been—he shut out thoughts of his long-dead wife. He had another, more current, tragedy with which to deal. Though he had yet to meet anyone who actually mourned Desmond Galbraith, seventh earl of Tavistock.

A plump woman, wrapped in a startling dressing gown of puce and gold, swept into the room, her impossibly yellow ringlets tumbling about her shoulders. She bore all the appearance of one dragged from much-needed slumber.

She smiled with lips tinged a bright red. "Mr. Frake? Of Bow Street? You must forgive Annie for deserting you in the hall. She is quite new, you see. She will be reprimanded, of course."

"Pray do not. I fear I gave her quite a shock." Annie. He liked the name.

His hostess seated herself on a sofa, then half-reclined. She waved him toward a padded chair opposite. "What may I do for you? I must confess, I cannot imagine what brings you here. No one has ever had cause to complain of my little house before."

"Nor has anyone now," he assured her. Again, he repeated the reason for his errand. To his surprise, tears welled in the woman's eyes.

"Tavistock? Oh, how dreadful. The dear man. You must know he has honored us with his visits from the very night we opened our doors. So often he has praised me for the quality of my suppers, for you must know I take the greatest pride in them, ordering only the newest peas and the freshest salmon and the finest wine I can afford. It never does to economize when it comes to a gentleman's stomach, does it? Tavistock." Her eyes filmed again. "Oh, how we shall miss him. Who could have done this dreadful thing?"

"That is what I am trying to ascertain, ma'am. Now, perhaps you could tell me if anything untoward occurred the night before last. Any argument or disagreement?"

"Oh dear." She clasped her hands together and stared into the empty grate. "No, I can think of nothing. But then we have several rooms, you see, and I try to circulate among them all. It would not do for my guests to feel neglected, would it?"

With this he agreed, hiding the reflection that this once, it might have been a good idea. "You must have help?" he suggested.

Mrs. Wickham brightened. "Indeed I do. Captain Palfrey and my own dear nephew run tables for me. Let me just send for them."

By the time these two gentlemen appeared, Frake had learned a great deal about the troubles of operating a discreet gaming establishment.

Captain Palfrey, a retired officer who walked with a decided limp, leaning on a cane, shook his graying head in answer to Frake's repeated question. "I only remember seeing him at supper that night," he said at last. "He seemed in excellent spirits, as I recall, and said for once the luck all ran his way. You don't suppose some foolish devil lost a fortune to him, do you?"

"He never said so," young Mr. Wickham protested. He disposed his lanky form in a chair beside his aunt. "For him, leaving a table without having scribbled a mountain of vowels would make it an excellent night. Hadn't a head for cards, though he liked to think he was all the crack."

"Who did he play with?" Frake added another note to his list.

Mr. Wickham and Captain Palfrey exchanged frowning gazes. "Lady Beatrix Underhill," Wickham said at last. "I remember her jumping away from the table when her husband entered the room. And that young sprig, what's his name? Only his second visit." He turned to his aunt. "You know, the one who fancies himself a tulip and is constantly sprinkling snuff all over the carpets?"

Mrs. Wickham closed her eyes. "Carncross," she pronounced after a moment's thought. "Sir Archibald Carncross."

Frake masked his reaction. So, Sir Archibald Carncross had gamed with Tavistock that night. Very interesting. He would have to learn more of that young gentleman's gaming habits.

Mr. Wickham named several others, all men of fashion of whom Frake had heard, but who had not been in attendance at the betrothal ball.

"You've forgotten Mr. Lambert," Captain Palfrey said suddenly.

"Mr. Kenneth Lambert?" Frake's eyes narrowed.

"That's right." Mr. Wickham nodded. "Spent the evening drinking himself into a stupor, if I remember rightly. I don't think he changed tables at all."

After cudgeling their memories for several minutes more, the two gentlemen produced the names of three more gamesters, none of whom interested Frake in the least. With thanks for everyone's cooperation, he saw himself to the door. Annie, he noted with a touch of regret, was nowhere to be seen. He donned his hat and set forth to interview some of the other ball guests.

Perhaps she should have taken Lady Carncross up on her invitation, Netta reflected. She hesitated in the hall outside the bookroom door, where Roland had closeted himself with Desmond's man of affairs. She couldn't like sharing the townhouse with him—his mere presence disturbed her, and that in itself she found disturbing. She was far too aware of him. Like a case of measles.

"Ah, there you are, my dear." Cousin Phemie fluttered up to her. "So much to do, I vow I do not know whether I am on my head or my heels. So many things to inventory for Roland. Dear Roland. I find it hard to think of him as Tavistock, though why I should is a mystery. I grew quite accustomed to Desmond in your papa's shoes."

Netta led the effusive little woman a few steps down the hall. "You are glad he is here," she stated.

Phemie beamed on her. "But of course. Are

not you?"

"I don't know," Netta admitted in a rush of candor.

"Now, dear," Phemie patted her arm, "you must not give credit to those vicious tales your Great-aunt Lavinia has told about him. Spiteful old woman."

Netta gave an evasive response. Lavinia's and Phemie's feud had existed for as long as Netta could remember, probably dating back to Lavinia's having been instrumental in Roland's being expelled from the family and England. "Cousin Phemie, you said something last night—" She hesitated, unsure how to continue.

"Yes, dear?" The gaze from the woman's gray eyes rested on her, her expression bright and helpful.

"About Desmond's threatening to turn you out of our household."

Phemie's mouth tightened. "Detestable boy. And I make no doubt he would have done it, too, and nothing you could have said would have made the least difference to him. He knew I had nowhere to go, but if that wasn't just like him—"

The door behind them opened, and Phemie broke off. Roland emerged with the elderly man who had for so long managed her family's affairs. He greeted Netta with a warm smile and words of condolence.

Netta responded, trying to ignore Roland and his sardonic expression. Why must he make her feel guilty that she did not mourn more deeply? She certainly experienced a great sadness at losing someone with whom she had shared her childhood. Yet at the moment, with the shock still new, uppermost in her mind loomed the relief that she did not have to wed him.

They made their way to the front hall, where Roland saw his visitor out. Phemie invited Netta to join her in the housekeeper's room to go over the inventory lists, but Netta declined, claiming urgent business. As soon as the little woman bustled off, Roland turned to Netta.

"Urgent business?" he inquired.

Netta straightened to her full, if meager, height. She would not let him overwhelm her — even if she did find herself annoyingly breathless. "I wish to speak with you."

His eyebrows rose. "A weighty matter, I perceive. In the bookroom?" He stood back for her to lead the way along the corridor.

Once inside, Netta crossed to the hearth, fighting her nerves. The myriad questions she wanted to ask jumbled inside her head. He was her second cousin, yet a virtual stranger. She knew only Great-aunt Lavinia's tales, her own fear-filled memories . . .

"What may I do for you?"

His deep voice sent a longing through her for she knew not what. "Why did you come back?" she blurted out.

"Is it so unnatural I should return to the land

of my birth?"

"Did you not like India? You spent more than half your life there."

"That does not necessarily mean I did so by choice." His tone held an edge.

She looked down at her clasped hands. "But why *now?* You've been gone seventeen years, with hardly a word except to Cousin Phemie."

"I was banished," he reminded her, "not sent on holiday."

With that she couldn't argue. She raised her gaze to his face, with its rough planes and chiseled angles. "You know perfectly well what I mean. You returned for Desmond's and my wedding, did you not?"

He leaned back against the desk. "In part. Nothing my Aunt Phemie wrote to me indicated any degree of attachment existed between you and Desmond." He looked down at one elegantly booted foot, then directly into her eyes. "It sounded to me as if you might be constrained against your will. If that proved to be the case, I intended to prevent it."

For a moment, she could only stare at him in open-mouthed astonishment as resentment rushed through her. Apparently, he misinterpreted her silence. A smile—somewhat condescending, she thought—just touched his lips.

"My Little Hen. Did you think your Big Cousin would do less for you?"

"Yes," came her blunt response. "Not one word did you vouchsafe to me through all those years, yet you honestly think I ought to welcome your interference now, and in a matter as important as my marriage?"

His smile never wavered. "Interference? Rather, I sought to look after your interests in your father's absence."

"I see. 'Big Cousin,' indeed. Did it not occur to you that I am no longer a child? I have long since cut my eye teeth and am quite capable of looking after myself."

"Are you? I admit, you do not seem as biddable as the circumstances might indicate."

Her lip curled. "Just try and 'bid' me do something and see what comes of it."

"I would not be so brave."

"Wouldn't you?" Her bravado wavered and she eyed him in uncertainty. "You seem to me very much the type of man who is accustomed to doing precisely as he wishes."

"Now we come to it," he murmured. "Do you, perchance, mean something like removing the only man who stood between me and a title? There is no need to answer, I see it in your face. You have only to add that oleander is native to India—where, as you have just pointed out, I have spent over half my life. And to save you the trouble of asking the next obvious question, yes, I have seen the effects of someone being so unwise as to cook food with oleander branches. The results were exactly as you observed with Desmond last night."

Netta turned away, feeling ill at the memory

of her cousin's agonies.

"What, Little Hen, have you no taste for plain speaking? I thought you would find it refreshing."

"I do." She mastered herself. "You said you don't want to be Tavistock. What do you want?"

His mouth thinned. "Does that matter now?"

She didn't answer, merely waited for him to continue.

He drew a deep breath. "I want quiet, to live retired, away from people. Not to be faced with a never-ending parade of problems and unwanted responsibilities."

"That sounds very dull."

"It may seem so to you, but after the difficulties of creating a life for myself on the other side of the world, it seems ideal to me." He raised challenging eyebrows. "Have I succeeded in answering your questions?"

"I don't know." For a long moment she stared at him, confused by his tension, his professed motives, and by her conflicting desires to both rage at him and seek refuge at his side. Instead of doing either, she retreated from the room, hurrying away down the hall. Sometimes, she assured herself, escape proved the best strategy.

She couldn't think clearly when he towered over her. It was hard enough when he filled her thoughts. Did he truly mean what he said about wanting a quiet life? How ironic that he should inherit the London townhouse while the country estate became hers.

The country estate. And she might have—probably *should* have—died along with Desmond.

Had Roland returned to England to obtain the title—and estate—before they passed beyond his reach with the arrival of an infant heir or two?

She reached the stairs and started blindly up, only to be startled by a strangled gasp. She looked up and saw Lady Beatrix Underhill above her. The woman clung to the banister as if she had halted a precipitous flight down. Her large eyes, wide with alarm, rested on Netta.

Chapter Five

"Lady Henrietta." Color flooded Lady Beatrix's cheeks, replacing the unnatural pallor of her normally olive complexion. The next moment, she recovered. "There you are." She came down the next few steps. "Can't imagine where that butler of yours took himself off to. Went to find you, but he's been gone this age and more."

"May I help you?" Netta regarded her in uncertainty, taking in the forest green velvet riding habit with its trailing skirt caught up in the woman's gloved hand. A high hat of mannish design perched on her dark hair, which she wore smoothed back from her squarish face. The aroma of roses hung about her. Netta found it overpowering, not at all like the pleasant scent Cousin Phemie concocted in their stillroom.

A moment passed before Lady Beatrix answered. "Came to pay a call of condolence."

Did she? The idea didn't seem likely. "Will you not come into the salon?" Netta suggested.

"Can't stay." Lady Beatrix shook her head.

"That's why I took the liberty of seeking you in the sitting room above. Should have only left my card, I suppose. Shouldn't have disturbed you at such a time. But when I learned about Tavistock, knew I must come."

That, Netta reflected, held the ring of truth. But *why*, precisely, had she felt she needed to call?

Lady Beatrix turned her considering eye on Netta. "Must say, glad to see you ain't all knocked to flinders over this. Bad business. Still, it's an ill wind and all that. Now, don't disturb yourself. Let myself out." With a brisk nod, she swept past Netta and down the remaining stairs.

Netta followed and saw her to the front door, then turned slowly back into the hall. Their acquaintance with the Underhills hardly warranted such a gesture of friendship as a condolence call. From Lady Beatrix's husband, in fact, she might expect a congratulatory message.

So what *had* brought Lady Beatrix? And what had taken her up the stairs?

Netta mounted the steps. On the first floor she hesitated, then decided to ignore the sitting room Lady Beatrix had claimed for her destination. She could think of nothing there that might draw the woman. But what would?

Something to do with Desmond's death.

Netta turned to gaze down the staircase with unseeing eyes. Desmond had kept his papers in the bookroom on the ground floor. But Lady Beatrix had gone *up*. To Desmond's bedchamber?

The shocking thought refused to be dismissed.

Had Lady Beatrix gone to Desmond's private apartment—for what purpose? Netta found herself halfway up the next flight before she realized she had moved.

Desmond's chamber stood just beyond the landing, a large sunny room overlooking the front of the house. She hesitated at the door. His body had been removed to the main drawing room, where even now the servants draped everything in enough black crepe to dress half of London. There must be nothing lacking in the display of mourning for the seventh earl of Tavistock.

Firming her resolve, Netta opened the door and stepped inside. Except for briefly last night, she had not entered this private retreat since her father's death—and Desmond's succeeding to both the title and the room. As she looked about, she found her surroundings distressingly unfamiliar.

Desmond had redecorated it to fit his taste—with comfort foremost in mind and every sign of luxury suitable to his exalted station in life. It put her forcibly in mind of him. Faint odors lingered, of sickness, of various potions and purgatives. Of death. And of roses.

Roses. So, Lady Beatrix had entered Desmond's chamber. But *why?* What had she hoped to gain—or find? Or had she come to remove something—such as any trace of her presence she might have left on an earlier visit?

The olfactory assault sent a queasy sensation through the pit of her stomach, and she crossed to the window and threw the sash wide. For a long minute she stood in the fresh air, breathing deeply, reordering her senses. She knew Desmond held her in no affection, that he indulged himself with a certain set of females referred to as the muslin company. She found it easy to believe he might have carried on a liaison with his enemy's wife in his own house. What she found difficult to accept was Lady Beatrix's participation in such an arrangement.

"What are you doing in here?" Roland's deep voice sounded from the doorway.

Netta spun about and felt her cheeks warm, embarrassed as if she'd been a child caught out in an indiscretion. Vexed with herself, she took refuge in attack. "Is there any reason I should not have come?"

Sardonic amusement glinted in his eyes. "I believe as executor it is proper for me to seal this room until I can go through its contents with Desmond's man of affairs."

As executor. And as new owner, she reminded herself, and found the thought foreign. Not her father's chamber anymore, not even Desmond's. Now it would be Roland's. She looked up to find his gaze still resting on her, his expression frowning. "If you must know," she said, "I encountered Lady Beatrix on the stair. She had been in here."

His eyebrows rose. "You are certain?"

"Can you not smell her scent?" Netta wrinkled her nose at the strong fragrance that still hovered in the air.

"Hers, is it?" He seemed to consider. "No, roses aren't like you. You prefer violets."

He'd noticed? That surprised her.

"What did she do in here?" He strolled to the hearth and bent to check the empty grate.

"I don't know."

He straightened, frowning. "How did she know which room was his?"

Netta's mouth tightened.

"Ah." His eyes glinted. "Pray, don't be missish, Little Hen. You cannot tell me you didn't know what he was like. Still," he added as they left the room, "it seems odd he'd bring her to his own house."

Netta made it through the rest of the day by avoiding Roland, first by mending one of her old mourning gowns, then by answering the cards of condolence that arrived with what should have been gratifying regularity. Only twice did she see Cousin Phemie. The woman had taken it upon herself to oversee the decking of the household in mourning, and bustled about murmuring in a disjointed manner. Netta stayed away from the drawing room where her cousin lay in state. All too soon — or was that not soon enough? — the funeral cortege would set forth for Ravenswood Court and the seventh earl's final resting place.

She at last dressed for dinner in the ancient but newly mended bombazine, then regarded her reflection in the cheval glass with distaste. Black always left her skin so very pale against the vibrant tint of her fiery hair. Almost as if she had been ill. Even her faint tracery of freckles faded, lending her a fragile, vulnerable appearance at odds with her nature.

She lingered in her chamber, even after Wembly finished arranging her hair. The prospect of seeing Roland again disturbed her. She closed her eyes, trying to sort out her confused emotions about him. She knew him from tales—from her own experiences—as the devil incarnate, yet she didn't fear him as she ought. She felt . . . anger? Was that the elusive sensation she hadn't been able to name? Or was it merely frustration tempered by a bit of fascination?

Had he changed from the cruel youth of Great-aunt Lavinia's stories? Seventeen long and undoubtedly eventful and difficult years had passed. They must have left their mark on him. Had they made him more devious, able to disguise his unpleasant nature—or had they tempered him?

Another question she could not answer. She had best go down to the salon; he and Cousin Phemie must be awaiting her by now. The prospect left her uneasy, and for a moment she actually toyed with the thought of having her dinner brought up on a tray.

Heavens, what nonsense was this? She was no schoolroom miss to cower from her formidable cousin. Or did she cower from the unpredictable tangle of emotions and reactions he created in her?

Now, *there* was a melodramatic thought if she'd ever had one! But still true, a little voice whispered in the back of her mind. She ignored it and turned her humorous regard on her reflection in the glass. "Definitely," she announced. "If I cannot bring Ravenswood to support itself, without a doubt I shall be able to earn my living in the writing of Cheltenham tragedies."

Feeling more her usual self, she descended the stairs. She would not give Roland the satisfaction of hiding from him. After all, what did she expect him to do? Murder her?

Very possibly, if he had already murdered Desmond.

Squaring her shoulders and tilting her chin upward, she marched down the hall and into the Green Salon where the family gathered before dinner.

Roland looked up from the side table where he poured himself a measure of amber wine, and his eyebrows rose. "Has something put you on end, Little Hen? You look as if you approached a guillotine."

Hot color flooded her cheeks. "I sincerely hope not," she said.

He set down his glass and picked up another decanter. "True. The world is rapidly running out of Galbraiths, is it not? Negus? Or do you prefer—" He broke off and inspected the contents of the third decanter. "Ratafia."

"Is that sherry you are drinking? I'll have that," she decided.

He filled a crystal glass and handed it to her.

Avoiding so much as a glancing touch of his

hand, she took it. She seated herself as far from him as she could and sipped the drink, then wrinkled her nose at the unexpected bitterness.

She returned her regard to Roland, who had paced to the hearth where he now leaned against the mantelpiece sipping his wine. She wasn't actually afraid of him, yet he filled her thoughts, setting her stomach churning. How she wished he had never returned to England.

And had Desmond cause to wish the same? she wondered.

She directed her assessing gaze over him, noting the breadth of his shoulders, the well-muscled leg that owed nothing of its perfection to padding. He dressed with elegance, she admitted, and showed to advantage in a drawing room. Something about the way he carried himself made her think he would not disgrace himself on horseback, either. A powerful man, this cousin she barely knew.

Was he also subtle enough to deal in poison?

He seemed too direct for that. She could imagine instead his breaking Desmond's neck in a fit of anger. But her father had always said Roland was clever, certainly clever enough to make his fortune and a new life for himself in India. Perhaps he learned other, more devious, arts there as well.

A slow awareness grew on her that he watched her, and once more warmth crept over her cheeks.

"Well?" he inquired. "Are you cataloging your reasons for despising me?"

"Have I any?" she countered, recovering.

A slow smile lit his eyes, easing his tension, investing the harsh planes of his face with an unexpected gentleness. "Little Hen," he murmured, and his lips twitched into a rueful smile. "Perhaps I should not be surprised, after all, at Desmond's coming to heel. You are the image of your mother."

Netta studied her glass. "She died trying to present my father with an heir."

"I know."

His tone held sympathy—not for her, but for her mother, Netta realized in surprise. "Of course, Cousin Phemie must have written you."

He confused her, thinking and behaving not as she expected him to, but in a very different way altogether. She felt drawn to him—and resisted. She took a too large swallow of the bitter drink and choked.

Cousin Phemie bustled through the doorway, her black crepe fluttering about her. She bent to kiss Netta on the cheek, and enveloped Roland in the warmth of her smile. "I am late. But there is no end to the many sad duties to be done. I have spoken to Cook, and he has decreed we must go to Gunter's for the funereal baked meats."

"Has he?" Roland's eyes kindled. "Does he not feel himself adequate to the occasion?"

"No, you must not take a pet, for indeed, I fear he is right. We must expect upwards of two hundred mourners, for though Desmond did not have as many friends as one might wish, his *position,* you know—"

"I do know." Roland's brow snapped down.

"The kitchen staff would be quite distracted, trying to concoct sufficient refreshments to entertain those who must surely come by. Cook fears he would not be able to set a decent dinner before you." She regarded him with anxiety.

A devil of amusement glinted in his eyes. "What, do you fear I shall take myself off to a club and leave you and Little Hen to face such meager gleanings at table? I could not be so shabby. Order what you will from Gunter's. And wine, I suppose. Is the cellar sufficiently stocked, or must we send to Berry Brothers and Rudd?"

Netta's lips twitched. "It is Christopher and Company now. Desmond prefers—preferred—French wines, which is their specialty."

Roland inclined his head. "I make no cavil."

"The cost, I fear—" Phemie regarded him in consternation.

"The estate can bear it."

"Can it?" Netta murmured, but only to herself.

Phemie sighed. "It is such a relief to have a gentleman take charge of all, is it not, my love?"

A fervent denial sprang to Netta's lips, but she bit it back.

Phemie accepted the glass of ratafia Roland held out to her. "Has my godson called?" She looked from Netta to Roland. "Mr. Kenneth Lambert?"

"Not to my knowledge." Netta took a contemplative sip of her wine. So much for Mr. Lambert's oft-repeated protestations of desiring to serve her by any means at his command. A love of gallantry often led gentlemen to make the most absurd remarks—especially when they knew the object of their supposed passions to be safely betrothed elsewhere.

Phemie plumped down into a padded chair and took a ladylike sip of her sweet drink. "To be sure, I quite thought—well, that is neither here nor there, is it?"

Roland drained his glass, then returned to the side table to pour another.

Phemie watched him through narrowed eyes. "You aren't smiling," she suddenly announced. "*That* is why you seem so very different. There, I knew I should hit upon it. You were always used to laugh, before. Does it not please you to be Tavistock?"

"It does not!" Roland halted his pacing. His features darkened, lending him a dangerous—or was that desperate?—appearance. "Of all positions I might wish to come into, this is the last."

"But—" Phemie regarded him in dismay.

He forced a poor excuse of a smile. "No, dear aunt, do not distress yourself. It is just that I have spent the greater part of my life in strife and doing what I must. I had promised myself a period of quiet. I find I have no taste for being tied down once more to responsibilities not of my choosing. I would rather be myself than 'Tavistock.' "

Again, with every word he spoke, he drove it

home to her that he would have preferred to inherit a country estate. And he still could. It would be easy to poison—She swallowed, then choked. "The sherry—"

Cousin Phemie looked up. "There, I told Desmond he should never have changed wine merchants."

Netta shook her head, still gasping.

Roland frowned. "It is a trifle bitter, perhaps, but surely not as bad as that."

Netta stared at him, her mind racing. Would he—*could* he—have slipped something into the wine, something like oleander? In another few minutes, would she, like Desmond, be rolling on the floor in agony?

But no, he had poured his own drink from the same decanter. And he had refilled his glass at least twice. She swallowed, and managed a shaky smile. "I—I merely swallowed wrong, and it did bite so."

"How very unlike Fenton not to have assured himself of the quality of the wine." Phemie shook her head of silvery blond ringlets, causing the black lace confection perched on them to slip. "Usually he takes such care when he decants a new bottle. The upset over poor Desmond, I make no doubt. We shall all go on much more comfortably once the funeral is over."

What an epitaph, Netta reflected. Yet the truth of Phemie's statement remained. They would go on much more comfortably in the future.

She found little appetite for the dinner shortly

placed before her. Phemie kept up a conversation, mostly one-sided except for Roland's occasional responses. Netta paid little heed. Exhaustion crept over her, a desire to retire to her chamber and sleep and sleep and sleep. In fact, it sounded a most excellent idea. As soon as the footmen removed the covers, she excused herself to Roland and Phemie.

Roland smothered a cavernous yawn. "Do you know, I believe it will do us all good to retire early. I, too, will bid you good night, Aunt Phemie." He stooped to kiss her cheek, then held the door for Netta to precede him from the room.

It must be the strain of Desmond's death, the lack of sleep the previous night. She could barely keep her eyes open. She mounted the steps and found her way to her room more by habit than conscious thought. Barely had she crawled between sheets before she fell asleep.

She awoke to a pounding headache and a room flooded with brilliant sunshine. With a groan she rolled over and covered her head with her pillow. Lassitude drained her of energy. She could easily stay here all day.

The thought revolted her. Normally she was up and doing barely an hour after Desmond dragged himself home from whatever gambling club he had honored with his all-night presence. Today she felt groggy—much, in fact, as Desmond described his own hung-over condition after broaching his fourth bottle scant hours before. Yet she had consumed no more than the one glass of sherry before dinner and a single glass of canary during the meal.

She swung her legs over the side of the bed and winced. Reaction to Desmond's death, she assured herself. She couldn't be sickening for something.

On her night table rested a tray bearing a roll and a cup of hot chocolate. Cool chocolate, rather. She sipped it, then set it aside. Not this morning. Instead, she nibbled on her roll while she awaited her abigail's answer to her summons.

Finally, dressed in the black bombazine and with her fiery hair under some semblance of control, she made her way downstairs. She avoided the breakfast parlor. The prospect of kidneys, eggs, and rare beef didn't appeal to her. What she would like would be a brisk canter through the Park to clear the lingering cobwebs from her mind. Fresh air, a bit of exercise—

Unfortunately, she had risen too late. Or had she? If she took her groom and avoided the main paths, perhaps she would encounter no one who would censure her need to escape the house for a little while. She went in search of a footman to send a message to the stable.

As she reached the ground floor, Roland approached down the hall, a scowl on his weathered countenance. Netta recoiled from the tangible wave of anger that emanated from him.

He looked up, as if sensing her presence, and the lines about his mouth tightened. "How did you sleep?" he demanded by way of greeting.

Netta blinked. As a polite conversational gambit, it lacked something in the delivery. "Quite well," she responded. "And you?" She tried a smile to show him how it should be done.

He ignored it. "As one dead. I was unusually tired last night, slept without stirring so much as once, and awoke unconscionably late with a blistering head. As if I had consumed several bottles, which I did not." He waited, eyebrows raised, watching her.

Her fingers strayed to her own temples, which still throbbed. "I thought it merely from the distress of the last day."

He nodded. "And so I might have believed, had not someone broken into the bookroom during the night and ransacked it."

Chapter Six

"Ransacked?" Netta stared at Roland, her eyes widening. Facetious comments about his having to be mistaken flitted through her mind, only to be dismissed. Roland, despite Great-aunt Lavinia's accusations, did not appear to Netta to be one who indulged in pointless hoaxes.

Instead, she started for the room. Roland stood out of her way, then followed along the hall. Reaching over her shoulder, he brushed against her as he thrust the door wide.

Awareness shot through Netta, of his power, his presence — of him. Startled, she moved away. He was the Big Cousin who dominated her, she reminded herself. Who treated her like a child. Who might want her dead.

And who was undeniably a man, in every fascinating sense of the word.

With an effort, she forced her attention from him. The bookroom had been ransacked, he had said. She had come here to see for herself . . .

She did see. Her gaze swept the cluttered apartment, taking in the papers that lay scattered across the Aubusson carpet, the desk drawers that stood open, their contents a jumble. Books lay strewn about the floor in haphazard piles, their shelves now almost empty.

"At least whoever it was did a nice, thorough job," she said at last. "Do you not just hate to see a task shabbily accomplished?"

A deep chuckle escaped Roland, though he winced as he advanced into the room. "Someone certainly has been looking for something. But what?" He raised inquiring eyebrows.

"What is Desmond likely to have kept in here?" she mused, more to herself than to him.

"Money? Jewelry?" Roland perched on the arm of a chair, watching her. "Documents?"

"Possibly all three." Or did he, perhaps, know? Again, nagging suspicions assailed her. Had it been Roland who tore this room apart? No, there would be no need for that. As executor of the estate, he had free access to anything he wanted.

She picked her way through the mess on the floor to the center of the room, then stopped to rub her aching head. Closing her eyes against the stabs of pain did little good.

"Do you not feel well?"

His voice sounded barely inches from her. She hadn't noticed him move, yet he stood before her, concern gentling his features. His intriguing features, which drew her in, enthralled her . . .

She stepped back, alarmed by her reactions. "It is no matter. I have the headache, that is all."

"I do also. And I might add that I slept as one

105

corned, pickled, and salted—or dosed with laudanum."

She stared at him. "Yes. As though we had been given laudanum. But how—The sherry! It tasted bitter last night. I remember thinking about it—then paid it no heed, for I noticed you drank from the same—" She broke off, vexed by what she revealed.

His mouth tightened. "I see. I drank, so you thought it safe after all. Allow me to set your fears at rest. I do not go in for poisoning. Someone else, though, appears to have gone in for a spot of drugging. And with us safely asleep and the servants in the attics, our housebreaker could proceed with impunity to tear the place apart with no one being disturbed. I believe we had best have in that Runner once more."

He rang for a footman, sent him on the errand, then escorted Netta from the room and locked the door behind him.

She raised her eyebrows. "Rather late for that, is it not?"

"I believe the Runner should see it as it is now. It would never do for some zealous housemaid to tidy things."

Together they made their way to the breakfast parlor. Netta took a chair near the window and stared out over the square and the garden beyond. Perhaps later she could escape there and walk for awhile alone. She could use a little time to sort out her chaotic feelings and impressions—a task that would have to be attempted far away from Roland's far too encroaching presence.

Roland brought her a cup of sweetened coffee, which she took with a word of suspicious thanks.

"Do you play piquet?" he asked.

"Yes. It was a passion of Papa's."

A reminiscent smile eased the harsh lines of his face. "He taught me the game when I was barely eight so he would have an opponent. Well, let us see if you do him credit." He pulled the bell rope, and when the footman arrived, sent for a deck of cards.

To Netta's satisfaction, she had not forgotten the subtle nuances of the play. Roland, though, held the obvious advantage of more recent practice and took the first two hands. The third went to her, winning a nod of approval from him. It pleased her to prove herself not so helpless to her "Big Cousin." Her headache, she noted, had faded.

They had barely started on a fourth game when a hackney pulled up before the house. Peering out the window, she saw the dapper figure of the Runner step out and pay the jarvey.

"He is here," she announced.

"That was quick." Roland swept the cards into a pile and started for the door. They reached the hall as Mr. Benjamin Frake turned his low-brimmed hat into the keeping of the butler.

The Runner saw them and nodded. "Your lordship. M'lady. Your good man here tells me you just sent for me. What's toward?"

"A break-in," Roland informed him.

The Runner's eyebrows rose. "Indeed, m'lord. That's interesting, very interesting indeed. If I may just have a look?"

At the bookroom, Roland drew the key from his pocket, fitted it into the lock, and pushed the door wide.

A soundless whistle escaped Mr. Frake, and he rocked back on his heels. "Well, well, well," he said, his voice soft and appreciative. He advanced into the apartment, his piercing blue eyes seeming to miss nothing.

Netta folded her arms, leaned against the wall, and waited. Roland, after a moment's pause, joined her. She cast a wary glance at him, then resumed her observation of the Runner.

Several times Mr. Frake stooped to pick up a paper, then set it aside into a neat pile. After perhaps five minutes, he nodded. "Someone made a cursory search, looking for one or more papers, which he may or may not have found. I believe we will now gather these together to see if we may discover what, if anything, is missing."

With three of them, the prospect seemed less daunting. Netta knelt on the floor with the others and began collecting sheets at random. When they had completed this and restored the books to the shelves, they carried the papers to a long table and sorted them into piles by subject. Most, Netta noted with dismay, proved to be tradesmen's bills.

As she added another daunting payment demand from Weston for a coat her cousin had never had a chance to wear, Cousin Phemie took a faltering step into the room. The little woman pressed a handkerchief to her temple, and the soothing aroma of lavender drifted from her.

"There you are, my dear." She seemed relieved to

see Netta. "And Roland. And Mr.—Frake, is it not? I cannot imagine what kept me abed so late, for you must know I always rise at an early hour. But I do not feel at all the thing, and I was wondering—Why, whatever is amiss?"

Netta rose at once. So, the ratafia had been drugged as well as the sherry. Someone, it seemed, took no chances. As she escorted her aged relative from the room, she explained.

"Merciful heavens!" Phemie regarded her in wide-eyed horror. Her hand fluttered to her pale cheek. "Do you mean we were poisoned—just like poor Desmond?"

"Not in the least," Netta assured her with a forced cheeriness. "Someone wished to be undisturbed with Desmond's papers, that is all. I daresay once we discover what has been taken, this whole dreadful business will be well on the way to being solved."

Phemie's hand trembled over her heart. "Such a shock. My poor system, for you must know I have the most delicate constitution—"

"Come, let me take you to Mrs. Garvey, and then you are to spend the day resting."

"But who—"

Netta silenced her gently. "I am sure we shall shortly learn all." Still murmuring encouragements and reassurances, Netta delivered Phemie into the capable hands of the housekeeper. Leaving the two women discussing possets and restoratives, Netta returned to the bookroom where the two men now studied the various piles.

"What have you found?" she asked.

Roland looked up, his piercing gaze resting on her, and she tried in vain to suppress the tremor of awareness that assailed her. Alarums clamored in her mind. This would never do. Surely she could not succumb to blatant masculinity and an intriguing aura of danger. She was not such a fool. She had best remain at daggers drawn with him—certainly it would be safer than being at "poisons poured." Her misguided attempt at humor left her shuddering.

"We have the results of his last night's gaming," Roland said.

Netta came forward. "He kept copies of his vowels?"

"Not in the least. He appears to have won."

"Desmond?" Shock replaced her disconcerting thoughts of a moment before. "No, you must be bamming me. There has never been a Galbraith who bet with impunity. Unless you do?" She looked at her cousin and realized how little she actually knew of him.

He shook his head. "I'm no gamester."

Mr. Frake cleared his throat. "I paid a call on the gaming house his late lordship visited on the night before his death and learned the names of those who sat at his table. Sir Archibald Carncross—and his vowels." He held up a small stack. "Lord Harcourt—and his." He held up another. "Mr. Edward Allington—and his." He gestured to a third pile. "We have found none from Lady Beatrix Underhill or from Mr. Kenneth Lambert."

Netta frowned. "Perhaps they won—or lost no more than they brought."

Mr. Frake shook his head. "Losses there were, m'lady. Deep doings at that house, very deep. I wonder if I will be able to ascertain the exact amount?"

"Then you believe someone broke in to—to recover their vowels before they must be redeemed."

Mr. Frake pursed his lips. "It does seem likely. And with your cousin dead, they must think themselves in the clear."

Netta glanced at Roland. "Did you tell him about the sherry?"

"I did." Roland leaned back in his chair.

Mr. Frake nodded. "Very clever, our man. Very clever indeed."

" 'Our man.' Do you think it Mr. Lambert, then? I do not believe he came near the house yesterday."

"But Lady Beatrix did." Roland came to his feet and strode about the now tidied apartment. "And she visited Desmond's chamber."

"Now, what is all this?" Frake demanded.

Briefly, Roland explained.

"Well, well, well," Frake muttered. "Do you believe she drugged the decanters when she couldn't find what she looked for? To give herself more time to search during the night?"

Netta shivered. Did that lady have a penchant for slipping drugs—or poisons—into beverages? But would she—or anyone else—murder Desmond to escape overwhelming debts of honor? Or did someone merely seize their opportunity once Desmond lay dead? She found she much preferred the thought of a debtor, rather than his heir, wanting him in his grave. And that realization dismayed her.

Fenton found them a short time later, going over the remaining papers. "Lady Carncross and Sir Archibald have called, Miss Netta. They are in the Blue Salon."

"I suppose I shall have to see them." Vexed, Netta rose.

"And I thought you quite enjoyed Sir Archibald's company," Roland murmured.

Netta cast him a fulminating look and exited the room with what dignity she could muster.

Sir Archy stood by the window in the salon, staring out onto the street and the garden beyond. Idly, he swung his ivory-handled walking stick. His mother perched on the edge of a Sheraton chair, her contemplative gaze resting on an assortment of knickknacks on the mantel. Inferior, Netta knew; Desmond had long since disposed of the Sèvres through discreet channels. She arranged her features into a polite expression of welcome and entered.

"Ah, my dear." Lady Carncross turned to her at once, all gentle smiles. "And how do you go on through this sad ordeal?"

"As well as can be expected." Netta seated herself on the sofa opposite.

Lady Carncross directed a meaningful glance at her son.

Sir Archy cleared his throat. "Black suits you, Netta. Very becoming." He strolled forward in a manner so nonchalant as to be awkward. Making a neat leg before her, he caught her hand and carried it to his lips for a brief salute. He retained her fingers, holding them in a warm clasp as he seated himself at her side. "Not too many depressing duties have fallen to you, I hope?"

"Cousin Phemie and Roland have been amazingly efficient." She drew away from him. "Still, there are any number of papers I must sort through."

His eyebrows rose. "Would have thought all that could be left in the hands of the executors or that Runner fellow. He—I don't suppose he's learned anything yet, has he? Must be dashed uncomfortable for you."

"It is," she agreed with considerable feeling. She forebore to tell him about the latest problem. Archy's vowels had not been among those taken.

That thought relieved her. She would hate to think her old friend capable of this latest crime. Lady Beatrix seemed the far more likely candidate for that.

Archy glanced at his mother, who made a shooing gesture at him. He cleared his throat once more. "Came to take you for a drive in the Park. Must be blue-deviled, just sitting about. Come with us."

Netta hesitated, then gave in to longing. She did want to escape and no one could attach any impropriety to her taking an airing with her country neighbors—both mother and son. "Let me just get my bonnet," she said, and hurried out the door.

She returned with both the chip-straw hat and a woolen shawl less than five minutes later. Her guests now awaited her in the hall, and their landau stood at the door. Archy handed in Netta and his mother, then took the facing seat himself.

Lady Carncross sighed. "Such a dear, obliging boy, is he not? Always eager to do any little service for his mama. I vow, it will be a lucky young lady he will wed. And mark my words, my dear, that day will not be long distant. It is my greatest fear some designing hussy with eyes on his position and fortune will entrap him."

Sir Archy blinked. "No, really, Mama, that's doing it too brown. Never marry to disoblige you, you know that."

"Dear boy." Lady Carncross beamed on him, then returned her attention to Netta. "Well, my dear, you look more the thing already. Fresh air. My doctor has told me times out of mind that nothing cures a fit of the megrims like a gentle outing." Her gaze rested on Netta's face, assessing. "There, it's shocking about poor Tavistock, of course, but I know you won't take it amiss if I say you are well out of that marriage. Too dominating, was Tavistock. No, a chit of your spirit wants a gentle husband." She looked once more at her son and nodded.

Archy leaned forward, bestowed a besotted smile upon Netta, and clasped her hand between his own.

Oh, no. Moodiness she accepted from him, gallantry she could not — especially when he did it so clumsily. He had never been much in the petticoat line; she'd thought of him as a friend, not a young mooncalf. She tried to draw her hand away, but he wouldn't let go. Instead, he cast an uncertain glance at his mama, as if checking for further instructions. Netta caught the encouraging nod of the woman's silvery head, and her irritation grew. With more firmness, she freed herself.

Lady Carncross didn't appear to notice. "Dear Archy. Such a matrimonial prize, with his air of elegance and fashion. I vow, the baronetcy will not weigh more than his person in a female's mind." She hesitated the merest fraction of a second. "It is such a pity he has no more estate than the Dower House to offer his bride."

Ravenswood, that's all they wanted. Ravenswood, with its unpleasant memories, its drafty halls, its rising damp, and the fireplaces that gushed smoke no matter how often she ordered them cleaned . . .

"I'll sell it to you," she declared.

Lady Carncross and Sir Archy exchanged a startled glance.

"Will you?" Archy stammered, his eyes wide and glowing.

An artificial laugh escaped Lady Carncross. "No, Archy, do not be taken in by a hum. I make no doubt once she has thought about it, dear Netta will regret her hasty words. You are merely worn down, my dear," she added to Netta, "drained by events. Such a strain upon your poor nerves. This is a good lesson. Never make hasty decisions when you are distraught. Does not your cousin Roland want Ravenswood?"

Netta's lips tightened. "He says he does not. Besides, it is mine to do with as I will. He has no claim upon it."

Lady Carncross nodded. "Think about it for a day or two, my love. We can talk about this more at a later date. Though I must admit, there are times I suspected Archy's grandpapa of staking Ravenswood in that absurd card game with *your* grandpapa with the express intention of losing it. He was forever going on about how expensive it was to maintain. Do you not find it so?"

Archy leaned forward. "But mama—" He broke off under his mother's quelling gaze, and shrugged. He turned a much more cheerful face toward Netta. "Great old barrack of a place, ain't it? Hate to think how lonely you'll be there."

A hearty hail saved Netta from replying. She looked up to see Mr. Kenneth Lambert, his muscular form enhanced by a riding coat in the new rich green shade called Spanish fly, astride a raw-boned gray. He pulled abreast, and their coachman reined his pair to a halt.

"Lady Carncross." He swept off his shallow curly beaver, revealing the thick waves of his mahogany-colored hair. "Carncross." He awarded a brief nod to Archy before his gaze came to rest on Netta, and his lips curved into a teasing smile. "And Lady Netta. It is no wonder the sun shines so brightly this day, for you have come out of doors where it may see you."

"Palaverer. Are you rehearsing your idiocies for the next ball?" Netta asked.

He covered his heart with his hat and shook his head, his expression crestfallen. "What need is there? You will not be able to attend." His restive horse sidled, and he muttered an oath as he replaced his hat safely on his head and recaptured his reins in both hands. "Young colt," he explained as the animal danced a few skittish steps sideways. "It seems he is not yet fit for society. Forgive me. Permit me to call upon you soon." With a cautious bow directed at them all, he allowed the horse to proceed a few steps forward, where it nearly lunged out of his control.

Lady Carncross shook her head. "These sporting mad bloods. One never quite knows if a Corinthian is being sincere, or if one is being made the object of subtle and unkind ridicule."

"Doesn't one?" Netta glanced back to where the colt now trotted away with apparent meekness. "He delights in teasing, it is true, but I have never thought him unkind."

Lady Carncross patted her hand. "Archy's father was such a one. Believe me, my dear, a gentleman devoted to hunting and pugilistic bouts makes a most uncomfortable husband. Much better to marry a man who shows to best advantage on the dance floor. It is infinitely more enjoyable."

By the time the Carncrosses returned Netta to Cavendish Square, she was relieved to escape the lady's hints and innuendoes. She thanked them for the outing, bade them goodbye, but offered them no encouragement to come inside. Even before the landau started forward, she ran up the stairs and into the house.

Fenton met her in the hall, relieved her of her bonnet and shawl, and informed her that Mr. Frake still roamed the premises.

"Still?" And she had thought her spirits low before.

The butler bestowed on her the encouraging

smile of one who had known her since infancy. "In his late lordship's room. Master Roland—his lordship, I should say—is in the bookroom."

She opened her mouth to inform the butler she had not the least interest in the whereabouts of Roland, then closed it again. After a moment, she thanked Fenton and headed down the hall.

The bookroom still looked disorderly to her, though now neat piles of papers replaced the haphazard scattering of the morning. Roland sat in a chair before the hearth, a glass of wine in one hand, a handful of bills in the other. He stared into the empty grate with unseeing eyes.

He could be vulnerable, this masterful cousin of hers. That surprised her, showing her another side of him, one he kept closed away. Dangerous, the little voice warned in her mind.

She should not catch him like this, off his guard. She shoved the door so that it banged closed behind her, warning him of her presence. "What is that Runner finding in Desmond's room?" she demanded.

With a visible effort, Roland focused on her. "I have no idea."

"What?" She opened her eyes wide in exaggerated surprise. "Why aren't you finding out?"

A slow smile tugged at his reluctant lips. "He did not desire my company. In fact, he specifically requested I *not* offer him my assistance."

"And you let him take the trick?" She shook her head. "You hold the long suit, you know. As executor, it is only right that you be present."

"I am also the most likely candidate to have mur-

118

dered Desmond. You, I might add, run a close second."

"I'm surprised he hasn't decided we brought about Desmond's death together."

"I feel quite certain the thought has entered his mind."

She sobered. "But we didn't."

"No," he agreed. "We did not. Nor did I kill him on my own. And neither can I believe did you."

"Thank you." She rallied. "But that still fails to explain why you are just sitting here. Why are you not up there?"

"I told you—"

She waved that aside. "How do you expect to learn anything down here?" She started for the door.

He reached it first and opened it for her. "In my defense, he locked me out," he said, following her.

So, he *had* tried to watch the Runner. That sat better with her impression of him as a man of action. But why had his seeming *in*action disappointed her? What Roland did or did not do should not matter to her in the least. Annoyed with herself, she marched up the steps, down the short hall, and rapped on Desmond's door.

After a moment, it opened to reveal Mr. Frake. He frowned at the sight of them, then he gave a fatalistic shrug as if accepting the inevitable. "Perhaps you can help after all. M'lady? M'lord? If you will come in?"

Netta crossed the threshold, bracing herself. Stebbing, Desmond's valet, stood before the wardrobe. A stack of neatly folded garments lay on the chair at his side. The man glanced at her, his expression blank, then resumed his labors. Everywhere lay organized piles—nothing the way Desmond would have left it.

A pang shot through Netta at this intrusion. Memories and shared childhood experiences tied her to Desmond, making up for the lack of sincere affection. Still, Lady Carncross's words sounded once more in her mind—*You are well out of that marriage* . . .

"Have you found anything of use?" Roland set her aside and advanced into the chamber.

"Not at first sight, I haven't," the Runner admitted. He turned to Stebbing. "Is there any place I have missed?"

The valet's brow furrowed. "His lordship didn't keep anything of value in this room. Only his less costly jewels, which he kept in his case in the secret compartment."

"The secret—" Mr. Frake's jaw jutted forward, and when he spoke, his words dripped sarcasm. "A secret compartment, is there? My, my, how kind of you to mention it. Would you care to show me where it is?"

The valet smoothed a crease from a velvet coat with unwavering precision. "Certainly, sir." He laid the garment aside with loving hands and turned to the ornate wooden frame at the head of the bed. His fingers brushed across the intricate carvings of fruit and came to rest on a cluster of mahogany grapes. With only a whisper of sound, a hinged door swung wide.

Stebbing drew out an enameled jewel cask, and a

bundle of small papers toppled onto the pillow. Mr. Frake swooped down on these, scooping them up.

"What are they?" Netta joined him at the bedside.

"Someone's vowels?" Roland regarded the stack through his quizzing glass. "Now, why did he keep these here and the others in the bookroom?"

The Runner untied the riband and leafed through the tiny sheets. "Lady Beatrix Underhill," he announced.

"But why—?" Netta broke off her question.

"Why, indeed?" The Runner turned to Stebbing. "Do you know anything of this?"

A muscle twitched at the corner of the man's mouth.

"Do you?" Mr. Frake repeated.

The man glanced at Netta. "Yes, sir."

Netta looked from one to the other of them. "Why?" she demanded.

The valet cast an anguished look toward the Runner.

A deep chuckle escaped Roland. "My dear Little Hen, you are causing the poor man embarrassment. It appears this is a subject not fit for your delicate ears."

Her eyes widened in comprehension. "I see." She drew out the words. "Yes, I see. And when did Lady Beatrix intend to redeem them?"

Stebbing didn't look at her. "After the ball guests had gone home, Miss Netta."

"So Desmond intended to exchange them for her favors, did he?" Roland's mouth thinned. "And

121

was the lady willing?"

"That I cannot say, m'lord."

Netta looked up from her contemplation of the counterpane. "I don't think she was. The way she looked at him—" She broke off. "I would have sworn she hated him as much as did—"

"Yes, m'lady?" Mr. Frake prompted her as she paused.

"As much as did her husband," she finished, wishing she had kept silent.

"Anything in particular lie behind that feud?" he asked.

"Something to do with pranks played on one another while at Eton. They have gone through periods in their lives when they could meet without coming to cuffs. Then one or the other of them would drag up some old recollection, and the battle would be on once more."

The Runner considered, then nodded as if he set the matter aside for later contemplation. He rocked back on his heels and tapped the vowels he still held with one finger. "Well, now. I must say as this here gives the lady a possible reason for wishing him dead before she had to redeem them."

"Or her husband," Roland pointed out. "If he knew of this, I doubt he would have been pleased."

"As you say." The Runner paced to the end of the room, then turned back. "And Lady Beatrix came to this room yesterday, looking for something. At least now we know what she sought." He frowned as he flipped one more time through the sizable stack.

"Dear me." Roland strolled to the mantelpiece

122

and propped his arm against it. "I fear I now have competition for the role of primary suspect."

Appreciative amusement glinted in Frake's eyes. "Well, now, m'lord, that's as may be." He turned back to the valet, who once more had resumed his labors at the wardrobe. "Is there anything else hidden in this room—or anywhere else?"

Stebbing turned a pained expression toward him. "Not to my knowledge, sir."

"Then these are the only vowels?"

"Yes, sir. Only Lady Beatrix's. His lordship kept the others in the bookroom, in his desk."

"Do you know whose they were?"

"Of course, sir." With elaborate care, he shook out a riding coat of Egyptian brown.

Netta fancied she heard the Runner's teeth grind.

"And whose were they?" Mr. Frake asked.

The valet paused a moment, his brow knit in the effort of memory. "Sir Archibald's. There were five from him. I remember particularly because there were so very few, not like these, or those of Mr. Lambert."

"Lambert?" Mr. Frake looked up quickly from his notebook. "I don't remember seeing any from Lambert when I went over the bookroom."

The valet raised a curious eyebrow. "Did you not, sir? I distinctly remember a stack of at least that many." He gestured toward the ones still held by Frake.

Once more the Runner rocked back on his heels, a thoughtful expression on his narrow face. "Well, well, well."

Netta crossed to the Runner and took the slips

from him. She leafed through them, mentally tallying the figures. A little over five thousand pounds? She counted again, then sank onto the bed, her head reeling.

"Little Hen?"

Roland's deep voice recalled her. She looked up at him. "Do you realize how much he must have won that last night?"

"A tidy fortune, I should say."

"A tidy fortune," she agreed. She turned back to the Runner. "The gentlemen of my family have always been gamesters, but rarely lucky ones. These—" She held out the slips of paper. "I cannot believe Desmond won so much."

Roland's eyes narrowed. "You suspect him of fuzzing the cards?"

Netta turned to him, seeking some denial in his features, that he would not believe it possible. She encountered only thoughtful agreement.

Roland's gaze strayed to Frake. "As our good Runner is fond of saying, 'Well, well, well.' "

Mr. Frake retrieved the slips from Netta. "Not in the habit of winning, then, was he?" He pursed his lips. "And what if one of his victims suspicioned his winning wasn't quite honest like? Might be angry enough to kill him in revenge—or more like to escape having to pay off an overwhelming and dishonest debt?" He met Roland's gaze and with deliberation enunciated: "Well, well, well."

Chapter Seven

Alone, once more, Mr. Frake stared out the window of the late earl's bedchamber, lost in thought. There were quite a number of reasons why someone might have wanted to put Desmond Galbraith's lights out for him. The first, and most obvious, to inherit his title and position.

Nor could he forget retaining an inheritance and estate, yet avoiding being leg-shackled to a right thatch-gallows. Frake could almost sympathize with that one. By all accounts, the seventh earl had been a queer cove—high in the instep and a loose screw to boot. Yet a young gentry mort could not permit herself to be cast out with her pockets all to let and without a roof over her head, as seemed to be Lady Henrietta's alternate fate. He'd already looked into the terms of her father's will. The old gentleman had really done his daughter a cruelty in that document.

He drew his briarwood pipe from his coat pocket, tamped the bowl, noticed it was empty, and instead chewed thoughtfully on the mouthpiece. Best concentrate on the problem at hand. Reasons to kill.

Where was he? Ah, yes. Number three. Revenge against a cheat. A regular Captain Sharp, this earl, it seemed. And four. Escaping having to shell out the blunt on an impossibly high debt of honor.

Honor. An involuntary snort escaped Frake at that one. Honor, indeed. There appeared to be lamentably little of that commodity in this case.

He shook his head. Too many reasons. He'd best concentrate on who had the best chance to slip that distilled oleander into the wedding goblet. With a sigh, he headed downstairs.

The second footman—what was his name, Jeremy? Yes, Jeremy—had been the one who brought the dashed thing to Lord Tavistock. No, better to think of him as Desmond. That way he wouldn't confuse him with the new earl, this Roland, who held the title now.

In the pantry he found Fenton, sitting at his table hard at work with the spoons and a bottle of silver polish. The butler eyed him with a certain measure of suspicion and distaste, a form of greeting all too familiar to the denizens of Bow Street. Fenton listened to his request, then with an air of great condescension summoned the footman.

A fair-haired youth with a long face dominated by a narrow nose arrived barely ten minutes later. He presented himself, countenance flushed, shifting from foot to foot. Frake closed his eyes for a long moment. Why did people act guilty the moment he said he wanted to speak with them? What deep, dark secret did this fresh-faced fellow hide? Had he been pinching the almond macaroons when the cook's back was turned? Or had he been slipping doses of poison to disagreeable masters? Frake sighed. Only time — and a thorough investigation — would tell.

"Now, then, lad." Frake offered up his most disarming smile. "Suppose you tell me once more what happened at that ball. What I really need to know, see, is who came near that wedding goblet."

"Yes, sir." Jeremy screwed up his narrow face in an effort of concentration. "I took it to his lordship, o'course, but I stood near it most of the time afore that."

"That's right," Frake agreed, all affability. Except, of course, for the last minute flutter, when in the excitement the footman forgot to collect the wedding goblet before going to his master. "Now, you just go over everyone else who came near it, all right?"

The tip of Jeremy's nose twitched. "His new lordship handed it to me." He cast a nervous glance at the butler, who had paused in his polishing to listen. Fenton returned to his task with vigor.

"He found it sitting on a table near the door closest to the kitchens," Frake prompted. "You told me Lady Beatrix Underhill stood near there for awhile." He consulted his notes. "Drinking champagne, she was."

Jeremy brightened. "That's right. Mr. Underhill brought it to her. I thought at the time he just wanted to stop her talking to Mr. Lambert."

Frake blinked. "Mr. Kenneth Lambert was there with her?"

Jeremy beamed, as if he'd performed a difficult lesson to perfection. "That was afore that Sir Archibald Carncross joined them."

"Sir Archibald —" Had everyone at the ball gone

near that dashed wedding goblet?

"Miss Wrenn shooed them away, she did. Wanted to make sure the goblet was ready when it was wanted. But Lady Henrietta, she told her not to worry about it, she'd seen it filled."

Frake closed his eyes and took a deep breath. "You didn't tell me none of this the other night."

Bright crimson flushed the footman's cheeks. "No, sir. That upset I was, drove it all clean from my mind. But I remember now," he added with the air of a shamed puppy hopeful of winning its way back into its master's good graces.

Frake flipped to the page listing those who could have poisoned the cup. "Let's review this once more. Lady Beatrix? The new earl? Mr. Joshua Underhill?" He looked up, checking for confirmation as he rattled off the name of each of his current suspects. Yes, every blessed one of them had gone near it. "Anyone else?" Like maybe the entire 42nd Highland Regiment, complete with bagpipes and drums?

Jeremy's face resumed its contortionist act. "Old Lady Bostwick," he said after a moment. "Thought it was more champagne." Frake added her name to the list, though a moment's reflection proved sufficient to disregard that bit of information. A notorious tippler, Lady Bostwick. Two more names joined the others, but it appeared the dancing had occupied the majority of the guests.

Well, that hadn't helped much, he decided as he watched the relieved footman scurry away. Muddled things up a right mess, it did. He hadn't eliminated any suspects, merely discovered any one of them could still be guilty.

Maybe it was time to try a new tack. He drew out his pipe and chewed once more on the mouthpiece, his unseeing gaze straying toward the ceiling. Any one of them could have put the poison in the cup. But who could have obtained the poison in the first place?

Any one of them, he answered himself the next moment. Any single blessed one of them. Oleander served as a common rat poison; it could be obtained in any suitable shop in London. He'd have to set the members of his patrol on the trail and have them interview every possible shopkeeper.

He tapped his teeth with the much mangled pipe stem. Of course, if his villain were clever, he wouldn't take the chance of being traced so easily. He might find the oleander from another source, such as his — or her — own stillroom. Now, did they distill it at Ravenswood Court? he wondered. Mayhap he'd just have a word with Miss Euphemia Wrenn.

He found that lady seated in the corner of the main drawing room. The late earl's body no longer lay in state; he now rested at the church in preparation for the funeral. Still, the heavy black draperies remained, giving the room an oppressive atmosphere. Miss Wrenn perched on the edge of a chair, gazing straight ahead at the lone black-bedecked table which now stood empty.

Frake didn't like to intrude on her mourning. He advanced quietly, and it took him a minute to realize a slight smile hovered about her lips. Moving slowly and making as little noise as possible so as not to disturb her contemplative mood, he drew up a chair beside her. A pleasing aroma of lavender hovered about her.

Modulating his voice with care, he said: "A great many changes you've seen over the years, I expect."

Miss Wrenn blinked, then nodded. "Oh, yes, a great many," she agreed. "And to think it has only been a few short years since it was Netta's father we laid out." A heartfelt sigh set her plump figure trembling and she dabbed at the corner of her eye with a lace-edged handkerchief. "He was the dearest man, you must know, Netta's papa. So sad, so very sad, his passing. An inflammation of the lungs, it was. Just like my own dear brother-in-law, who was his cousin and Roland's papa."

"Yet his will seems to have caused Lady Henrietta a measure of trouble." Frake brought the conversation back where he wanted it.

"Such a disappointment." She clasped the wispy bit of muslin between her hands. "I tried to talk him out of it, time out of mind I told him how unsuitable it would be. But there was Netta to be considered, he said, and no way to provide suitably for both her and his heir. So very improvident, the Galbraiths."

"Was he?" Frake prompted as Miss wrenn drifted into silence. "Improvident?"

Her reminiscent smile returned. "Gamesters, you must know. All of them. It is in the Galbraith blood. So very unfortunate. They are forever placing the most hopeless wagers. Netta's papa once told me he found no pleasure in a bet he felt certain he would win."

"And so he lost." Frake reached for his Occurrence Book, then changed his mind and made a mental

130

note instead. No point upsetting her mood by making this look official like. "And this Desmond was the same."

"Oh, no. He was much worse." Miss Wrenn's fingers clenched in the fine muslin. "He was forever 'under the hatches,' as he would say. Why, Netta and I positively dreaded coming up to London, where he would seek the tables every night."

"Then you would be surprised to learn he had won a great deal the night before he died?"

"Won? Why, I should not believe it at all. No, not at all." Miss Wrenn shook her head. "Now, you must not try to take me in with such a Banbury tale, for it will not fadge. So sad, their luck. Indeed, it is no wonder the Galbraith fortunes have been so greatly reduced. Quite run off their legs, I fear."

So Desmond most likely fuzzed the cards. The question then became, did one of his victims catch him? And did that victim—Mr. Lambert, perhaps, he of the missing vowels?—take stern measures to assure he didn't have to pay up?

At the moment, though, he had another question to answer. He cast a considering eye over Miss Wrenn. "Lavender," he pronounced. "An excellent scent. Do you go to Yardley's?"

Delicate color touched her faded cheeks. "Is it not delightful? Yardley's. They do make a lovely scent, do they not? But I blend this one myself. From my own garden! At Ravenswood, you must know. Dear me, yes. I do love my garden."

So easy. Mr. Frake leaned forward in genuine interest. "Do you, now? My mother has one she swears goes back to the time of Queen Elizabeth. A knot garden."

"I should not be surprised if it did. Such a treasure, to be sure. Mine only dates to Queen Anne, I believe. But it is such a pleasure. I have added a great number of the most useful plants."

"Do you distill many essences?"

"It is my hobby." Pride shone in her face.

Frake nodded. "My mother always seemed to have a remedy ready for everything, from influenza to the rheumatics."

"Herbs are so very useful, are they not?" Miss Wrenn cocked her head to one side, her eyes bright. "I vow, hardly a day goes by that dear Netta and I are not hard at work on our tinctures and tisanes — so very enjoyable, and so useful. Why, we are forever bringing out a bottle of something for one of the servants or ourselves."

Frake fingered the pipe in his pocket and tried to match her enthusiasm. "Do you know, my mother even makes up some potion to kill the rats in the barn."

"There, is it not amazing how many uses one can find for herbs?" Miss Wrenn's entire countenance glowed. "I make one, too. Not my grandmother's receipt any longer, though to be sure it was a most excellent one. I wonder which herb your mama uses? Yew, perhaps?"

"Is that what you use?" With care, Frake kept any trace of tension from his voice.

"Oh, no, not anymore. Dear Roland, so very thoughtful of him. He knows my garden is quite my delight. He sent me an oleander plant when he first went out to India, you must know. A distillation of that is quite excellent for vermin."

"And Lady Henrietta knows all about these herbs, too, you say?"

"Such an attentive pupil." Miss Wren nodded in vigorous agreement. "Why, her knowledge must nearly equal my own by now. Just like dear Netta to know her duty as the lady of the manor."

"Indeed." Frake drew out his pipe and tapped it against his leg.

"Oh, yes. Such a delightful time we have in our stillroom, Netta and I. Whenever Desmond takes— took—one of his pets, we would just hide ourselves away. He almost never ventured in there, you must know."

The ladies probably gossiped between themselves about how difficult he could be, all the while they handled poisons. It would almost be unnatural if the possibility of killing a different type of rat hadn't occurred to them. The means at hand, the motive abundant . . . He blinked his eyes back into focus to find Miss Wrenn staring at him, her expression aghast.

"You think—Oh, you *dreadful* man. But we *never* keep anything on hand that could *harm* anyone. No. Oh, no. We wouldn't. We—we only make up what we need to give to the head groom. We would never keep such a thing around. The—the oleander that killed poor Desmond could *never* have come from my stillroom." She fluttered to her feet, wrung her hands for a moment, then ran for the door.

Frake watched it swing shut behind her. "It couldn't, could it?" he muttered. "In a pig's eye it couldn't."

133

* * *

Netta paced the length of her chamber, conscious of the silken rustle of the gown she had just mended. It made her uncomfortable. She would be glad to put off her mourning. At least she need not attend the funeral on the morrow. She would, though, be expected to accompany the funeral cortege to Ravenswood, where her cousin would be laid to rest in the moldering old vault.

The door burst open, breaking off her depressed line of thought. Cousin Phemie, her complexion scarlet, scuttled into the room like a distracted hen.

A cry of relief escaped the little woman at sight of Netta. "There you are at *last,* my love. I have searched everywhere for you."

"Whatever is the matter?" Netta hurried forward to receive her tearful companion into her arms, and led her to the high-backed chair positioned near the hearth.

"I want to go *home.*" Phemie wrung her handkerchief between her hands and sniffed. "I — I am quite worn down with all these sad preparations. I only want to return to Ravenswood."

To return to Ravenswood, to escape all the turmoil and botheration and uncertainties. . . .

To escape Roland and his disconcerting presence.

Part of her, to her dismay, cried out against leaving his fascinating vicinity, but her more rational self came to her rescue. Netta couldn't think clearly when he was about. Her mind went all muddled when he smiled, and she tended to forget he had an excellent reason to want her dead. She would be safer under a different roof.

They would go because it would be for the best. Today. Right now. They could avoid —

"We cannot," she exclaimed, dismayed. "It would be too shabby of us to leave Roland to entertain everyone alone. You know how many will insist on coming to the house after the funeral."

Phemie clasped her hands. "We must cancel it. Indeed, that would be the very thing. Then dear Roland may set forth from the church tomorrow morning and come directly to Ravenswood. Yes, that will be much better. I shall tell him at once."

Before Netta could protest, the little woman darted out the door. Well, and why not? she reflected. They could announce that the gathering would now take place after the interment rather than the funeral and feel sure that few if any would travel so great a distance. It would make the arrangements much easier.

Until Roland came to Ravenswood tomorrow.

Well, she would face that problem when he arrived. In the meantime, it would do her good to get away from him, even if only for one day. She could depart at once, for she would need time to prepare for the possible guests on the morrow. Then she wouldn't have to be part of the lengthy and depressing cortege that would escort Desmond on his final journey. That thought raised her spirits.

It would take just under five and a half hours, perhaps a little less, for the Brighton Road was in excellent condition. They need pack no more than the essentials, then she could remove from the townhouse . . . and leave Roland behind. Longing for the freedom of the country filled her, and she went in search of the Runner.

Mr. Frake, it seemed, held no objections to her immediate removal. She found him all kindness, not even questioning her reasons. Stopping only to summon the traveling carriage, she returned to her chamber to oversee the packing.

Cousin Phemie awaited her there, appearing strained. "Dear Roland says the Runner might not quite like it."

Netta's heart went out to her. The poor dear, she looked so drawn and tired, she had undergone so much in the couple of days since Desmond's death. "He has just granted his permission. Never fear, we may leave as soon as you can be ready. Do but hurry, and we may be on the road within the hour."

A tap sounded on her door, but on her call to enter, Fenton, not her abigail, crossed the threshold. "Lady Carncross and Sir Archibald are below, Miss Netta," he informed her.

Netta swallowed her exasperation, then experienced a tinge of guilt. They came out of the best intentions. And her maid could proceed with the preparations without her.

Dismay showed on Cousin Phemie's face. "Will you see them, my love? I vow, I am quite distracted. I fear I shall not be up to receiving them with you."

"No, see to getting everything ready." Besides, she could probably send them packing more easily by herself. She tidied her hair, then once more descended the stairs.

Her guests sat beside each other on the brocade sofa, Archy listening, nodding in accompaniment to his mother's low-voiced words.

Lady Carncross broke off as Netta closed the door behind herself. "Here we are again, my dear. I know you must be wondering what could bring us back so soon. But with such a sad occasion on the morrow, I thought perhaps there might be some way in which we could be of assistance. Indeed, I had meant to offer our services when we saw you before, but your comment about selling Ravenswood quite put it out of my mind."

"Mine, too." Archy captured Netta's hand and carried it to his lips.

Lady Carncross, Netta noted, wore the same gown she had on her earlier visit for the drive in the park. Archy, though, sported a new coat with a dashing waistcoat. He preened under her gaze.

She moved away. "I fear you were right, Lady Carncross. I find, upon reflection, I am not quite ready to sell Ravenswood. While my memories may not all be pleasant, I did grow up there, and now it is all I have."

"But to be buried in the country! Surely you would rather remove to a small house in Bath where you might always be sure of finding entertainment."

Netta wrinkled her nose. "I should prefer Brighton, I believe. But situated at Ravenswood, I have the advantages of both town society and the country."

Lady Carncross's mouth thinned. "Ah, well, my dear, there is no need to make hasty decisions. At least we will still be able to see a great deal of you. How pleased Archy must be at that prospect. Are you not?" She prodded her son gently.

"What? Oh, yes, delighted." He smiled. "Must

know I've always had a fondness for you. Seems odd, not having Desmond in the picture anymore."

Not having Desmond in the picture anymore. It struck Netta fully for the first time, startling her, that she was now free to marry where she wished — if she wished. No more constraint.

She turned away, hiding her sudden feeling of elation — of freedom. "In fact," she said, covering her reaction, "you find Cousin Phemie and me on the verge of departing for Ravenswood."

Lady Carncross nodded wisely. "Yes, of course, the interment. You are quite right to go ahead. There must be any number of unpleasant tasks awaiting you. So young to bear such a responsibility. We will not take your answer as final, my dear. You may find that without a gentleman to help you with the estate, it will prove more than you can manage. Rest assured, though, dear Archy will render you every assistance possible. Although sadly not, himself, in the possession of an estate, his father trained him with diligence in management practices. He is quite remarkable, is he not? A young gentleman with such a flair for fashion — quite an asset to any lady's drawing room, I am sure, and always so popular at balls and soirees — yet a capable landlord. Such a lucky lady she will be, the one upon whom his fancy lights."

"Do you indeed wish to manage an estate?" Netta regarded her old acquaintance with a measure of surprise.

He managed a look of intense interest. "Very much so."

"I am surprised you have not long ago purchased

138

another property."

"And leave Ravenswood?" Lady Carncross laughed. "Do you know, even though it no longer belongs to the Carncross family, I still feel it is where we must remain. There, now, I must not keep prattling on. If you are indeed preparing for the journey, you must be wishing us at Jericho by now. We will see you within a day or two, you may depend upon that, my dear. You and dear Miss Wrenn must come to dine at the Dower House. Nothing formal, of course, because of your mourning, just what my late husband would have called taking your pot luck. We will call upon you as soon as we are settled in."

Archy recaptured her hand. "Until then, dear Netta."

He pressed a fervent kiss onto her fingers, squeezed them, and gazed at her with an expression that put her forcibly in mind of a worshipful puppy. Startled, she shied away.

He stepped back, maintaining that besotted gaze, though now it seemed more piercing. "You're sure this cousin of yours won't be pestering you for the place?" he asked.

"You need have no fear." After all, she had enough for them both.

Apparently satisfied, he ushered his mama from the room with such a flair that Netta stared after them for several seconds after the door closed. Perhaps she should have continued to let him think she meant to sell him Ravenswood. Then at least she wouldn't be subjected to this playacting. Unless he did indeed wish to marry her? No, he'd seemed so relieved at mention of her willingness to part with the estate. Shaking her head, she went to check on the progress of the packing.

She found Cousin Phemie now in her own chamber, neatly folding a gown into a trunk. A maid knelt beside her, just closing the lid on another.

The little woman managed a wan smile. "There, my dear. Except for my hatbox and dressing case, I am finished. Will you ring for a footman to carry these down?"

"Of course." Netta crossed to the bed and pulled the rope that hung there, then hurried on to her own chamber.

There Wembly looked up from Netta's dressing case and directed a quelling look at her. "Rather sudden, Miss Netta," was all she said.

Netta, aware she had offended the good woman, set about soothing her. "A whim of Miss Wrenn's, and truly, I feel it is for the best. We will breathe easier in the country. Let us only take what we need for the moment. We may send for the other things later."

"Yes, Miss Netta." Somewhat less stiff, the abigail resumed her work.

As Netta followed the first of her cases down to the main hall, Roland strode out of the bookroom and came to a halt. "You are quite certain you wish to leave now? Is it not too late?"

Not if she could help it. From the first moment she had seen this dangerous cousin of hers across the ballroom — was it only two nights ago? — she had known he meant trouble for her. Well, if running away was what it took to protect herself, then run she would.

"Little Hen?" He regarded her with a quizzical look, as of one who has spoken and received no answer. "Will it not grow dark before you can reach the estate?"

She dragged her attention from his intriguing features to his words. "No, not if we leave at once. Cousin Phemie is—is quite anxious to have the house in readiness to receive you tomorrow." Well, that was close enough to the truth. She could hardly say she avoided him for her peace of mind.

He drew out his watch. "It lacks but ten minutes until two," he said, more to himself than to her. "You will not reach Ravenswood much before seven-thirty."

"I dispatched a groom earlier, so all will be in readiness for us."

"I see," he said after a moment. His dark countenance gave no clue as to his reflections. "I will wish you a safe journey, then." He strode away.

And what would she have done had he asked her to stay? She considered a moment, then dismissed it as a pointless exercise. He had no reason to want her about.

Their carriage pulled away from the house less than fifteen minutes later. She was glad to leave Roland, Netta assured herself. She barely knew him; she had reason to both despise and fear him. Yet she didn't, that irritating voice reminded her. He dominated her thoughts, making her aware of him as a man, not as a possible murderer. What a—a goosecap she was!

A murmur from Cousin Phemie caught her attention, and she glanced at her companion. The little woman perched on the edge of her seat, wringing her hands together, her gaze fixed on the window.

"Whatever is the matter?" Netta touched Phemie's chilled fingers.

Cousin Phemie shook her head, not vouchsafing a single word. Not until they drew out of London did she speak, and then only to beg Netta to have John Coachman whip up the horses. Netta, not at all amiss to speeding the journey, did as Phemie asked, but her concern grew. Why should her elderly companion, who normally preferred a plodding gait, now wish something different?

At the second posting house they reached, Netta overruled the little woman and insisted upon taking some refreshment. Rather than drink the tea and eat the cakes placed before her, though, Phemie paced the inn's private parlor, casting such frantic glances at the mantel clock that Netta at last gave up and allowed them to proceed.

To wile away the hours, Netta worked on a knitted woolen baby shawl intended for a christening present for an old friend married last Season and now in the family way. Phemie held her own yarn, but as the time slipped by, Netta noted that not one stitch changed needles. The little woman stared out the window, her fingers clenched so that her knuckles turned white.

"Is it not a relief just to be away from Tavistock House?" Netta watched her companion's distress.

"What?" Phemie started, then turned to her. "Oh, yes. Certainly. Though I do wish we would reach

Ravenswood."

Netta, noting Phemie's obvious unease, heartily agreed with her. They would not arrive one moment too soon, as far as she was concerned.

At last, by the fading light of the westering sun, they turned from the Brighton Road onto the lane which, in less than a mile, would lead them home. Cousin Phemie tucked her knitting away in its bag and clutched at the door as if she would throw it open the moment they stopped. Finally they turned through the iron gates onto the gravel drive, passed the Dower House set in its garden on their left, and proceeded the last five hundred yards to the front door.

Before the carriage pulled to a complete stop, Phemie fumbled with the catch, swung the door wide, and jumped to the ground. Netta, alarmed, scrambled after her. Haskins, the elderly retainer who remained in charge, barely opened the front door before the little woman burst past him.

With a bewildered apology to the startled man, Netta followed across the stately hall and down the passage leading to the kitchens. Phemie dashed through the first pantry and into the stillroom, where she scanned the shelves. With a cry of triumph, she grasped several bottles and tucked them under her arm.

Netta positioned herself squarely in front of her. "Cousin Phemie, will you not tell me what this is about?"

"No time, dear. Later, once we are safe."

"Safe? From what?" Perforce, she stood aside as the little woman pushed past, headed for the "secret" door set in the side of the chimney, the quickest route to the garden beyond.

"Get the others, there are still two I cannot carry," Phemie called over her shoulder.

"Two of *what?*" Netta cried, bewildered.

"The oleander, my dear, what else? We must destroy every one of these horrid bottles before *he* discovers them."

"I'm afraid you're a little late, Miss Wrenn." The Runner's voice, filled with satisfaction, sounded from the doorway behind them.

Chapter Eight

Netta spun about to face Mr. Frake, startled. Half-formed questions bombarded her mind, none of which she could utter.

Phemie squeaked in dismay and clutched her burden to her full bosom. One bottle slipped and shattered on the flagstone floor, scattering shards of glass and liquid. Tears filled her eyes. "Oh, you dreadful, dreadful man," she managed before giving way to a convulsive sob.

"Cousin Phemie?" Netta rallied and strode across to the little woman. She pried her fingers loose from the bottles and set them on a table.

"Oleander?" The Runner nodded toward them.

Netta checked a label. "Yes. But why—" She broke off, her eyes widening. "Do you mean—Oh, how horrid. You cannot possibly believe the oleander that killed my cousin Tavistock came from *here!*"

"Well, now, m'lady, that does seem likely. If the person who did it had access to this place, of course.

There might be an easy way to find out. How many bottles did you have?"

Netta went to a small writing desk in the corner of the room. "We keep an inventory."

"There is a bottle missing," Phemie wailed. "Oh, Netta, this is too dreadful, too, too dreadful."

"Yes, of course it is. How do you *know* one is missing?"

She sniffed. "Because I gave one to Farley—he's Desmond's head groom," she added for the Runner. "He wanted to scatter it for the rats. There were seven bottles left, and now there are only six."

Netta straightened up from their tally book. "She is quite right. Here, you may see for yourself where she made the entry for Farley." She held out the slim volume to the Runner.

He took it, examined it a moment, then looked up at Cousin Phemie. "Did you know about this here bottle afore you went up to London?"

"Indeed, I did not." The little woman sniffed, then sought in her reticule for a handkerchief.

"Then why did we race down here like this?" Netta asked. "Please, Cousin Phemie. What is this about?"

"It—it's all because of that Terrible Man." She pointed an accusing finger at Mr. Frake. "He—he wanted to know all about our stillroom, and he made me feel so horridly guilty when I said we had oleander, I thought the best thing to do would be to get rid of it before he came snooping around here and accusing one of us of—of killing poor Desmond."

Netta turned on the Runner. "Of all the impertinent—" She broke off. It was not in the least impertinent. The man merely did his duty—unfortunately a bit too well. She sagged as her argument evaporated about her.

"Just so, m'lady." A touch of amused understanding lit his eyes. "Now, Miss Wrenn, if you'll just answer a few more questions for me?"

"More questions? Oh, you do not believe me, not at all." Phemie burst into tears.

"Cousin Phemie." Netta took her elbow and gently led her to a chair. "Do not distress yourself so. You must do your best to tell Mr. Frake what he needs to know if you want—" she hesitated over her choice of phrases "—this matter concluded."

"This matter." Phemie's tone scorned Netta's words. "It served Desmond right for the shocking way he treated us." She ended on a wail and dissolved once more into tears.

The Runner waited, Occurrence Book in hand, until her sobs subsided. "Now, Miss Wrenn, if you're able? You maintain you did not take that bottle of oleander yourself?"

"I did not." Her shoulders trembled. "Nor did I kill him, however much he might have deserved it."

"I see." The Runner jotted down a quick note, and his gaze strayed to Netta.

"You *wicked* man," Phemie breathed. "How dare you assume it was Netta? Why, any number of people could have had access to our stillroom. Could they not, my love?" She turned to Netta, then back to the Runner, her eagerness to diffuse the blame apparently equaling her anxiety. "Why, only the morning before we left for town, that Lady Beatrix Underhill called on some pretext or other. I cannot

147

remember aright. It was while Mr. Lambert helped you in here, do you remember Netta? Dear Kenneth — " She broke off, aghast.

"Mr. Kenneth Lambert," Mr. Frake mused. "Interested in herbs, is he?"

"He is my cousin's godson, you must know, Mr. Frake." With difficulty, Netta kept herself under control. "He maintains rooms in Brighton and is a frequent caller. And though he has assisted us upon many occasions, I would hardly call him 'interested' in herbs."

Mr. Frake jotted down another quick note. "Back to Lady Beatrix for a moment, if you will. Can you tell me anything about her visit?"

Netta actually smiled. "Mr. Underhill's uncle — his *wealthy* uncle — lives in Brighton. He tends to summon them whenever the whim takes him. They had been here at least a fortnight at that time, for she came to pay off a gaming debt she had incurred with Desmond some ten days previously. I have no idea where they played. I remember being surprised, for most often it is — was — Desmond who loses — lost."

"Yet she came in here?" The Runner looked up from the page on which he scribbled.

"Desmond was from home at the time, and she did not wish to come back again. You are well-aware that her husband and Desmond did not get along."

"Yes, m'lady. So she came in here and gave the money to you?"

"And I gave it to Desmond when he returned."

"Was she here long?"

"Not very. And to save you the trouble of asking your next question, I suppose she could have taken a bottle without my noticing. Though I cannot see why she would want to. She would hardly plan to kill him then, when she had lost no more than fifty pounds to him."

"And Mr. Lambert? Did he call for a particular reason?"

Netta fought a losing battle against the color that warmed her cheeks. "Only to see his godmother. Then he stayed to bear me company for a little. I suppose he, too, could have taken a bottle, though I cannot think why he would."

Mr. Frake nodded, more to himself than to her. "Can you remember what you spoke about?"

The warmth in her cheeks intensified. "The engagement ball." She had hated to cause Mr. Lambert pain. He had known for some time she was as good as betrothed to Desmond, yet still he courted her. . . . She caught the Runner watching her and looked away. "Have you other questions?"

"Does anyone else come in here?"

"The servants, of course. Desmond — rarely. This is *our* sanctuary, you see."

"Any other friends visit in here?"

Netta frowned. "Archy — Sir Archibald Carncross, of course. He lives in the Dower House across the gardens. He is a frequent visitor here, and he has often helped us collect herbs."

"Yes." Phemie's eyes brightened. "Why, he must know their properties as well as do we!" She regarded the Runner with a look of triumph.

"Mr. Underhill?" Mr. Frake looked from one to the other of them.

"Certainly not!" Phemie exclaimed. "Desmond

would not permit him in the house, not since that terrible quarrel over that hunter last year."

The Runner frowned and made another note. Cousin Phemie rose and sniffed. "If you have no further need of me, I shall retire to my chamber. Netta, my love, I would like a plate of broth brought up to me on a tray. Will you tell Cook—oh, he is in London, still, is he not?"

"I shall see to something." Netta glanced at the Runner, got his nod of permission, and ushered her elderly cousin from the room.

Mr. Frake watched the ladies depart, his speculative gaze on their retreating figures. At least he knew where the poison had come from. Unfortunately, it sounded like any blessed one of his suspects could have taken it. Except Underhill, of course. Unless his wife helped him.

And except for the new earl, Roland. He drew out his pipe and chewed on the mouthpiece. Or *did* that leave his lordship in the clear? He went in search of the old retainer who had admitted him.

As he reached the hall, he encountered Lady Henrietta, who stood at the foot of the heavy carved stair, watching her elderly cousin ascend. His footsteps echoed across the marble tiles, and she turned.

Her fine brow creased into a frown. "What may I do for you now?" Her voice held only resignation.

"Your butler, m'lady. If I might have a word with him?"

"Butler," she breathed. "I suppose I shall have to engage a new one. And a footman, I suppose. Well, Roland had better not try to steal my housekeeper."

Her bright eyes kindled. "And he may find his own cook, as well. He shall not have either of them."

Frake gave a gentle cough. "The man who admitted me?" he asked. "Elderly? Walked with a slight limp?"

"Oh, Haskins." Her expression remained vexed. "My father's valet. He has retired, of course, but he remains here with his wife and one maid while the rest of the staff goes up to London with us."

"Haskins," Frake repeated, memorizing the name. "And where might I find him, m'lady?"

"In the butler's pantry, I should imagine. This way." She swept ahead of him, accompanied by the rustle of her silken skirts.

Frake kept pace, his gaze scanning the rooms. Grandeur prevailed. Her father's idea of decorating, or did it date to her grandfather? Or perhaps the Carncross from whom that gentleman won this estate in a card game? Heavy carved pieces of furniture stood as if at attention about the rooms through which they passed. Oppressiveness, not comfort, he decided.

For the first time, he put some credence to this Roland's tale of not wanting anything to do with the estate. He couldn't help but wonder what this young lady would do with the whacking great mausoleum. All it needed was a specter or two—a murdered bride, maybe, or a withered, faceless nun. A smile just touching his lips at his whimsy, he returned his thoughts to the matter at hand.

They wended their way along a dark corridor, passed through a heavy door that creaked on its hinges, and entered the servants' hall. An ancient table dominated the narrow room, stretching most of its considerable length. A motley assortment of chairs surrounded it, and a single moth-devoured tapestry of dubious color and design hung on one darkened wood wall.

A coat of whitewash would go a long way to cheering the place up a bit, Frake reflected. He glanced at Lady Henrietta, but she didn't seem to notice the depressing atmosphere. Raised here, he reminded himself.

The hollow echo of their footsteps accompanied them as they crossed to a small doorway on the far side. The tenor tones of a youth's voice reached them, followed by the lower, gruffer syllables of an aged man.

"They are in the kitchens," Lady Henrietta announced, and headed down the hall.

The tantalizing aroma of fresh bread drifted out to welcome them. Now, this was more like, Frake decided as they entered the cook's domain.

Despite the gloom that pervaded the rest of the house, here a cheerful hand prevailed. Gleaming copper kettles and bowls hung from the walls, and bundles of herbs dangled from the rafters. The elderly Haskins sat in a chair, slicing apples into a pan. A youth—Frake recognized Jeremy, the footman he had met at Tavistock House—sat on a wooden table, swinging his legs as he munched on a piece of fruit. He leaped to his feet, a vivid blush rising to the roots of his sandy hair as he saw them.

A plump woman of matronly aspect stood on the other side, folding a crust into a tart pan. Her eyes widened at sight of the intruders, she dropped her pastry and dusted her floured hands on her apron. "Miss Netta." She beamed on her mistress.

Haskins rose slowly, a frown on his lined face. "Did you ring, Miss Netta? If that dratted bellpull isn't working again —"

"I didn't." She came forward, smiling. "Mrs. Haskins, I fear we must hire a girl from the village. And a man, too, I shouldn't be surprised. Just until we know which of the staff will remain with us and which will take service with my cousin."

Mrs. Haskins's lips tightened and she nodded. "And right glad I'll be to have someone, Miss Netta. Miss Lavinia has been in a rare taking since young Jemmy here brought the news of Master Desmond."

Lady Henrietta winced. "I should go to see her, I suppose."

"Now, don't you trouble yourself none about her now. Sleeping, I make no doubt. *You* know how she is."

"I don't." Frake looked at the woman, then at Lady Henrietta.

The young lady introduced him to the servants. "And Great-aunt Lavinia — Lady Lavinia Galbraith — is my grandfather's eldest sister. She has become somewhat — eccentric — over the years. She only leaves her chamber at night."

Frake nodded. He'd already heard tell of this woman, how she'd petted and cosseted her great-nephew Desmond. And how she'd hated her other great-nephew Roland. Talking to her should prove enlightening. For the moment, though, he turned to Haskins.

"Did anyone visit the house between the time the family left for London and the night his lordship died?"

The valet considered. "No one who would be of interest to you, sir. Only a tinker offering to repair any damaged pots."

Someone in disguise? "Did he stay long?" Frake asked.

Haskins glanced at his wife.

"He didn't so much as cross the doorstep," the woman responded. "Didn't need him."

"So no one came." Frake spoke to himself.

"Only Mr. Roland — his lordship, I should say," the retired valet corrected himself.

"Mr. Roland?" Frake looked up, intent.

"What was *he* doing here?" Lady Henrietta demanded.

"He stayed for two nights before going up to London," Mrs. Haskins said. "He'd just come from the north, the Lake District I believe he said. So surprised as we were, for we had no notion he was come back from India. So many years." The woman shook her head, her faint smile lingering. "Could have knocked me over with a feather, you could have. And so dark and grim as he'd become. But when he smiled I knew him in an instant, so like his old self he was."

"So Mr. Roland was here." Frake tapped his graphite pencil against the rim of his notebook. Now, why had that gentleman given the impression he'd only arrived in England in time for the engagement ball? It appeared he'd spent several days, if not a week or more, in the country. And why the Lake

District? He jotted down a quick note to ask about that.

Next, why had he come to Ravenswood? A likely answer presented itself. Roland would know about the stillroom, and he could have guessed about the oleander—Miss Wrenn herself had admitted it was Roland who sent the original shrub from India. And like as not that gentleman knew just how deadly that gift could be.

Frake thanked the servants, then trailed Lady Henrietta out to the main hall, still rolling the new information over in his mind. He almost walked into the young lady, who stopped abruptly and turned to face him.

"Are you anywhere nearer to knowing who killed Desmond?" she demanded.

"Well, now, m'lady, we don't seem to have narrowed it down any."

"*He* did it." A rasping, high-pitched voice sounded from above.

Frake looked up to the banister which ran the length of the gallery over the hall and encountered a baleful glare from a wizened face that renewed his faith in specters haunting this house.

The frail figure hobbled a step closer to the railing. "I warned you what would happen if Roland ever set foot in this country again. Murder most foul and vile, and all for the sake of my brother's title. He was evil as a child, and he is evil as a man. He could never fool me, no, try as he might, he could never twist me to his bidding as he did with that fool Euphemia."

Frake raised his eyebrows and glanced at Lady

Henrietta. "Is she always so melodramatic?" he whispered.

"Usually more so. She has yet to hit her stride with you." The young lady took hold of the carved oak newel post and looked up. "Great-aunt Lavinia, you should not say such things. Now, you must meet Mr. Frake, who is from Bow Street and is investigating Desmond's death."

The elderly woman snorted. "I know that, gel. Think you just because I don't leave my room until midnight means I don't know what's toward?" She waved her cane in their direction. "Roland killed Desmond, you mark my words." She turned her baleful eye on Frake. "Come to arrest him, have you? Well, he ain't here. Nor will he ever be, not if I can help it. Wild and cruel he was as a youth, beating both Netta and Desmond. Only little children, yet he'd strike out at them. You just look at Netta's wrist if you don't believe me. She'll bear the scar for the rest of her life."

She fell silent, staring at them, and vagueness replaced the piercing regard in her eyes. Quietly she muttered to herself and waved her cane in an offhand manner. An eerie laugh, akin to a cackle, escaped her, and she wandered off, still muttering.

Lady Henrietta drew a shaky breath. "My great-aunt, Lady Lavinia Galbraith."

Frake met her gaze, and he nodded. "Sad what age does to a person. Was she telling the truth?"

"About the scar?"

"Yes, m'lady." It pleased him she didn't pretend to misunderstand.

She hesitated. "I can't remember, it happened so long ago."

"But?" he prompted as she fell silent. "Could it be true?"

For a moment, fear flickered across her expressive countenance. "Oh, yes," she breathed.

Sleep did not come at all for Netta that night. Too many questions remained unanswered, too many possibilities haunted her. She knew too little about Roland. Why did he come here before going up to London? Surely not to visit Great-aunt Lavinia! He must have known, though, that he could find a deadly poison or two amidst Cousin Phemie's herbal pharmacopoeia.

Or perhaps he had come merely to lay a few personal ghosts before facing his relatives in the flesh.

Her lips twitched in self-derision. It seemed she could provide him with an innocent reason as well as a guilty one if she wished. But *why* should she so wish?

She rose at an early hour and spent the morning with Mrs. Haskins, selecting a simple fare for the funeral feast. This accomplished, they left the maid to begin roasting the meats while they went off to inspect the linen cabinets and review the number of servants necessary to keep a manor house of medium size functioning.

Perhaps she should sell it back to the Carncrosses after all, Netta reflected after a wearying hour. How, without the additional Tavistock income, could she possibly pay the salaries of so many people? Yet which positions could she eliminate? Certainly not the laundry maid, nor the single footman she must retain. Nor could only one groom handle the stable. These thoughts plagued her while she helped slice vegetables and oversaw the arrangement of the tables.

Depressed and drained, she curled into a chair in the library for a quick rest and stared out the window at the sunlit shrubbery below the terrace. A beautiful day — for a funeral. All too soon — by late that afternoon — the slow-moving cortege would arrive at the house, and Desmond would be laid to his final rest in the mausoleum constructed by her grandfather. Three earls it would contain.

She closed her eyes and wondered whether or not the current owners of their lost estate at Larkspur tended the ancient family vault containing her more distant ancestors. Larkspur, of which she'd only heard wistful tales. Larkspur, in the Lake District — a district which Roland had apparently visited before coming here.

She straightened. What had taken him there? So far, Roland had attained the title. Did he try to obtain the ancestral estate as well? Would the present owner, if he refused to sell, be found poisoned one morning by an heir who might be more willing to part with it? These thoughts kept her uncomfortable company as she returned to help in the kitchens.

At last — and all too soon — the black-draped carriages of the funeral procession pulled into view. Netta made her way to the Gold Drawing Room where Haskins and Jeremy had laid out the cold collation. There she sat, staring with unseeing eyes out the window at the bright spring afternoon, and thought of Desmond. Yet not her childhood's playmate, nor even the man whom she nearly wed, filled her mind. She mourned their unhappy past, the fact she could not recall a single joyous memory.

"Little Hen?" The deep voice sounded behind her.

She hadn't even heard the door open. She blinked back the unshed tears that hovered on her lashes before she turned, but with a sinking heart she realized he had seen. Vexed — embarrassed — she looked away once more.

"It is done." He crossed to the window and examined her view.

"Thank you."

He nodded without looking back at her, and she took the opportunity to dry her eyes. After restoring her handkerchief once more to the black reticule which dangled at her wrist, she stood. "Was it — difficult?"

His lips twitched. "You might say that. It is not a pleasant duty. I believe that Runner hoped Desmond's murderer would be overcome by remorse upon the occasion of the interment and confess his vile crime, but only disappointment awaited him."

Netta crossed to the hearth and picked up a china figurine of a horse. "Are many people here, then?"

"Only me."

"Only — oh!" A gasp of laughter escaped her. "Poor Mr. Frake. How unkind of you not to oblige with a confession, then."

Roland shook his head. "It quite wrenched my heart," he agreed, "but I fear I could not."

Or would not? Her smile faded.

"Do not take it to heart that no one has come." He spoke quickly, as if seeking to offer comfort. "You could not really expect anyone to travel so great a distance and at a moment's notice."

"We quite pinned our hopes on that, if you must know." If only there had been a way of preventing him from coming as well. She met his frowning gaze, and a frisson raced up her spine, leaving her tingling in its wake. Yes, it would have been so much better for her already disordered senses if he had stayed in London.

Yet perhaps now, with him here at Ravenswood where she had known him before, her tangled emotions might sort themselves out, begin to make some sense. For she *had* known him, though she'd been so very young. His dark, dangerous appearance matched her vague memories, but his manner — no, his manner did not. She could sense his strength and determination, but not the cruelty Great-aunt Lavinia assured her he possessed.

Roland crossed to the table. "It seems a shame to let this spoil. Will not your cook be offended?" He selected several slices of cold rare beef and placed them on a plate.

"Actually, the wife of my father's retired valet."

His brow snapped down. "Where is your cook? Or your housekeeper?"

"In London. We leave only a few servants when we remove to Tavistock House."

He added several slices of ham and a small assortment of cheeses. "I see. One staff, two households. I will send word for them to return to you at once."

She blinked. "But will you not need people?"

He gestured with the roll he held. "My man may interview applicants. If you can recommend a dependable agency? And until all is ready, my Aunt Phemie has invited me to remain here."

"To remain—" She broke off, dismayed. Or was she pleased? That thought startled her. No, she would much rather he returned to India! The stress of Desmond's death must have affected her more than she realized. That could be the only explanation for this fascination Roland exerted over her. He treated her like a little sister, yet the emotions that assailed her were far from fraternal.

He poured a glass of wine and held it out to her. "Canary, I believe. Would you care for some?"

She reached for it, but as her fingers closed about the stem, she froze. The wedding goblet, with its deadly oleander. The sherry, which might have been drugged for some more deadly purpose than just to allow someone to ransack the bookroom. What if someone—what if Roland—wanted her dead? Would there be some drug or poison in this as well?

She set the glass on a table and, with a murmured excuse, fled the room.

Chapter Nine

Netta pushed a bite of baked sole about her dinner plate, her appetite gone. Mrs. Haskins had tried her best to conjure a meal from the numerous remains of the funeral feast, with creditable results. Roland, seated at the head of the table, consumed a hefty portion. Even Cousin Phemie, seated at Roland's left, ate every morsel on her plate, then accepted another serving. Only Netta refrained.

The decision she had reached that afternoon filled her mind. And the sooner she shared it with the others, the happier — and possibly safer — she would be.

She waited until Roland and Cousin Phemie paused in their conversation, then blurted out in a tone louder than she intended: "I plan to go to Brighton in the morning and make a new will."

Cousin Phemie's fork clattered to the table and a gasp escaped her. Her hand fluttered before her throat. "Oh, my love, you must not speak of such things."

An ironic gleam lit Roland's eyes. "Now I wonder what could have brought this on?"

"Do you?" She met his gaze with defiance. "If something—untimely—should happen to me, Cousin Phemie and Great-aunt Lavinia would not be provided for. It must distress you, Roland, to know you would be the only one to benefit from my death."

His eyes gleamed. "It does indeed. I should imagine our good Mr. Frake must also find that fact fascinating."

"Dear Netta—" Phemie wrung her hands. "Pray do not talk so. Roland could never wish you harm, my love."

"Certainly he would not. And if he did, it would be particularly foolhardy of him to try anything now when I have stated my intention to make a will. If I met with a tragic accident before I could do so, Mr. Frake would naturally draw the most tiresome conclusions."

A cackling laugh sounded from the door, and Netta jumped. Lavinia, her frail form enveloped in a trailing lace shawl, stood only a few feet away. Netta hadn't heard the aged woman come in. It was as if she had just appeared or had been hiding behind a curtain.

Lavinia thrust her chin forward. "That will settle Roland's hash. No need to murder Netta now."

Netta flushed, embarrassed at having her thoughts expressed in so blunt a manner.

Roland merely smiled. "I assure you, Little Lady Hen is quite safe. Murdering her has never been an ambition of mine."

Lavinia hobbled forward and waggled a bony finger under his nose. "Like murdering Desmond was? You'll not hurt any more of us. You've taken my Desmond, I'll not let you get away with anymore. You never could have done it if they held the ball here where I could have watched you. Should have gone up to London, knew I should, as soon as you came back."

"How dare you speak to Roland like that?" Phemie flared, eyes blazing.

Lavinia raised the lorgnette that hung about her neck and peered at Phemie. "Phah! Old fool. You always were one, Euphemia. Not a lick of sense. You'd let the devil himself wrap you around his finger."

"What — what a vile thing to say."

Lavinia snorted. "Taken in by his cozening ways. You let him get away with all his cruel pranks just because he knew how to turn you up sweet. And now he's murdered Desmond and still you're protecting him."

Phemie flushed. "I'll not have you say such things. You have always sought to do Roland harm. It was you who had him sent to India, don't you deny it."

"I don't," came the venomous response. "He should have died there."

"Oh!" Phemie gasped. For a moment her mouth worked, then she rose to her feet. "You are a wicked, evil-tongued creature, Lavinia Galbraith. You have no idea what Roland is really like, you never gave him a chance. You believed everything Desmond told you, even about Daisy!"

Lavinia's mouth spread into a yellow-toothed

grin. "No better than she should be," she muttered.

"Daisy?" Netta turned from her battling relatives and raised questioning eyebrows at Roland.

"Good Lord," he said. "Wasn't that your maid, Aunt Phemie? I remember some dust up about her being turned off. That must have been ages ago. Before I left."

Phemie sniffed. "Turned off without a character, the poor child, and all because she wouldn't let Lavinia into my room to take my pearl necklet. And not a thing I could do to help her."

Netta, fascinated, returned her regard to her elderly great-aunt. "What role did Desmond play? He could have been no more than seven."

"Saw her up to no good with a footman," Lavinia informed them.

"Yes," Roland mused, "so he did. And no one happened to ask Desmond what he was doing in the servants' quarters peeking through keyholes. I'd quite forgotten that."

Phemie quivered. "*I* have not. Nor any of Lavinia's other slights and maliciousnesses. I've endured her spitefulness for nigh on five-and-twenty years, but I tell you, Netta, I'll not have her in the house another night, wandering about when all decent folk should be in their beds asleep."

Roland grasped Phemie's trembling hand. "You can hardly throw her from her home." He retained his calm, but with obvious effort.

So much for Roland's precious peace around here, Netta reflected. She could see the tiny lines of strain forming about his eyes. Perhaps the strife would drive him from the house. That would be best — at

165

least until they discovered the identity of Desmond's murderer. Too many doubts plagued her, as did her own conflicting emotions.

Phemie sniffed, on the verge of tears.

At once, Netta came around the table to her. "Do not distress yourself so, Cousin Phemie. You know you do not mean that."

"I do!" Phemie glared at her adversary.

Lavinia chuckled. "Weak, that's what you are, Euphemia."

"Netta, how can I—" Phemie wailed.

"Please, Great-aunt Lavinia." Netta threw her a pleading look. "Now, Cousin Phemie, you know we all share this house."

Phemie sniffed again and groped for her reticule. Roland drew a handkerchief from his coat pocket and gave it to her. With a muffled "thank you," she took it and blew her nose. "Very well," she said at last. "It will be better, though, if Lavinia and I contrive not to meet. Yet how we shall manage this when Ravenswood is of no very great size, I cannot say. But I shall live the remainder of my days in my own apartment if necessary."

"I am sure it will not be." With one arm about her cousin's shoulders, Netta led the woman from the room. Lavinia's gleeful cackle followed them down the hall.

Once in her own chamber, Phemie dissolved into tears. Netta rang for her abigail, then set about the difficult task of soothing her cousin's overwrought nerves. She bathed hands, sprinkled lavender water on a fresh handkerchief, prepared a hot brick, and by the time the maid arrived, Phemie had ceased to bewail Lavinia's perfidies, and meekly drank the draft of laudanum which Netta pressed on her.

"Sit with her," Netta instructed the uncertain abigail. "It has been a somewhat trying day."

"Yes, Miss Netta." The maid settled in a chair by the fire and anxiously watched as her elderly mistress lay back against the pillows in her bed.

When Phemie's breathing at last slowed and deepened into sleep, Netta slipped from the chamber. Roland must have finished his dinner by now, and Lavinia either prowled the house or had returned to her apartments. Netta started across the hall to her own rooms only to pause, too restless to remain confined between four walls. She wanted to get out, escape for a little while. The moonlit gardens beckoned.

She hurried the few steps to her bedchamber to fetch a woolen shawl, then ran down the steps and through the great double doors leading to the ballroom. The path stretching away from the terrace beyond the library window might be the more direct route, but Roland might have settled in there, and she didn't wish to meet him.

Or did she? No, she did *not*. She told herself so several more times for good measure and firmly ignored that nagging little voice she was beginning to hate.

Resolutely, she let herself out onto the paving stones and directed her steps along a gravel walkway toward the rose garden. The sweet scent drifted out to welcome her, and she slowed her pace, enjoying the silence of the warm evening. As she reached the side of the house, the pale illumination of a branch of candles lit the long French doors into the library. She'd been right; Roland had sought refuge there.

She fought the urge to go up and tap at the glass. Why did he fascinate her so? Because she couldn't understand her tangled feelings about him? A sudden memory filled her, vivid in its every detail, of her running toward him, laughing in delight, throwing herself into his arms. She could have been no more than five, trusting him — loving him — implicitly. Part of her longed to do so again, to experience his comforting strength.

Yet another, probably more rational, part of her urged her to flee before it was too late. But from what? Had she true cause to fear him? All she knew for certain was that he filled her thoughts more than he ought.

She turned down another path that led past the shrubbery maze. She couldn't really believe him to be a murderer. Yet he gained the title, and just before Desmond's marriage and the potential arrival of an heir who would place him that much farther from the succession.

That might all be no more than a fortuitous circumstance — or an infernal nuisance, as Roland would have it. He seemed to mean that, too. She had detected no satisfaction in his manner, no air of possessiveness as he had stood in Tavistock House. Only distaste.

She walked on, disturbed at how quickly she sought to clear Roland. She didn't really know him; she had every reason to distrust him. Yet in spite of all common sense, something within her longed to believe in him.

She followed the path to the line of trees separating the Ravenswood garden from that of the Dower House. Through the leaves she caught a glimpse of candles glowing in one upper window. The younger children, retiring to bed. She hoped, for their sakes, their measles were almost gone. With a slight smile for her own remembered agonies with that complaint, she headed back toward the roses.

If only she could banish Roland from her mind. His dark features persisted in haunting her, accompanying her every step. Frustrated, she wandered along the shrubbery paths, pulling off an occasional leaf and twisting it between her fingers.

As she picked another, the hairs prickled up the back of her neck. She glanced over her shoulder, suddenly alert, aware of every sound. Had she heard something — like a footstep or an intake of breath? She strained her eyes, trying to see through the darkness of the moon-cast shadows.

Nothing. Yet she couldn't rid herself of that eerie sensation that someone hovered nearby, waiting, following. Shivering, she chided herself for a missish fool. She took another two steps, only to freeze as a twig snapped behind her and to her left.

She spun about, searching, but could make out nothing. Only her overwrought nerves, she assured herself. Still, she glanced toward the manor. She had wandered several hundred yards from it, and the path back meandered through the shrubbery — right past the spot from where that sound had come.

This was nōnsensical. She would go and look and no doubt find some night-time creature out foraging. She took a step forward, and at once a branch rustled, as if someone leaned against it. A shadow wavered, and sheer terror defied her attempts to move. A shape—a very human shape—drew back into sheltering darkness. Not her imagination, after all.

She swallowed, her throat dry. "Who is it? Roland?"

Only silence answered her call, so ominous in its completeness as to leave her ill with dread. The person waited between her and the house. To reach it, she would have to pass him. She backed a pace away, then turned and hurried along the gravel walkway. If only the moon would shine brighter or be nearer to full. . . .

Footsteps crunched along the tiny stones behind her. No longer did her stalker take pains to move without noise; he openly kept pace, yet did not try to close on her. At least, not yet . . .

She broke into a run and ducked down a side path, her heart beating so loudly it drowned all other sounds except her rasping breath—and the footsteps that continued to follow. She doubled back along another narrow walkway and found herself once more within the living, leafy walls of the shrubbery. She'd been cut off from the house, trapped in here. She wouldn't be able to circle around and reach safety.

The crunching on the gravel behind her slowed, then stopped, as if her pursuer guessed her predicament. She stood very still, not wanting to breathe, not wanting to make any sound that might betray her whereabouts. He'd have to find her—but pathetically few hiding places offered themselves. She would see him coming, but what consolation would that be? If she screamed, he would only have to move faster — although more than likely no one at the house would hear.

The footsteps resumed, and she backed away. There had to be a way out; hadn't there been a gap in the hedge? She'd asked the gardener to plant a new shrub, but had he done it? Her hand, extended behind her, encountered the prickly branches of the hawthorns, and she eased along the line of bushes.

She faced the house; she could see the head of the statue near the entrance where the leafy greenery hadn't quite grown tall enough to cover it. The gap she remembered would be to her right, perhaps ten — or was it twenty? — yards away. If she could crawl through it, she might be able to reach the Dower House. Sir Archy's servants would help her. She only had to reach them.

If she ran, now, as fast as she could, had she a hope of reaching the gap before her follower caught her? She searched through the darkness, straining her ears for any sound from him. There, a rustle of leaves. He drew closer, with uncanny stealth, while she dallied in uncertainty.

Without conscious decision, she found herself running headlong. There, the leaves thinned. Even in the dark she could see the bare spot. If she could only get there . . . She dove at it, wincing as the spiny branches clawed her cheeks, gouging at her arms.

Fingers grasped her silk skirts, clinging, holding her back, then she ripped free, only snagged in the shrubs. Gasping, she struggled on hands and knees, yanking her gown free of the last entangling twigs. As she scrambled to her feet, her pursuer crashed into the shrub almost on top of her.

She fled, blind with panic, stumbling in the narrow confines of her skirt. From behind came low-voiced curses and the breaking of branches as he broke through. He'd be on her in minutes.

She dragged the bedraggled material up to her knees and blundered headlong through the spinney. Twigs scratched her, catching at her shawl, snatching tendrils of hair from her chignon until the pins scattered, cascading the heavy waves about her shoulders. The thudding footsteps neared. She wouldn't be able to reach the Dower House. His hands would close upon her in only moments. Her gasping breath broke on a sob. She wouldn't make it.

She stumbled over a gnarled root, caught her balance by grabbing the twisted trunk, and yanked herself onto a side path. As she raced along it, a rushing sound made itself heard over the pounding of her heart. What—the river. The folly would be just ahead. If she could just reach that, she might be able to . . .

She ducked a low branch and raced on, following the rambling turns of the rustic walkway. Then the folly loomed up ahead, calm and serene in the moonlight which filtered through the leafy branches. She could make it.

And what, then? Be trapped? Await her pursuer within? He'd expect her to try to hide there. She ran past, then on inspiration flung herself down the steep bank, scrambled over the rocks and into the river, at last crouching among the sheltering roots of a giant pine, up to her neck in the swirling, icy depths. She leaned her face against the rough bark, hanging on to keep from being swept away by the current, and willed her racing heart to slow. She could only hope the sounds of the rushing water drowned out the ragged gasps of her breathing.

Her pursuer blundered past on the path above and threw open the door of the folly. For several minutes he remained within, shoving the few chairs and table about as if he sought her hiding place. She gripped the trunk all the tighter, shuddering. She could see nothing, only the rocky bank with the edge of the folly above. Then the door opened once more and footsteps descended the three steps, then came down the bank.

Netta cringed, willing herself to disappear into the shadowy darkness. She could let go, be swept away by the black, swirling waters — and be battered by the boulders and fallen trees which long ago had sunk the toy boats she had launched.

The snapping of twigs stopped, and she risked a peek. A dim shape, nothing more than a darkness against a greater darkness, stood on the edge of the bank, barely ten yards away, studying the river. A man — or could it be a woman in disguise? She couldn't tell, certainly not enough to identify the person.

He started forward, as if searching. She held her breath, pressing her cheek into the bark until she longed to cry out with the pain. Why didn't he give up and go away?

I'm not here, the thought filled her mind, and she fought the urge to shout it out loud.

He stood only a yard from her now, on the opposite side of the pine. She could hear the panting breaths — yet she couldn't see who waited there with her murder on his mind.

Endless seconds passed, then at last he turned and scrambled among the rocks and tree roots in the opposite direction. Gathering her courage, she peered around the trunk, but again could only make out a shadowy shape. He continued his search for some distance, stood for several minutes, then clambered up the bank once more to the path above. To her relief, the footsteps receded.

Still, she didn't move. Too terrified, she realized in disgust. Or was that too prudent? What if he waited, just a little ways away?

She remained where she was for a very long while until her racing heart slowed and the tension eased from her muscles with the ebbing of her fear. She continued to tremble, but now with cold and reaction. She allowed more slow minutes to creep by until the cold drove her from her hiding place. Dripping and freezing, she pulled herself up the side of the bank, using tree roots as steps and handholds.

Once more on the path, she hugged herself. She must have lost her shawl somewhere — though if she'd had it in the river with her, it would do her little good now. She'd better get back to the house — or better, the Dower House, in case her pursuer still lurked in hiding, waiting to intercept her. With caution, trying not to make a single sound, she started down the path.

The door to the folly stood open. She caught her

174

breath, then released it in a silent, shattering sigh. He must have left it that way. He hadn't gone back in — had he? She crept past.

A shadowy shape loomed against the darker background of the interior. A scream tore from her throat and she broke into a run. With every step he gained on her, then an iron-strong arm wrapped about her waist, dragging her back into his imprisoning grasp.

Chapter Ten

A gasping cry escaped Netta. She struggled, kicking at her captor's shins with her water-logged slippers. He didn't seem to notice. He spun her about, gripping her arms with painful intensity, and she stared into Roland's grim face.

"Little Hen—" He breathed her name, the sound ragged.

Gravel crunched behind them, the footsteps of someone approaching along the river path from the other direction. Roland tensed but didn't release her. Her knees buckled in relief, and only his grip kept her from falling to the ground.

A bulky figure rounded the bend. Roland looked behind him, and the shifting of his broad shoulders blocked the new arrival from Netta's sight. She pulled, but his grip tightened in response. The footsteps stopped, followed by a moment of silence.

Roland moved then, though he did not release her. Netta stared past him at Mr. Josiah Underhill.

"Underhill?" Roland exclaimed. "What are you doing here?"

The man regarded them with an expression of mixed shock and disapproval. "Might ask you the same thing. Lady Henrietta, you're all wet!"

"And shivering," Roland agreed. His hands dropped from her and he lifted a white fabric from where it hung over his arm. Her shawl. He draped it across her shoulders and she took hold of it. "I found this on the path. I was about to ask you what happened." He stripped off his coat and wrapped this about her as well. "I thought I heard someone scream earlier, and came out to investigate. Was it you?"

"I—I don't know." Her voice sounded strangely calm to her own ears. Roland—or Underhill—or someone else? She clutched the smooth wool of his coat. For all she knew, she might well have screamed. She looked up and realized both men watched her, waiting for her explanation. "I went out into the garden, and someone chased me."

Mr. Underhill's eyebrows rose, his expression skeptical. "What the devil for?"

"My sentiments exactly," Roland agreed, "though perhaps I should not have phrased it in quite so reprehensible a manner in the presence of a lady."

Underhill ignored him. He considered a moment, then shook his head. "Load of rubbish. Who'd want to go and chase her?"

"In case you have forgotten," Netta said through teeth clenched against their chattering, "someone murdered my cousin only a few days ago."

"Demmed good thing, too, if you want my opinion." Underhill frowned. "But what has that to do with you?"

"That person most likely meant me to die as well. If Desmond hadn't swallowed the entire contents of the wedding goblet, I would have taken the poison, too."

Roland's brow snapped down. "Did you see who followed you?"

She hesitated. "No," she admitted. "Did you not see anyone?"

"No. I heard nothing but that scream, near the house. I wandered about for a bit, then came out to the folly. I was about to return when I saw you on the path." He frowned. "You are quite certain you were pursued?"

Her jaw clenched. "Not in the least. I jumped in the river for a lark — or possibly out of boredom, considering how dull we have been these several days past."

"Don't see any point in that," Underhill protested.

"I meant chased by someone who intended you harm," Roland snapped.

She shivered. "I am very sure he intended me that. I led him a merry chase, I promise you, even *through* the hedge."

Underhill shook his head. "All sounds rum to me."

Roland cast him an enigmatic glance, but all he said to Netta was: "Let's get you back inside before you take an inflammation of the lungs and save any would-be attacker further effort."

She hurried ahead, stifling the urge to run. Her every instinct told her to trust Roland—yet how could she? On the very night she announced she would make a new will—with only him to gain from the current arrangement—someone tried to kill her. If only she knew what sort of man he actually was. Had he come to her rescue, as he claimed—as she wanted to believe? Or did this Big Cousin who haunted her thoughts want her dead?

"You never told us what brought you here." Roland's voice sounded calm—quite normal—as he followed a pace behind with their visitor.

"What?" Underhill sounded surprised. "Oh. That demmed Runner fellow of yours."

"Of mine?" Roland's voice held a musing note. "Yes, I suppose I am his main interest at the moment. Has he been bothering you as well?"

"Been asking questions among m'staff. Upsetting 'em. M'butler threatened to quit this morning. Said it's not the sort of thing to which he's accustomed. Demmed haughty fellow. Gave him the sack."

Netta slowed, falling into step on Roland's other side, and cast the two men a sideways glance.

Underhill waggled a finger under Roland's nose. "You keep that fellow under control, or there'll be trouble."

Roland's expression remained bland. "For whom?"

Underhill snorted. "All the same, you Galbraiths." He glared at them both. "Bid you good night."

"A moment." Roland held up one hand. "What has brought you all the way to Ravenswood? I had thought you in London."

"Hah! Summons from m'uncle. Lives in Brighton," he explained.

"How obliging of you to comply with his requests."

Underhill glowered. "Holds the purse strings." With a curt nod, he stomped off.

Roland stared after him for a long moment. "You said this assailant of yours pursued you *through* a shrub, Hen?"

The deep undertones of his voice set a fluttering inside her, and she took a hasty step away from him. With an effort she brought her thoughts to his question. "And down the bank to the river."

His frowning gaze swept over her disheveled appearance, and he touched her cheek with a surprisingly gentle finger. "You are bleeding. Come, let us get you within doors and see what other injuries you have sustained."

"Just scratches." She moved out of his reach and hurried toward the house.

He kept pace with ease. "You seem to have suffered somewhat from the experience," he mused.

"Indeed?" She regarded him with fascination. "It must have escaped my notice."

His smile flashed. "Underhill, on the other hand," he went on, "appeared not to have so much as a hair out of place."

"Oh." That stopped her. "Then it could not have been he who followed me, could it?" Or Roland.

Relief, out of all proportion, washed over her.

"Unless he had another coat near at hand. Could he have had time to straighten his appearance?"

That brought her back to earth. He could—and so could Roland. Either man could have worn an overcoat and simply removed it.

Roland took her arm and led her toward the house. "I wonder what our Runner will make of all this?"

Netta wondered, also, though she thought she could hazard a guess. Roland made the most likely suspect. It was simple, reasonable—so why didn't she want it to be so?

Once inside the house, she escaped from Roland and made her way to her room to bathe her scratches. In response to her abigail's shocked exclamations and questions, Netta admitted the truth, then wished she hadn't as Wembly went off into a fit of the vapors. Netta at last calmed her, argued down the shaken woman's proclaimed intentions to remain at her mistress's side closer than a sticking plaster, and at last sent her off to her bed. Still, Wembly remained rooted outside the door until Netta assured her she had turned—and removed—the key, then at last the abigail took herself off. With a sigh of relief, Netta sat down and composed a letter to the Runner.

She awoke in the morning to stiff muscles and painful scratches. With the assistance of the grim-faced Wembly, she applied ointment to the worst, then donned the bombazine round gown. Her maid, in spite of Netta's adjurations not to do so, followed her down the stairs. At the last landing, Netta dismissed her firmly and went to deliver her letter into the hands of Jeremy.

She found the breakfast parlor deserted except for the aged valet, who checked the flame beneath a warming pan. She looked about the apartment, noting that no dirtied dishes rested on the sideboard. "Has no one else come down, yet, Haskins?"

"Yes, Miss Netta. Master Roland breakfasted over an hour ago."

"And my cousin?"

"Miss Wrenn is keeping to her apartment, Miss Netta."

Netta closed her eyes. So the little woman intended to make good her threat about avoiding Great-aunt Lavinia. Netta would have to coax her down. But first, at least, she could have her breakfast in peace.

She had taken no more than four mouthfuls when Haskins reappeared and announced the arrival of Sir Archibald Carncross. Netta's surprised gaze flew to the mantel clock; it lacked fifteen minutes until ten. Concerned by a visit at such an unprecedented early hour, she went to him at once.

She found him pacing the North Salon, his expression frowning, his appearance staggering in his attempts to outshine any Pink of the Ton. From the top of his pomaded curls to the soles of his gleaming Hessians, not a flaw could be found in his dress—aside from its inappropriateness to the country setting. Netta regarded him with the first stirrings of amusement she had felt since going for her walk last night.

"You could turn heads on Bond Street." She advanced into the room. "How do you go on, Archy? I did not expect to see you. I had thought you settled in London for a little longer."

He touched the starched point of his shirt collar, which reached to his cheekbone. "Thought we should keep an eye on you. All alone here with That Man." His tone capitalized the words. "Fellow told me he has no interest in Ravenswood. If that don't beat the Dutch! I mean, not want an estate? Says he'd sell it in a minute if it were his. Dashed silly thing to say, don't you think?"

"I don't know." She sank onto the sofa. "He says it harbors unpleasant memories for him. That could very well be true, you know."

Archy leaned forward, peering at her. "Dash it, Netta, what have you been about? Your cheek is scratched."

She managed what she hoped to be an unconcerned smile. "Oh, it's been quite an adventure, I assure you. Someone chased me through the garden last night."

"By Jove." He settled in the chair next to her. "Did you see who it was?"

She shook her head. "And that puts me quite beyond the pale, I make no doubt. What a poor honey I was. I was actually more concerned with getting away."

"So I should think," he agreed with considerable

feeling. "Chased you, by gad. Have you told anyone?"

"You may be very sure I have. Including that man Frake from Bow Street."

For a long moment he worked his lower lip between his teeth. "Best thing you could have done," he pronounced at last. "Bound to keep you safe. Well, what I mean is, should like that chance m'self."

Netta blinked. "Would you?"

He clasped his hands in his lap, then unclasped them and reached for hers. "Know this is sudden, Netta. Only realized m'self how I felt about you when I was about to lose you to Desmond."

She moved away. "You need not feel any chivalrous duty toward me, you know."

He tried to look affronted, but didn't quite succeed. "No such thing. Assure you! Honored if you'd be my wife."

She leveled an assessing gaze at him. "Has this venture your mama's blessing?"

"Well, of course it does. You know how she feels."

"Indeed I do." About Ravenswood, at least, if not about herself. Did they regard her as a necessary evil in order to regain the estate for their family? Lady Carncross obviously brought pressure to bear on her son. She could not imagine Archy proposing to her without a parental push. Nor had she any desire to wed one whom Desmond had freely disparaged as a young nodcock. She would have to

184

let Lady Carncross know his suit would not prosper.

He still regarded her with the intentness of a hopeful puppy, and she forced a smile she was far from feeling to her lips. "As you say, this is quite sudden. I am not even out of deep mourning, yet. But you need have no fear — I shall not allow myself to be pressured into any hasty decisions."

"You mistake." His hands gripped together once more. "Very much desire this marriage. No need to give me your answer now, though. Know you've been permitted to consider no man but Desmond. Must grow accustomed to your freedom." He rose, claimed both her hands and carried them to his lips, then swept her an elegant bow. "Won't press you, have no fear. May I call again tomorrow?"

"Of course." When had he ever bothered to ask before? She saw him out, then returned to her now-cold breakfast. She couldn't help but wonder if he knew his mama's real reason for promoting this match. Most likely he did. Well, she would deal with this problem at its source and at the first opportunity that presented itself. Once his mama knew the situation to be hopeless, she felt certain she could rely on Lady Carncross to discourage his pretensions.

She replaced her cup of tea, but had time to do no more than take a bite of toast before Haskins again appeared at the door. Netta turned resigned eyes on him.

"Mr. Frake, Miss Netta," he announced in tones of deep disapproval.

"Oh, thank heavens." Only he couldn't have received her letter yet; she would have to tell him. She swallowed the rest in two mouthfuls and hurried from the room.

The Runner sat in the estate room, pouring over an account book with a puzzled frown on his brow. He looked up as she entered, and he rose, laying the volume aside. "Not a sizable fortune," he said by way of greeting.

"Rather you should call it a competence."

His gaze narrowed on her. "Now, how would you be getting such a nasty scratch?"

She touched her cheek. "Someone chased me through the garden last night. I only escaped by climbing down into the river."

"Did you now?" He rocked back on his heels, regarding her through wide, innocent-seeming blue eyes. "Now, why would someone want to go chasing you?"

Skepticism. She should have guessed. And she had not a shred of evidence to corroborate her story, only Roland and Mr. Underhill to say they had seen her dripping wet and shivering, though they could not say for certain how—or why—she had gotten that way.

She glared at him. "I suppose you think I made the story up, that it's all an elaborate hoax on my part to throw suspicion from myself."

"Now, m'lady, I didn't say no such thing."

"You don't have to say it. It is obvious from the way you are looking at me. But I'll have you know that if that were the case, I'd have been at

186

pains to assure a better audience."

His generous mouth twitched into a smile. "You could easily have drunk some of that poison your betrothed swallowed, couldn't you? You think someone wants you dead as well?"

"The thought did just cross my mind."

"Would anyone gain by your dying?"

She turned away, suddenly reluctant to tell him. It made no sense, her trying to protect Roland. If he were innocent, then she had no need. If he were guilty — That prospect tore at her.

"His new lordship, wouldn't it be?"

She swallowed. "He would inherit everything," she admitted. "Which is why I intend to go into Brighton this morning and make a new will." It dawned on her with distressing clarity that her motive for this lay not so much in protecting her own person but in reassuring herself that Roland, at least, had no reason to wish her harm.

Frake pursed his lips. "Did you mention your plan to anyone last night?"

She admitted it, her heart sinking. Why did the Runner have to make Roland look so *very* guilty? Only it wasn't Mr. Frake's fault, she realized.

The Runner shook his head, as if saddened by the information. "Well, now, m'lady, perhaps it might be best if you remain within sight of others at all times. Don't you think? Now then," he went on without waiting for her response. "About this trip into Brighton. When was you thinking of going?"

"At once."

He nodded. "Think I'll go along with you, if you don't mind. Wouldn't object to having a word with your solicitor."

Half an hour later, with Miss Wrenn beside Netta in the ancient landau and the Runner on the facing seat, they set forth. The brilliant morning sky promised warmth, while a gentle breeze assured it would not become too hot. The starkness of Netta's unrelieved black felt inappropriate. Perhaps she could purchase a riband to smarten up her bonnet a little. Even a black one would help.

She leaned back in her seat, closing her eyes, raising her face to the sun. It would be more appropriate, she supposed, if she went to make her will in the pouring rain or in the depths of drear winter. Anytime but this lovely spring morning. Yet perhaps, in the spirit of spring, she made a gesture that would assure her life. That thought brought her no pleasure. She could not — or was that *would* not? — believe Roland wished her dead.

A journey of no more than thirty minutes along the excellent road brought them to the red glazed-brick paving of the Steyne. The coachman eased his team past the Pavilion and drew up at last before one of the more recently constructed buildings.

Netta eyed it with interest and a touch of trepidation. Never before had she visited a solicitor's office. Always, Mr. Wickstone came to Ravenswood to consult with her father or Desmond.

Mr. Frake jumped down and handed her out.

Phemie followed, casting an uncertain look at the structure. "I make no doubt he would have come, had you sent for him," she repeated for perhaps the tenth time that morning.

"I want this settled." Clutching the strings of her reticule, Netta marched up the steps into a narrow corridor, then ascended the flight within. At the top she discovered another hallway and proceeded along it until she found a door on which a lettered sign announced she had found Mssrs. Wickstone and Wickstone, solicitors.

Mr. Frake knocked, then opened the door and ushered Netta and Cousin Phemie inside. Netta glanced about the comfortably sized vestibule, with its window looking out over the street, two doors leading, presumably, to offices, and a selection of wooden chairs. A desk stood to one side, currently vacant.

One of the inner doors opened, and a slender man of indeterminate years peered at them from over a pair of wire spectacles. "May I help you?" he asked.

Frake stepped forward. "Lady Henrietta Galbraith, to see Mr. Wickstone."

A deep voice sounded within, and the clerk turned to relay the information. In a moment, the large, familiar figure of the senior Mr. Wickstone emerged, his expanding girth blocking the doorway. His jovial aspect showed concern.

"Lady Henrietta, do come in. What has brought you? You had but to send for me, and I would have come at once."

"I had to come to Brighton, and I thought to save you the trouble." She allowed him to lead her into the inner sanctum, where he pressed her into a high-backed chair.

Cousin Phemie hesitated, then took one of the chairs in the waiting room. Netta saw the Runner take up a position at her side before the solicitor closed the door.

Mr. Wickstone leaned back on the edge of his desk. "What may I do for you?"

Netta drew a deep breath. "I wish to make a will."

He frowned. "Now, you must not refine too much upon your cousin's death. Still, you are wise to concern yourself with the estate."

The process, to Netta's dismay, took more than an hour while the solicitor took notes on her wishes, made suggestions, discussed at length the needs of Ravenswood. While agreeing that Miss Wrenn and Lady Lavinia would be comfortable with the bequests left to them, he could not but shake his head over her determination to leave the Ravenswood estate and its income to charity. At last, though, he promised to have a formal copy drawn up within two days, and escorted her back to the waiting room.

Two days, and then she should be safe—or at least free of her suspicions of Roland. After that, if any attempts were made on her life, she could be certain it was not he. Couldn't she?

Mr. Frake rose as she came out and announced his desire to speak with the solicitor concerning the late earl's affairs. With a promise to meet Netta and Miss Wrenn at the lending library when he was done, he disappeared into the inner office.

Before they reached the door to the hallway, it swung wide, and Mr. Kenneth Lambert strolled in. He stopped at sight of them, and his generous mouth widened in a broad smile. He bowed over his godmother's hand, then carried Netta's fingers to his lips, the expression in his eyes a caress. "I didn't know you had returned to Ravenswood. I had thought you established in London until this dreadful business is over."

"The Runner assured me he saw no reason for us to remain. Did you not hear the announcement at the funeral?"

He squeezed her hand, his expression one of regret. "The pressing nature of my own affairs, I fear, prevented me from attending. I assure you, nothing else could have dragged me so far from your side at this distressing time."

"There is no need—"

"How I regretted," he went on as if she had not spoken, "not being able to offer you my support. Though perhaps that is just as well, for in the eyes of the world, at least, the desires of my heart must seem precipitous." He glanced at his godmother, but Phemie had retired to the window and stared out with apparent fascination. Lambert lowered his voice and spoke with an increased urgency. "I know it is wrong for me not to regret Tavistock's untimely passing, but it had always caused me pain to know you were bespoken to such a man."

She bit back the retort that it had not been easy for her, either.

"I hope you have now had time to come to terms with your unexpected freedom. May I call upon you at Ravenswood soon? At that time perhaps I might speak more openly to you of my hopes." He pressed a fervent kiss onto her fingers.

She drew her hand back, startled and dismayed to realize she had permitted him to retain it for so long a time. Such unseemly behavior. So very fast. And a trifle exhilarating. Only he was not the right man.

Mr. Wickstone's door opened, and the solicitor came out, accompanied by Mr. Frake. The Runner stopped in his tracks and beamed. "Mr. Lambert."

Lambert's smile turned brittle. "Ah, the Runner chap. What's the name—Frake? Yes, Mr. Frake."

The Runner rocked back on his heels. "Lucky thing, running into you like this. I had planned to call at your lodging. A question, if you will."

"Yes?" Lambert toyed with the riband from which his quizzing glass hung.

"About your gaming debts to the late earl. Quite substantial, as I believe." Frake shook his head. "It seems a wonder to me that anyone could pay such an amount. It must have been weighing heavily upon you. Quite relieved you must be by his lordship's death."

Chapter Eleven

Benjamin Frake regarded Mr. Kenneth Lambert with an affable smile. Interesting, what a person's first reactions could reveal. He waited, his keen gaze missing nothing.

The Corinthian stiffened, then with deliberation raised his quizzing glass and regarded Frake through it. "You will be so kind as to explain yourself."

"Oh, aye." Frake repressed a smile. "A sizable number of vowels. Now, I wonder, can you tell me the exact sum?"

Lambert inclined his head. "You have only to look at them—as it seems you already have."

Frake clucked his tongue in regret. "Now there you are mistaken. They appear to be missing."

"Missing?" Lambert's eyebrows rose, and he looked at Lady Henrietta.

Frake gave the young lady an almost imperceptible nod.

"Someone broke into the bookroom," she explained. "Your vowels may have been taken, for we could find no trace of them."

Lambert's lip curled. "I see. I assure you, I did not perform this perfidious deed. I had no need, you see. The amount I lost—contrary to this Person's assertions—was quite trifling compared to what it might well have been."

"And that was, sir?" Frake schooled his features into a look of innocent hopefulness.

Lambert cast him a pained glance. "Really, my good man—"

"For the investigation." Frake shrugged, his expression one of "what else can I do?"

Lambert's lips tightened, then relaxed into a supercilious smile. "It was somewhere in the vicinity of three hundred pounds, I believe. Ah—and you need have no fear. Even if they have been lost, I shall of course redeem them."

Frake made a show of jotting the information down in his Occurrence Book—along with the fact that Mr. Lambert's manner now appeared just a shade too casual, not at all in keeping with his irritation of a moment before. No, not at all. And that amount he named was as nothing compared to that owed by Lady Beatrix, and less than a quarter the sum of the scattered vowels belonging to Sir Archibald Carncross. Well, well, well.

Now, would a gentleman of fashion such as this one ransack the dead earl's bookroom in order to reclaim his vowels before he was required to repay an impossible amount? Mayhap he would. And might he even have killed his late lordship to avoid a crushing debt — and perhaps to rid himself of his rival for a certain young lady's hand as well? Interesting possibility, that.

He returned his Occurrence Book to his breast pocket. "I won't take any more of your time, Mr. Lambert. For the moment." He doffed his hat. "Lady Henrietta?"

Miss Wrenn turned from the window. "Dear Kenneth." She came forward once more. "You will call upon us at your earliest convenience, will you not?"

Mr. Lambert bowed over her hand. "I shall be at Ravenswood ere you know it," he assured her.

Ere you know it. Frake shot a glance at the man. What about "even if they don't know it?" Like last night, perchance? If Lady Henrietta didn't lie about being pursued through the gardens, then it seemed likely someone wanted her dead.

Stewing over the possibilities, he ushered his charges from the building, then checked his watch. The carriage would not call for them for another hour yet. He might as well see the ladies safely to the lending library, then take a long walk and have himself a think.

"Did not dear Kenneth look tired, Netta?" Miss Wrenn emerged first onto the street. "I vow, I am quite glad he has left London, are not you? Such late hours as gentlemen keep at their clubs. Shall we have him to dine?"

"When we are out of mourning," came Lady Henrietta's firm response.

Miss Wrenn sighed. "I don't wish to sound pettish, my love, but it would be so very pleasant just to have a guest for dinner. Surely, after a week or two, that could not be considered shocking."

Lady Henrietta returned a vague answer, and they fell silent as the three of them strolled along the sunlit street.

Cooler here than in London, Frake reflected. The salt tang of the sea permeated the air, refreshing and pleasant. Another block and they neared the building housing Donaldson's Circulating Library.

A raven-haired young woman came down the steps, garbed in a forest green velvet riding habit. She glanced casually in their direction, and Frake got a clear view of her squarish face. Lady Beatrix Underhill. The woman turned at once and hurried along the street.

Seemingly, he'd have no reason to return to London, Frake mused. This placed the last of his suspects here in Brighton—here, where any one of them could have stalked Lady Henrietta last night. But why had Lady Beatrix been so anxious to avoid them? She could not have missed seeing them. Again, interesting.

Netta remained silent on the return to Ravenswood, her thoughts far from Cousin Phemie's rambling chatter. The Runner once more occupied the facing seat, but he, too, seemed intent on his own reflections. He had not spoken beyond common courtesies since rejoining them after their luncheon at the Old Ship.

Nothing made sense, nothing was the way she'd expected. Not the murder, not Roland, not her own emotions. Of all the gentlemen of her acquaintance, she had thought Mr. Lambert her favorite. Now he seemed frippery, a mere Bond Street Beau. She discovered in herself an unexpected preference for a gentleman who could face hardships and carve his own way in the world in spite of his high birth.

She closed her eyes, trying to bring Roland's powerful, rugged features to mind. Was he a murderer or just her overprotective Big Cousin? Logic warned her to run from him, instinct urged the opposite. She needed to be rid of these doubts.

She'd been raised to fear him—she had *reason* to fear him. Her fingers traced the three-inch scar across the back of her wrist. So why didn't the mere thought of him send her into panic?

Because she'd fallen under his spell the first moment she saw him the night of the ball. Because he personified every romantic fantasy in which she had ever indulged. Because she could not make the connection between this dynamic, compelling man made for daydreams and the wicked, cruel cousin of her nightmares.

No person could change that drastically, not even in seventeen difficult years in another country—on another continent. The Roland of Greataunt Lavinia's tales would have become more determined, more devious. Able, perhaps, to fool her this completely?

What was the truth? What had really happened

that day when her father cast him out of their lives? If she could understand that, perhaps she could understand everything that led up to it—and everything that happened now.

She'd been only five, her memories shaky, colored by emotion. They'd been in the nursery, playing . . .

By the time they reached the house, her temples throbbed from her efforts at recollection. Phemie bustled at her side, bemoaning Netta's sad affliction, and seemed bent on accompanying Netta to her chamber with a selection of medicines running the gamut from pastilles, laudanum, feathers to burn, and handkerchiefs soaked in scent. Hiding her exasperation, Netta declined all her companion's suggestions with gentle firmness.

"There is something you could do for me," she told Phemie, hitting on how to be free of the unwanted solicitude. "Will you oversee dinner?"

"Dinner?" Phemie stopped in her tracks. "But what if That Woman comes downstairs?"

"How often has Great-aunt Lavinia left her chambers before midnight?"

Phemie sniffed. "She did yesterday."

Netta tried a cajoling smile. "Please, Cousin Phemie. You know Mrs. Haskins cannot manage on her own, not with most of the staff still in London."

Again, Phemie sniffed. "But dear—"

Netta touched her aching head and needed no acting to produce a convincing wince. "I know you would not wish to set an inferior dinner before Roland. Or an inferior table."

That gave Phemie pause. She considered a moment. "Violet is the most skimble-skamble maid, is she not? How I do miss Fenton. I vow, no one sets a table to perfection as does he. Will he come back to us, do you think? Or remain at Tavistock House with Roland? Oh, I do hope he does not. Servants take so dreadfully long to train just as one would like, do they not?" The little woman peeked up at her, her expression uncertain. "But you know how so many of them prefer the London House."

"All the more reason to keep an eye on Violet." Without giving her companion a chance to answer, Netta made good her escape, determined to reach her destination with no more delays.

The door to the schoolroom suite in the West Wing stood closed. She hesitated, bracing her nerve. Nothing lurked within except memories, which she came to awaken. Memories and possibly understanding.

She thrust the door wide and advanced several steps into the long room, then paused. Dim light filtered through the unwashed window panes, doing little to dispel the darkness. Ghostly shapes hovered against the walls, which resolved themselves into furniture long shrouded beneath Holland covers.

Old beloved toys peeked out from a chest too full for the lid to close tight. She knelt before it and lifted out a dark-haired doll, gowned in the fashion of twenty years before. Yvette, she had called her, after the little French girl she had met in Brighton the day—

She held the doll close. The day *Roland* gave it to her? Could that be true? For years she'd called it a present from Cousin Phemie, had come to believe it, because—because her father had forbidden Roland's name to be mentioned in the house!

She sat back on her heels, startled by the realization, hoping this might trigger a flood of memories which might explain so much. They didn't come. With a sigh, she laid aside Yvette and picked up one of the painted wooden soldiers that lay beneath. Desmond's. No help there.

She rose and walked about the chamber, touching the bookcase, the door into the schoolroom, the chair where she had curled up by the window to read. In the middle of the room she came to a halt, closing her eyes, trying to recapture images and impressions of that horrible day.

Unfocused fear rippled through her. A child's scream—her own—filled her mind. Her knees gave way and she sank to the floor, folding her arms about the neck of an old hobby horse for comfort and support. Someone had broken its ear. Tears filled her eyes as she ran her finger over the spot filed smooth against splinters.

An image of Desmond flashed through her mind, aged about seven, twenty months her senior. He waved a wooden sword at her and his childish taunts filled her mind. He came at her—no, the image faded, to be replaced by a youthful Roland, grasping the seven-year-old Desmond, scooping him off his feet. She was screaming, hysterical, blood covering her gown. Great-aunt Lavinia, her mahogany hair loose about her shoulders, was shouting something, striking Roland with a vase, then beating him with Desmond's toy sword, driving him away . . .

The scuffing of a heel startled her, and she looked up, past blending into present. Roland, his dark hair now touched with gray, his expression closed, stood before her. She rose on shaky legs, her fingers still clutching the hobby horse.

Anguish, buried deep and long, overwhelmed her. Without understanding why, acting only upon instinct, she struck him with every ounce of strength she could muster.

Chapter Twelve

For a long moment, Netta stared aghast at the flaming mark left by her hand on Roland's cheek. Then a gasp of shocked laughter escaped her. "Oh, Roland, I didn't mean—" She broke off, her eyes widening in amazed realization. "I *did* mean it!" she exclaimed.

He rubbed the spot. "Somehow, I had gained that impression."

She shook her head. Sudden tears burned her eyes as long-ago emotions overpowered her. She turned blindly, and more by instinct than plan found her way to her childhood refuge in the chair by the window. She curled up on it, hugging herself, regarding Roland with accusing eyes.

"You left me." She felt—must sound—like the little girl of five that had awakened within her. "You swore you'd always be here, then you ran away and left me to *them*."

"Good God." He stared at her, taken aback. "My poor Little Hen. Did my leaving truly distress you so much?"

"I worshipped you." She fumbled in her reticule

for a handkerchief and swiped at her eyes in irritation. "Heavens, what a—a peahen I am being. I am sorry, Roland."

His frowning gaze still rested on her. "I didn't precisely leave by choice, if you'll remember. What did you expect me to do, take you with me to India?"

She managed a watery smile. "That would have been quite ineligible, would it not?" She leaned back against the cushion and allowed her gaze to travel about the room. "I came here to try to understand—everything."

"Did it help?"

Her lips twitched. At least her determined attraction to him, in defiance of all logic, made more sense in light of her childish adoration. But so many questions remained unanswered. She looked up and found he still watched her. "What brought you up here?" she asked.

He hesitated a moment. "Curiosity. I followed you."

"And?"

A slow smile eased the harshness of his mouth. "I find that the past haunts you as much as it does me."

"What really happened?" She searched his face for answers, for clues to what it meant to him.

He ran a hand through his thick, dark hair, rippling the patch of gray at his temple. A strange intentness shone in his eyes. "What do you *believe* happened?"

"I don't know anymore." Her gaze drifted toward the window, and she looked out across the rose garden that sprawled toward the river. "I only have impressions of that day, not real memories. Desmond had that wooden sword, then you were there, and I was screaming and bleeding, and Great-aunt Lavinia started hitting you—" Remembered fear choked off her flow of words.

"And they told you I attacked you, and Lavinia drove me off. I suppose they repeated that over and over until you believed it?"

The grimness in his voice caused her to turn so she could see him. The lines about his face had deepened, giving him a strained, tired appearance. She swallowed. "Now I want the truth."

"Are you likely to believe me?"

"Would I have come here—would I have asked you—if I didn't want to know?"

His expression remained closed. "That wasn't my question."

"How can I answer that until I've heard what you have to say? For all I know, Great-aunt Lavinia's tale may be true and it doesn't matter one whit that I was used to make a hero out of you. Children are apt to do that with the unlikeliest people, one gathers."

"That has put me in my place, hasn't it?" Humor flickered across his countenance, only to fade at once. "All right." He drew a deep breath, and his gaze roamed about the shrouded chamber as if

204

to prompt his memory. "I wasn't here when it started, though I was coming to take you to ride old Bartholomew."

Her pony. Long-forgotten details sprang back to her mind. "He used to be yours, did he not?"

He ignored her interruption. "I heard you screaming as I came along the hall. I burst through the door in time to see Desmond hit you with his sword and you strike him back. A right wisty caster, as I recall. You could sport your canvas in those days, my girl." He rubbed his still-reddened cheek. "I see you have not lost the knack."

His gaze rested on her. A gleam flickered in the depths of his eyes before he looked away to the hobby horse in the middle of the room. "Lavinia was there, watching you I suppose while the nurserymaid ran some errand. She pounced on you, started beating you. Her bracelet broke, and the rough metal tore your wrist. When I tried to stop her, she started throwing things at me."

Netta's fingers traced her scar while she digested this new interpretation to her memories. It made sense, it seemed right, yet — "Then why were you sent away?"

"Lavinia told your father it happened the other way around, that I'd been there first, that she'd tried to save both you and Desmond."

"But why did Papa believe her?"

He crossed the room to another window and gazed out. His shoulders seemed to slump, as if

205

with exhaustion. "It had gone on for years, these stories, her poisonous tongue." He shook his head and a curious smile tugged at the corners of his mouth. "Do you know, I actually welcomed escaping this house, going to India. Though I confess to worrying what would become of you. Have you other questions?"

"Not at the moment. Only—"

"Yes?"

"If you had returned home to murder anyone, I should think it would have been Great-aunt Lavinia," she said in a rush of candor.

A rueful smile tugged at his lips. "I shall leave her to Cousin Phemie. Come, in case you did not hear it, the gong to dress for dinner sounded some ten minutes ago."

He strode from the room with his pantherlike grace, his figure tall and straight. Netta trailed after him, somewhat bemused. She believed him—and to her consternation, she realized a measure of her childish adoration for him had returned.

Roland parted from her at the corridor leading to her chamber, and Netta continued on her way, lost in reverie. From this she was roused by her abigail, who awaited her with the information that if she didn't bestir herself, she would be late. Netta scrambled into the black silk, now repaired after her escapade in the garden, and shook loose her long hair. This she instructed her maid to fasten at the nape of her neck with a black riband.

Grabbing up her shawl, she hurried down the stairs to the salon.

Roland stood before the hearth, an impressive figure in a coat of black velvet over knee breeches. He gazed into the deep ruby wine in his glass, presenting a partial profile to her. She hesitated, wondering what thoughts filled his mind. Recriminations against the family that discarded him? Regrets for the life he might have—should have—lived? Or memories of the difficult years of his exile? He might well have cause to despise both the title and this home of his youth. And every member of his family, also.

He looked up, and his gaze met hers. An infinite sadness lurked in his hazel eyes, and her heart twisted within her. Without thinking, she moved toward him, drawn as she had been that night at the betrothal ball. She started to hold out her hand to him, then let it drop to her side. Did he despise her, too? Or would she forever remain to him the little child of five of whom he had been so carelessly fond, who had followed him about like a tantony pig?

He looked away, then crossed to the side table. "Sherry? Or would you prefer something else?"

"Have you checked to see if the decanters have been drugged?"

That brought a slight smile to his lips. "I stood over Haskins myself while he opened fresh bottles." He poured some of the amber liquid into the cut-crystal glass and passed it to her.

She twisted the stem between her fingers. "I really ought to apologize, you know."

He had turned away, but glanced at her over his shoulder. "For what? The sins of the past? They are in no way your fault, I assure you."

"The sins of the present are. Except for Cousin Phemie, you have not precisely received a warm welcome home. And after what the family has already done to you, it hardly seems fair."

"Life is not fair." He spoke the dictum in the off-hand manner of one who had repeated it often. Still, sadness lurked in his eyes, giving the lie to his air of not caring.

She sipped her wine. Returning to Ravenswood, facing his unhappy memories, facing his relatives—none of it could have been easy for him. Except for facing one particular relative, who had welcomed him with the joy he deserved. Which reminded her. "Where is Cousin Phemie?"

Roland's lips twitched. "Making good her threat not to remain where she might encounter Lavinia."

"I'm surprised you haven't done the same. Does Cousin Phemie know the truth?"

"Yes." He studied his wine. "Have you never wondered why she has remained in this house, with Desmond and Lavinia?"

Netta blinked. "I assumed she had nowhere else to go. She has been my companion—"

"Protector. She has made quite certain you would come to no harm."

"I—see." She found it hard to envision the ineffectual little woman in that role, yet knowing Cousin Phemie, she would have tried very hard. No wonder she had always seemed to regard Desmond and Great-aunt Lavinia as the enemy. To her, they were. This was proving to be a very enlightening day. "Is there anything else I ought to know?" she asked.

He studied the wine in his glass, and the furrows in his brow deepened. "A great deal, my child. And a great deal you should not. And sometimes," he added with a wry twist to his lips, "I fear they are one and the same."

"I am not a child anymore. And what ever do you mean about their being the same?"

He shook his head. "It is nothing that need concern you, my—Little Lady Hen."

She bit back her irritated rejoinder that she would rather be the judge of that; she knew how futile it would be. Obstinacy was a trait shared by most Galbraiths. No amount of threats or cajolery would win an answer from him unless he chose to give it. And at the moment, he obviously did not so choose. She instead contemplated the problem of convincing him to stop thinking of her as a child.

Haskins entered announcing dinner, and Roland led her across to the dining room. Jeremy remained in attendance on them there, making it impossible for Netta to do other than keep the conversation within the bounds of the commonplace. To her further dismay, Roland excused himself to her as soon as they finished the meal and removed to the bookroom to deal with his personal correspondence and paperwork he had neglected of late. One searching gaze of his closed countenance assured her he would not welcome company. She retired to her bedchamber with a book, but though she curled up in her bed with the volume open, she found after nearly an hour she had not turned a single page.

The morning brought renewed determination. She would come to know her long-absent second cousin better—and whether he wished it or not, he would come to know her. She smiled as she donned the black bombazine and allowed Wembly to arrange her hair. Yesterday, for the first time, Roland had permitted her to glimpse his true feelings, to see within the defensive wall he constructed about himself. Today, she would begin to show him she was no longer a child to be teased and protected, but a woman to be—

That brought her up short. What *did* she want from Roland? As a five-year-old, she had adored him, wanting nothing more than to spend time in his company. And now? She wanted the same, she realized. The same—yet very different. Warmth surged through her, a longing to feel his strong arms about her, to know he wanted her with him as well. Never had she felt that way about another man.

But if he felt anything for her, he kept it very well disguised.

She descended the stairs, eager to see him, yet shy. He was her "Big Cousin." He might well be satisfied with keeping exactly that relationship with his "Little Hen"—and nothing more.

In the main hall she encountered Haskins, who informed her Master Roland had ridden out more than an hour before. No, the elderly man assured her, he had no idea when his lordship, as he should say, might return. Stymied for the moment, Netta went in search of breakfast, then took the gardener on a tour of the terrace and the roses to discuss weeding and the preparation of a new flower bed.

She returned to the house to find Haskins arranging the newly arrived mail on a salver. Very little, she noted. Three cards addressed to herself, probably of condolence, and a number addressed to Desmond's estate, which bore all the appearance of tradesmen's bills. These she left for Roland.

A heavy booted footstep sounded in the hall behind her, and a thrill raced through her. He strode up, striking in a riding coat of deep russet, leather breeches, and gleaming boots. Chestnut hairs clung to him, as did the pungent aroma of the stables. He'd grown up into a compelling, powerful man, this Big Cousin of hers.

He tossed his hat onto the table and examined the salver's offerings. "Bills?" Resignation sounded heavy in his voice. He broke the seal on one after the other, examining the contents, then going on to the next.

At the fourth, he paused. "The devil," he muttered.

"What is it?" Netta tried to peer around his broad shoulder.

He held it out to her: a demand from a small gaming hell off St. James's Street for payment of nigh on twelve thousand pounds.

Netta's fingers clutched the page, and a moment passed before she turned her dismayed gaze on Roland. "So much?"

Roland glanced at Haskins, who watched them with interest. The man coughed and took himself off.

Reclaiming the sheet from her, Roland smoothed it out. "Twelve thousand." He tapped it with one finger, considering.

"He would have to sell out of the Funds," Netta said, dismayed.

He glanced at her. "He already had, more than a year ago. Did he not tell you? For this he would have had to sell his cattle and perhaps a painting or two. Or would he have been able to settle this account after your marriage?"

"My father did not leave a fortune, you must know. You are standing in my inheritance. My income will derive solely from the tenanted farms."

"No funds and no hope of obtaining any. And then this sudden winning streak."

Their gazes met.

"You think someone knew he—he gulled them, and took revenge?"

"I believe Mr. Frake will be interested in this." With that, he collected the other demands and headed for the bookroom to continue his efforts in winding up the estate.

Depressed, Netta went in search of Cousin Phemie, then spent a contemplative hour or two with her over the mending basket. Somehow, her thoughts never strayed far from Roland.

Shortly after one, Haskins came to inform her that Master Roland sent his compliments, and would she join him in the bookroom, as Mr. Frake had arrived. Netta thrust the sheet she darned into the pile of unfinished work and, with an apology to Phemie, hurried down to where the men awaited her.

As she entered the book-lined chamber, Roland looked up from the ledgers that lay scattered across the desk and stood. For a moment his expression lightened, then closed over once more.

The Runner smiled as he rose to his feet. "Well, m'lady, this is a pretty state of affairs. Very pretty, indeed. It would seem more than likely your cousin pressured those who owed him money to repay it, so as he could cover this here demand."

She hesitated, her hands clasped before her. "Mr. Frake. In light of the sizable amount of that debt, I cannot help but wonder about Lady Beatrix's vowels—" She broke off, embarrassed.

Roland's lips twitched. "The thought occurred to me as well. It does seem very unlikely Desmond would forgive a debt of over five thousand pounds in exchange for a single evening with the lady. Ah — I trust I do not too deeply offend your sensibilities?"

"I have lived beneath the same roof with Desmond since infancy," Netta reminded him. "Plain speaking was what you might call his specialty. He long since cured any tendency I might have had toward missishness."

"Did you have any?" Roland regarded her with a touch of amusement.

A tantalizing tingle crept along her spine at this promising gambit.

"No, m'lord, it don't seem likely about Lady Beatrix." Mr. Frake, with both tone and purpose firm, brought the conversation back to the matter at hand. "Yet the Underhills ain't flush in the pocket neither."

"Do you mean they can't redeem the vowels?" Roland turned to him, his attention once more on the problem.

"Well, now, m'lord, that fact does spring to mind."

Netta stifled a sigh and rejoined the conversation. "Do you think Desmond asked something else of Lady Beatrix, then? But what?"

"I could ask her ladyship, excepting I might hear some Banbury tale, more than like. Still, I can but try." He nodded to Roland, sketched a

214

bow to Netta. "I'll be letting you know when I find something out. Right now, I need to think." With that, he took himself off.

Netta stared at the closing door, then turned to Roland.

His expression softened. "Don't look so distressed, my dear. More than likely Desmond only hoped to pressure her into finding the funds."

"It isn't that. Did you not notice Mr. Frake offered to tell us what he learns?"

Roland leaned back against the desk, his hazel eyes glinting. "I believe we are no longer his primary suspects. What a novel situation. This calls for a celebration." He crossed to the cabinet on which rested a silver tray bearing several decanters and glasses. "Sherry?"

She accepted his offering but didn't take a sip. Instead, she swirled the contents. When she looked up, she found him watching her. "Will you answer a question for me?"

His eyebrows rose, signifying neither assent nor denial, merely curiosity.

Probably the best for which she could hope. "Do you want Ravenswood?"

He stiffened. "Good God, no! I have no desire for this place. In fact, I have already made an offer to repurchase Larkspur."

"Larkspur? So that is what took you to the Lake District. You will be Tavistock indeed."

The lines on his face deepened. "I care nothing for the title. Desmond might have kept it with my blessings. But our ancestral estate should return to the Galbraiths. I shall not be so foolish as to gamble on an ideology. I support no Pretenders."

"And Ravenswood?" The thought of him leaving, going so very far away, dismayed her.

"Do with it as you will: I want no part of it. It holds nothing but unpleasant memories. Sell it to Carncross if you wish to be rid of it. He is eager enough to reclaim it."

Had Archy approached Roland? After, perhaps, she changed her mind and refused to sell? Poor Archy, he must be quite devastated. And so too would she be when Roland departed.

For perhaps the hundredth time, Frake paced along the gravel path that ran the length of the manor. From somewhere nearby, he could hear the sound of a spade turning the soil. He shielded his eyes from the bright sun and spotted the gardener he had seen earlier near the stable, now hard at work on a planting bed.

Why didn't he ever get the simple, straight-forward cases? The wife who bashed in her husband's skull with an iron skillet. The elderly, embezzling clerk who stabbed the employer who had just discovered his dishonesty. Or perhaps the earl who was murdered by his heir for the sake of the title?

No, not this time. At least, not as obviously so as it had seemed at first.

Of course, he'd find the routine work of an uncomplicated case to be boring. He preferred a challenge. And a challenge was what he had here. He still had the heir, of course, and a fine motive that was. Nor could he forget the reluctant bride, now free of a distasteful bridegroom and in possession of a comfortable little country seat.

Nor did it stop there. What of the elderly cousin whom the victim threatened to toss out of his home? Or that Sir Archibald and his mama, and their desire to repurchase Ravenswood? Or Mr. Underhill and his long-standing feud? Or Lady Beatrix's mysterious method of reclaiming her vowels? That last would probably prove all a hum, but it did lend itself to delightful speculation.

And that brought him to gaming. He turned on his heel and strode into the house, where Haskins informed him that Lady Henrietta had retired to the music room. He found her sitting at the pianoforte, idly strumming the keys, her attention obviously elsewhere. He cleared his throat, and she spun about.

A touch of disappointment flickered across her expressive face, then vanished behind her polite smile. "Have you thought of another question?" she asked.

"Well, now, m'lady, not as such. I'd just like to go over something with you again, if I may?"

She gestured for him to be seated.

He perched on the edge of the chair. "About your late cousin's gaming. Did his luck run in spurts, as you might say? Might he have reason to hope he'd come about?"

"Galbraiths rarely win."

"And your cousin in particular?"

She picked up a sheet of music and fingered it. "My cousin, in particular," she agreed. "He had notoriously poor luck — and judgment, I fear." She looked up, meeting his gaze squarely. "If you are asking me if he fiddled the cards those last two nights he played, I fear nothing seems more likely."

"Well, now, m'lady, I think I've taken that for a fact. What I wants to know is, do you think those he played with realized it?"

She granted him a wry smile. "The Galbraith ill-luck is legendary. My father always swore Sir William Carncross — Sir Archy's grandfather — cursed the family after we won Ravenswood."

Frake pulled his pipe from his pocket and tapped the bowl in the palm of his hand. "Do —" He broke off as the door opened and Mr. Kenneth Lambert, dressed with impeccable elegance, strolled in.

Miss Euphemia Wrenn trotted at his heels, beaming her pleasure. "Do see, my love, who has called, just as he promised. So kind of him to relieve our dreariness."

Lambert bowed low over Lady Henrietta's hand and carried her fingers to his lips for a lingering kiss.

A sigh of rapture escaped Miss Wrenn.

Lambert straightened, and transferred his smiling gaze to his godmama. "I know you are busy. There is no need for you to linger. I shall take the most excellent care of your charge." He accompanied the words with a broad wink, then turned his haughty stare on Frake.

Frake rose, putting his pipe away. "I'll just get back to my notes, then, shall I? M'lady?" He nodded to Lady Henrietta and exited the room.

Miss Wrenn scurried after him. "So much the gentleman," she sighed. She pulled the door not quite closed behind her.

Through it, Frake could see Lambert leading Lady Henrietta to the leaded window alcove overlooking the rose garden.

"There." Miss Wrenn peeked through the crack. "He will offer for her again, I am quite certain of it," she murmured to herself, sounding quite satisfied.

"Again?" Frake's interest perked up, and he positioned himself beside Miss Wrenn.

That lady blinked at him. "Oh my, yes. Dear Kenneth, he has begged Netta to put aside her duty to her family and marry him at least twice that I know of. Of course, he had no way of knowing how things were left in her papa's will."

"Suitable match, is it?" He kept his tone purely conversational.

"Very agreeable it would be for both of them, you know. Such a gentleman as he is. Such a misfortune."

"What is?" Frake pressed, mustering his patience.

"Why, that he has not a greater fortune. Not that that will weigh with dear Netta, of course, but it is so disagreeable for a gentleman, is it not? I shall be so glad to see him comfortably established with an estate."

"And what advantage is there in this alliance for Lady Henrietta?"

"Advantage?" Miss Wrenn stared at him, bewildered. "Why, he is a most excellent gentleman. Such a dashing husband as he will make. Quite a leader of society, I am sure. I will see my beloved Netta happy at long last."

"Will you?" Frake muttered.

Lambert's words didn't reach them, but Frake could see Lady Henrietta draw her hand from the gentleman. She rose, turning away, but Lambert caught her arm, drawing her back.

She shook her head. "I am aware of the signal honor you do me." Her words sounded clearly. "Indeed, every eligible young lady of the polite world would be envious if they but knew. But I do not seek marriage at the moment."

"I have been too precipitous upon your period of mourning." Lambert's voice rose. "If you could but give me hope—"

"It would be wrong of me, for I fear we should not suit."

He stepped back, his bearing stiff. "I see," he

220

said after a long moment of silence. "Is there someone else?"

"Of course not." Her tone sharpened. "Do me the honor of believing what I say."

"You have been leading me on, madam."

"Really, Kenneth, I have done no such thing. I have always made it clear I could offer you nothing but friendship."

"I thought it was because of Tavistock." He sounded angry. "You should have explained—"

She strode toward the bellpull. "Jeremy will show you out."

Lambert's jaw tightened. "There is no need. I shall not distress you further, madam."

Frake grasped the stunned Miss Wrenn's arm and hauled her bodily into the next withdrawing room. No sooner had the door closed behind them than the one to the music room slammed with Lambert's departure.

Frake let out a low whistle. Lambert's debts—at Desmond's hands. His ardent pursuit of Lady Henrietta—which apparently he had felt would reach a happy conclusion if not for Desmond. Well and well and well.

Chapter Thirteen

Netta turned her mare onto the path following the stream. Lacy patterns of light and shadow fell across her as the advancing sun passed behind a line of towering elms. Birds sang their challenges to one another overhead, and the babble of the water rushing over the stones filled her; but none of this brought the peace she sought.

Kenneth Lambert appeared to be Mr. Frake's current favorite suspect, and that thought distressed her. She couldn't believe him guilty—or could she merely not face the possibility that someone had committed a murder over *her?*

That idea had to be preposterous. More lay behind this mystery of Desmond's death than any gaming debts or estates or marriage aspirations. Someone stalked her. Mr. Lambert certainly had no reason to want her dead. How could anyone?

She guided the mare over the stone bridge and urged her into a controlled canter. The exercise eased her tension, stimulated her thinking.

Did anyone want her dead? Perhaps her being pursued through the garden had been nothing more than a ploy to make the Runner believe Roland guilty, after the estate, while all the while someone murdered Desmond to avoid gaming debts — or something else. She could see the unpleasant Mr. Josiah Underhill devising such a hateful scheme of terrifying her and carrying it out with relish.

Her mount lengthened its stride into a gallop, and Netta tried to block the upsetting possibilities from her mind. She needed to escape, if only for a little while, to restore her normally humorous outlook. It had been sadly lacking of late.

She allowed the mare her head for another ten minutes, concentrating her energy on guiding the animal over the uneven ground. They cleared a low hedge, landed on the verge at the side of a narrow lane, and Netta reined in, bringing the mare to a walk. She patted the steaming neck and, with reluctance, headed for home.

She wished she knew why someone had wanted poor Desmond dead, why someone had chased her like that. She wished Roland would find her as fascinating as she found him, and knew this last less likely to be granted than her other wishes.

She fell to contemplating this cousin who had lived so very different a life from hers. This beloved cousin. A pleasant warmth rushed through her, followed at once by the ache of longing. His harsh features and powerful build filled her mind.

She wanted to see a gleam light those hazel eyes when they rested on her. Instead, she received no more than a fond smile. At least he had not tousled her hair as he had done so many years ago.

A familiar voice hailed her, breaking into her thoughts, and she looked up to see Sir Archy astride his glossy black trotting toward her. His slight frame swayed in his saddle; no playful tricks from this docile creature. Archy rarely rode if he could drive.

So what brought him out?—his mama, of course. Netta remembered catching a glimpse of Lady Carncross standing at the window as she'd passed down the drive on her way to the streamside path. She must have sent him in pursuit. Mentally she braced herself and waved in response.

He pulled abreast of her, beaming. "Thought I saw you earlier. Driven you out of the house, have they?"

"Who?"

"That cousin of yours and the Runner. Seem to be haunting the place, both of them. Tell you what, you come back to the Dower House with me. Drink a cup of cat-lap with my mama. Likes you, y'know. Always glad to have you visit."

Netta managed a smile, sought an excuse, but any plausible ones evaded her. With a word of thanks she accepted her defeat, and Archy turned his mount to accompany her back, his air the conquering hero personified.

They left their mounts at the stable behind the garden, then followed the path between the flowering rhododendrons to the narrow terrace that ran the length of the Restoration house. As they neared, Netta caught a glimpse through the French windows of a petite figure in yards of lavender crepe peering out at them. Lady Carncross vanished at once. Netta repressed a sigh and prepared to enter the snare.

Archy swung the doors wide, bowed her through, and Netta entered the quiet elegance of the East Salon. Lady Carncross sat in a brocade armchair at the far end of the chamber, her embroidery draped across her lap. To her right, above the hearth, hung the portrait of the late Sir Cuthbert, Archy's father.

"My dear!" The little lady laid her intricate work aside on a low scroll-footed mahogany table and gestured for Netta to take the seat opposite her. "How delightful of you to come to relieve our tedium."

"How do the children go on?" With luck, the topic of the infectious complaint suffered by the four younger scions of the household would divert the determined woman from matrimonial plans for her eldest.

"Poor little Tom." Lady Carncross rose to the bait. "He is still confined in his sickroom, you must know. But Richmond will be permitted to come downstairs tomorrow and resume his studies with his tutor."

Netta fought back her smile. "How fortunate for him."

"Now they are so much better," Lady Carncross went on, apparently not noting Netta's sarcasm, "I hope to see you and dear Miss Wrenn here very soon. For a nuncheon, perhaps?"

"Al fresco?" Archy brightened. He took a chair by the window, but his gaze stayed on Netta.

His mama clasped her hands in delight. "The very thing. There, it is settled. In three days' time, so little Sukey may join us."

Netta managed a noncommittal response and promised herself to have another engagement by then.

Lady Carncross beamed on her. "Poor dear Archy, you must know he has been positively chafing, not being able to call upon you as he would wish. But tell me, how do you go on with that dreadful cousin actually in the house with you?"

Netta stiffened. "Roland, do you mean?"

Her hostess laughed. "Now, my dear, you must not take offense. We have known you since your cradle. And I can remember when your papa sent him away. Now get off your high horse, my love, and assure me his presence does not distress you overly."

Meddling wrapped up in the guise of kindness. Netta forced herself to relax. "We do well enough. There is a great deal to keep him busy, winding up the estate." She could wish it kept him less busy and that he would bother her with his presence more often.

"Ah." Archy nodded his head. "You'll be glad when it's all finished, no doubt of that." His expression clouded. "Not pursuing you with unwelcome advances, is he?"

They wouldn't be unwelcome at all, Netta realized. Prudently, she kept that reflection to herself.

"To get the estate," Archy clarified. "No telling what he might do to get that."

"No, there is no fear of that." She kept the regret from her voice. "He has made an offer for Larkspur, which I believe will shortly be accepted."

"So it's true, then." Archy threw a triumphant glance at his mama. "Still, can't see why he wouldn't jump at a chance to get Ravenswood as well."

A crease formed in Lady Carncross's brow as her gaze rested on Netta. "You do not seem glad," she accused.

"Of course I am. I should hate to be forever pestered about the estate." And would they catch her pointed meaning? "In fact," she added for emphasis, "I quite look forward to a period of peace. This has been quite a stressful time." She stood. "Now, I must be getting back, or Cousin Phemie will be imagining the most dreadful things happening to me."

"Of course, my dear. Archy, you will see her out?"

Netta could not help but see the encouraging gesture which accompanied this. Resigning herself to listening to Archy's rehearsed gallantries with a measure of tolerance, she allowed him to lead her to the terrace.

"Ride back with you," he offered.

"What, do you fear I shall become lost on a journey of barely above two hundred yards?"

He pursed his lips but made no retort. They reached the shrubbery, but before they rounded the corner of the hedges, he drew out a handkerchief, shook it with care, and laid it on the gravel path. Grasping her hand, he sank onto one knee.

"Archy!" she protested, pulling back.

"No, dash it all, Netta, got to listen. Asking you to marry me. Know I took you by surprise before, but you know how it is. Wanted to, any time these past two years. Only there's always been Desmond."

And Desmond wanted Ravenswood. She detached herself. "No, please Archy. I'm conscious of the honor—indeed, I am quite flattered—but you know as well as do I, we should not suit."

He gazed up at her, his expression earnest. "Any chance you'll change your mind?"

"You may assure your mama there is none."

Honest regret flickered across Archy's face, fading to a sadness that lingered in his eyes.

It startled Netta. She had never thought him more than passingly fond of her. "I have always regarded you as my dear friend," she said, "and I

228

know we can continue in that light. Can we not?"

He rose. "No wish to embarrass you." He stuffed the handkerchief back into his pocket and led her around the hedge. At the stable, he allowed the lad to throw her into the saddle, then, with a short, dejected wave, turned and walked back to the house.

Netta urged the mare forward, disturbed. She ought to be in alt, she supposed. To receive two offers in one day. Yet she felt no desire to preen herself on this feat; she could take no pleasure in causing anyone pain. Mr. Lambert had seemed deeply chagrined in the face of her refusal. And Archy appeared honestly dismayed and dejected — though he probably no more than feared his mama's disapproval. She had best prepare herself to receive in the near future a visit from Lady Carncross, intent upon changing her mind.

She left her mount in the groom's care and returned to the house by way of the herb garden and the little door set into the stillroom chimney. Inside their sanctuary, she encountered Cousin Phemie hard at work sorting and drying a batch of freshly picked sprigs. Netta joined her, and this occupation kept them busy until the gong sounded to change for dinner.

Netta found herself lingering before her mirror over her preparations, adjusting a curl so it hung in a different position over her eyes, wishing she could subdue the vivid red of its color.

229

"If you wish to look your best for his lordship—" her abigail began.

"Why on earth should I?" Heavens, was she so transparently obvious? Did Roland know—and find it amusing, perhaps? That possibility caused an unpleasant tug in the pit of her stomach. Covering her confusion, she swept out of the chair, grabbed up a shawl, and arranged it over her arms before Wembly could help. Without so much as another glance at her reflection, she hurried from the room.

Both her cousins awaited her in the salon. Roland, handsome in a coat of mulberry superfine, stood at the sideboard pouring ratafia for Phemie, who sat on a sofa with the shawl for which she knotted a fringe. Roland looked up as she entered, and a touch of warmth flickered in his eyes.

Yes, that was what she wanted—or at least it was a beginning. She advanced a step and felt as if she floated. How very broad were his shoulders, how elegant his manner and dress, how compelling his brilliant eyes as his gaze rested on her. She swallowed, which reminded her to resume breathing.

He came toward her, holding out a glass of wine, and she focused on the cut crystal with its ruby-colored liquid. As she took it, she allowed her fingers to brush his hand, aware of the touch, of the unfamiliar sensations it caused.

He pulled away as if he had encountered hot

230

steel instead of her fingers. He poured more madeira for himself, then strode to the hearth and drained his glass in one gulp.

What caused that? Had she just betrayed that she had come to care for him — and he rejected her? Did he, after all, find the thought of her distasteful? She couldn't bear it if he did.

Her heart yearning, she studied his back, the way his dark hair curled with a mind of its own just above the nape of his neck. She bore a scar outwardly on her wrist. Did he bear ones of his own, deep within? Did his rejection by his family haunt him, make him resent even her? How could she ever overcome that?

Dinner, for once, passed all too quickly. Netta found her attention wandering from the dishes set before her to study the deeply etched lines about Roland's eyes. He looked at her as seldom as possible, concentrating instead on describing to Cousin Phemie a journey he had taken to a holy city in India. She wished he would include her, smile at her as he did at his aunt. She might also wish for the moon, she realized.

At last, with Haskins and Jeremy waiting to remove the covers, Netta rose to leave Roland over his port. Cousin Phemie bustled after her into the hall where Netta stopped abruptly, a scant two paces from the wild-haired figure who stood before her.

Great-aunt Lavinia grinned, baring her yellow teeth, and gathered her shawl about her nightgown. Her gnarled fingers clutched her cane. Leaning forward, she hissed: "He only wants Ravenswood, my girl. Mark my words." She nodded vigorously in an impressive Cassandra-like performance. "He's only using Larkspur as a blind. There never was a Galbraith with an ounce of practicality in his blood. He couldn't have made a fortune. So what, pray, does he hope to use to buy Larkspur? Hmmm?"

Netta drew back, startled.

Lavinia waved her cane. "He knows he can't woo and wed you. He'll have to kill you for the inheritance. Don't be daft, girl. He's already killed Desmond, why should he not rid himself of you, as well?"

"Oh!" Phemie surged forward. "You dreadful, hateful wretch! How can she say such things? You—"

"Cousin Phemie." Netta attempted to soothe her, in vain.

"I will not be quiet!" Tears started in Phemie's eyes. "I have tolerated this—this *Medusa* for as long as I can."

"Phemie," Netta tried again.

"Fool!" Lavinia laughed, a harsh, grating cackle. "Do you wish to die, to molder in your grave like my Desmond?"

Netta shuddered and turned away.

"Rather melodramatic, Great-aunt Lavinia," Roland said from the doorway. "You would have been quite the rage in Cheltenham had you ever wished to tread the boards."

Lavinia glared at him a moment, disconcerted, as if knocked off her stride by the interruption. With a muttered curse, she gathered her momentum once more. "Keep your distance, Brutus," she cried. "I'll not let you murder me as well." With a triumphant swirl of her shawl, she spun about and hobbled off.

Cousin Phemie, unnaturally pale, clenched her hands. "How could we have lived with that viper for so long?"

Roland laid a hand on her shoulder. "Do not let her distress you. It's the death of Desmond that has affected her so."

Netta drew a steadying breath. "Do you know, she actually had me frightened for a moment. Is it really all just an act? A performance?"

"Most of it, I should think." Roland recovered Phemie's shawl, which had fallen to the floor. "She was used to have both a violent temper and a love of dramatizing herself. I see she has not changed over the years. Let her be. She enjoys her eccentric ways, and she has so few pleasures left at her age. I, for one, will no longer take offense. Try to do the same," he advised Phemie, "and you will not mind her as much."

Phemie sniffed. "Dreadful woman," she repeated. She shook herself free of Roland's restraining hands. "I shall go to my chamber now. I find I have the headache."

Netta saw her cousin up the stairs and into the

hands of her abigail, then went back down. Yet though she tried the bookroom, the withdrawing room, and the music room, no trace of Roland could she discover.

Disappointed out of all proportion, she went back to the bookroom, selected the thin leather-bound volume of *Marmion,* and curled into a chair before the grate in which a small fire burned. Not that she waited for Roland, of course. Still, she wouldn't mind if he happened to walk through the door.

For once, the poem failed to hold her attention. Her gaze wandered, and lost in thought, she stared through the French windows across the moonlit garden.

A movement among the shrubs caught her attention, a dark shape ducking deeper into the shadows. She sat up, straining her eyes, her pulse quickening in alarm. A moment later she saw it again, and this time no doubts remained. Someone crouched low, running just beyond the edge of the terrace.

She sprang to her feet and pulled the bellrope, all the while trying to keep the figure in sight. In another moment he—or she?—would be out of her range, disappearing around the corner of the house. To do what?

She cast a frantic glance at the door, but no one came yet. She didn't have time to wait for reinforcements, not if she hoped to gain some clue to the intruder's identity. Yet she didn't want to risk confronting a possible murderer. Neither could she just let whoever spied on her quietly disappear . . .

She could turn the tables on the person, be the stalker instead of the prey. Perhaps she could determine in which direction the intruder went. Gathering her courage, she slipped out the French windows and set off in silent pursuit.

At the corner of the house, she paused, straining her ears. She heard nothing at first, then the unmistakable sound of crunching gravel reached her. Only about fifty yards away, perhaps in the shrubbery. Holding her breath, she inched forward, afraid to make any noise that might alert the intruder to her presence. She should have waited for the energetic Jeremy to help her; yet if she had, the intruder would have gotten away, unseen, unidentified.

She left her shelter and ran lightly for the hedge that surrounded the terrace off the ballroom. Just a bit farther to the rose garden. She paused to listen once more, and from somewhere ahead came footsteps on paving and the rustle of leaves. What did he do? Check to see if everyone had retired to bed? She drew her shawl closer about her shoulders and crept on.

By the moonlight that seeped through a low cloud covering, she glimpsed the rose bed ahead of her. If she wanted to remain unseen by anyone who might glance back, she had better retreat to the hawthorn hedge nearer the house. She slipped through the shadows, reached the outer edge, and froze as gravel crunched only a few feet behind her. She gasped, but before she could draw back, a strong arm grabbed her and a hand shot over her mouth.

"Be still." Roland's deep voice hissed in her ear.

She sank against him, relief leaving her weak. For a long moment he held her, his chin just brushing the top of her curls, his fingers closing about her shoulder in what might almost be a caress. Awareness welled within her, of his strength, of the rapid beat of his heart. Of the pungent odor of a cigarillo that clung to him.

He drew his hand from her mouth, and his touch trailed across her lips and cheek. She turned her head, leaning against his shoulder, all thought fading away except a yearning to remain with him like this for a very long while.

His breath caught, and he pushed her away, his hands on her shoulders. "What brought you out here?" he whispered.

It took a moment for her disordered senses to cooperate. With an effort, she pulled herself together. "There is someone out here." Someone who might have murdered Desmond, who might wish to murder her. "Did you see anyone?"

"I'm not sure. I came out to blow a cloud. Then I thought I saw movement in the shrubs."

She peered into the darkness, very glad of his powerful presence at her side. "Where did he go?"

"I don't know. I don't even hear anyone now.

Stay here." He slipped from her side, his passage so silent it might have been no more than an illusion.

She shouldn't let him go alone—she didn't want to *be* alone. She started forward, then realized he had vanished. Not so much as a shifting shadow met her searching gaze. More unsure than ever, she inched along the hedge. If she made any noise now, she might confuse Roland's search. She followed first one leafy path, then another, seeing and hearing nothing. Then someone ran, crashing through small branches and twigs, and a moment later hoofbeats cantered off into the distance.

Roland . . . Netta broke into a run, dashing headlong around corners in the twisting path until she lost all sense of direction. She halted, listening, trying to control her breath which came in short gasps. Where—? The steady crunch of boots on gravel reached her, and she hurried forward, rounding another bend, colliding with him.

His arms wrapped about her, steadying, and she clung to him, burying her face in the smooth wool of his coat, welcoming even the distasteful aroma of his cigarillo. As if of their own volition, her arms wrapped about his waist, and she held him with all the desperation of her pent-up fear and nerves.

"He escaped." He spoke against her hair. "I couldn't see who it was."

"A man?" She looked up into his face. His warm breath fanned her cheek.

"Or a woman." His voice sounded tight.

She pulled closer to him. "At least you aren't harmed. I was so afraid for you."

For a moment he didn't move. His gaze rested on her face, his expression unreadable in the moonlight, but his eyes glowed with an intensity that set her pulse racing. Gently, he stroked a curl back from her forehead, his fingers lingering as if loath to break contact.

Hesitant, as if against his will, he traced the line of her cheek to the corner of her lips. Then with a soft groan, he lowered his head, claiming her mouth with his own. She clung to him, lost in an unfamiliar whirl of sensation, knowing only that this was what she wanted, what she had longed for, what only he could bring her.

Abruptly he set her from him, muttering something she couldn't quite catch. He turned away, running an agitated hand through his hair. "You had no business setting foot out of doors alone. You are not to do so again under any circumstances. Is that understood? It is far too dangerous."

"In more ways than one," she murmured. She still trembled from being in his arms. That was one assault—both to her heart and to her person—she would be willing to repeat at any time. But he didn't seem to feel the same way.

"Come." He grasped her arm just above the elbow. "Best get you inside." The strain sounded heavy in his voice as he propelled her forward.

She hung back, still shaken. "Roland—"

His brow snapped down. "Have I made myself clear? You are not to go out alone, even in daylight."

He marched her toward the terrace, and she went with him blindly. Had she been wrong? Had she imagined his reactions? His kiss had meant the world to her; had it been a mere nothing to him? Big Cousin comforting Little Hen?

They entered through the South Drawing Room. Several candles illuminated the gilt-trimmed apartment that would hold comfortably upwards of thirty people. She searched his face as he bolted the door behind them and blew out the first of the flickering lights.

Nothing of her own chaotic emotions showed on his features. She could see concern—but no more than he would naturally experience over the intruder. He was not one to wear his heart on his sleeve, but surely she should be able to detect something, some residual glow in his eyes—if there ever had been any in the first place.

He extinguished each of remaining candles as they passed. Darkness closed about them, wrapping them in an ever-shrinking cocoon. His arm brushed against her shoulder with every step, sending aching need through her. Yet he seemed to be oblivious to her presence.

From the small table by the door he collected his chamberstick, which he held aloft as he ushered her out. Again she peeked up at his face, and his eyes gleamed in the warm glow that fell over them.

A cold lump formed in her stomach. It hadn't been any inner passion that lit his face when he'd held her in the garden. It had been moonlight, nothing more. She had imagined the whole thing. Everything—except her own reactions. She huddled into her shawl, feeling a fool, feeling betrayed—though she knew he was not to blame.

He accompanied her to her room and didn't leave until she shut and locked the door. She closed her eyes, listening to his retreating footsteps, wishing everything could be different.

This accomplished nothing. With determined briskness, she prepared for bed and crawled between sheets. For a very long while she lay awake, staring into the darkness of the canopy above her.

A scratching noise disturbed her sometime later. She rolled over, her mind bleary with newly achieved sleep. The sound repeated, this time identifiable as her unyielding door latch.

Her eyes flew open, but she could see little in the dark reaches of the room. She turned up the oil lamp that burned low on the bedside table, then froze as the scratching came once more, banishing the last vestiges of drowsiness. Someone stood just outside, trying to open the locked door.

She swallowed, her throat dry, unsure what to do. Confront the person and possibly get killed in the attempt? Cower in her bed, waiting for the door to burst wide and her assailant to descend on her?

No, she would summon help, she answered herself as her rational thinking shook free of its paralysis. She drew herself into a sitting position and with a trembling hand tugged on her bellrope. She could only hope her abigail would not come alone. She sank back on her heels amidst the covers, her hands clenching the comforter, and stared at the door.

"You! What are you doing?" From down the hall, Great-aunt Lavinia's scratchy voice rose on a querulous pitch.

Great-aunt Lavinia. Horror filled Netta, and fear for her elderly relative galvanized her into action. She scrambled out of bed, searching on the nightstand's top for the key.

"Here, you get away from—" Lavinia began, and broke off on a strangled cry.

A dull thud followed, then silence.

Chapter Fourteen

Panicked, Netta rammed the key into the lock. After an agonizing moment it turned. She dragged the door open, burst into the hall, and came to an abrupt halt.

At her feet lay Great-aunt Lavinia, wrapped in her shawl, her nightcap askew. A knife protruded from her bony breast. Netta swallowed a rising wave of nausea. Blood soaked the white muslin of Lavinia's bedgown and pooled about her.

Netta clutched the jamb, dizzy, her gaze focused on the carved ivory handle of the blade. She'd seen it before in the bookroom, lying on the desk. Roland had brought it back from India with him . . .

"Netta, dear?" Phemie's trembling voice sounded as if from a great distance.

Netta looked up. Across the hall, in the open doorway of her bedchamber, stood Cousin Phemie. Netta gasped in relief and ran to her, and the little figure enfolded her in a comforting embrace.

"There, there, dear." Phemie stroked her hair.

"It's all over now, nothing more to worry us. Just you go back into your chamber and wait, and I'll return in a moment. Such a dreadful chill for this time of year, is it not?" She disappeared within, only to reemerge a minute later, wrapping a warm woolen shawl about her shoulders. "Now, Netta, what are you thinking of, just standing here?" She took Netta by the arm and tried to lead her forward.

Netta pulled away, too shocked to respond. "We—we've got to summon help. I pulled the bell-rope," she added, remembering.

"Did you, dear?" Phemie patted her hand. "You always were such a practical one. I daresay someone will be along in just a moment, then." She eased Netta into her bedchamber. "Pray, do not distress yourself so. We shall all get along far more comfortably, now."

Netta sank into the armchair, hugging herself, chilled with a cold no fire could disperse. "We—we'd better warn whoever is coming. If it's Wembly—" No, her abigail should not be forced to come unprepared upon the horror that awaited outside the door.

"To be sure, how thoughtful of you, my love. I'll go." Phemie bustled out, humming to herself.

Netta stared after her, startled by her companion's composure. She would have expected the little woman to have gone off in a fit of the vapors. Instead, she acted as if someone had done her the greatest favor. She seemed so serene, with not a single silver hair out of place beneath her lace nightcap and her dressing gown fastened to the neck.

Netta's gaze strayed to her mirror. Yes, she herself looked as if she had tumbled from her bed. With hands that still shook, she straightened her cap, tucking stray curls in at random. Her own dressing gown lay across the foot of the bed where she had discarded it hours before. When had Phemie found time to neaten herself?

Then memory of the way Phemie had stood in her doorway flooded back. She'd been going into her room, not coming out. To get her shawl—or for some other reason? Netta closed her eyes tight. She had seen no one else, could not remember hearing any retreating footsteps. Could Phemie have taken all she could from Lavinia and stabbed her? The two had fought constantly for as long as Netta could remember, their antagonism growing more bitter with every passing year.

No, Netta rejected the thought at once. Greataunt Lavinia died because she saw whoever it was who tried to break into Netta's room. Which meant that person had something to hide—such as Desmond's murder. But why did this person want to kill *her?* This could have been no mere attempt to mislead the Runner.

She roused herself enough to light a fire from the kindling and dried moss that lay in a scuttle by the grate, then returned to her chair where she waited, trying not to listen to the distressing sounds in the hall. Cousin Phemie must have roused the entire household. Some time later

Wembly, pale and strained, brought her a glass of brandy and hot tea. Netta thanked her and sipped the drink until Phemie once more came into the room.

"You should get between sheets, dear." Phemie shook out her comforter and smoothed the bed.

Netta hunched lower. "What is happening?"

"Haskins has sent the groom into Brighton to fetch that Mr. Frake. I thought we should move Lavinia—so distressing to have her just lying there, is it not?—but Roland would not permit it. Dear Roland. I am sure he knows best."

"I must be numb," Netta said. "Great-aunt Lavinia has been murdered! Yet I hardly feel anything at all, as if I were devoid of emotion." Except a longing for Roland's presence.

"Now, dear." Phemie perched on the edge of the bed. "You are in shock, I make no doubt, but you will see how well we will go on. You just sit there and relax, my love, and leave everything to me. I told you I wouldn't let Desmond harm you, and now that old harridan and her evil tongue can't do so, either." Phemie leaned back against the pillows, humming softly to herself.

Dawn crept across the sky and seeped into Netta's chamber before the Runner at last arrived. She remained in her chair while he made his preliminary investigations, then rose as he knocked and entered. Roland followed, his dress impeccable, his expression haggard. His gaze sought hers, and for a moment his strength buoyed her. He leaned against a bedpost, waiting.

"Well, now, m'lady," Mr. Frake said by way of greeting. "Why don't you tell me what's been happening." He pulled up a smaller chair, drew out his Occurrence Book, and bestowed a comfortable, encouraging smile on her.

Netta took a deep breath and told them of waking to the sounds of someone trying to open her locked door and of Lavinia's interruption. Roland's mouth thinned, but he made no comment.

Mr. Frake cocked his head to one side and clucked his tongue. When she finished her tale, he shook his head. "I'd best tell you at once, m'lady. I've gone all over this here house with Haskins, and there's no sign as anyone forced an entry." His thoughtful gaze strayed toward Roland.

The furrows in that gentleman's brow deepened. "Which is your way of saying one of us killed my great-aunt. Why do you not just accuse me and be done with it?"

Or Phemie . . . Netta's stomach clenched. No, there had to be another explanation. "Did you try everything? What of the secret door?"

Mr. Frake raised his head. "What 'secret door'?" he demanded.

"The one built into the chimney of the stillroom. It doesn't always latch properly. I went through it only yesterday—or the day before? It might have remained unlocked."

The Runner drew a deep breath. "Secret doors," he muttered. "Just how secret is this?"

Roland frowned. "Lord, I'd thought that boarded up ages ago."

"Oh, it was, dear." Phemie smiled brightly. "But it was the easiest way into the herb garden, so I had it opened."

"When?" the Runner shot at her.

She tilted her head to one side. "Was it thirteen years ago? Netta, do you recall? No, I remember now. It was the year after Roland left, that summer when your poor Cousin Maria stayed with us for a week. Do you recall how you and Desmond were used to tease her with it, forever popping out into the garden when she least expected it?"

The Runner glared at her. "Does anyone else know it exists?"

Netta fought an hysterical desire to giggle. "As my cousin says, it is the easiest way into the stillroom. We all use it."

"Anyone outside the house, that is," the Runner clarified.

Netta considered. "Anyone who has visited us while we were in the stillroom, I should say."

Mr. Frake checked his notes. "Sir Archibald? What with him living so close, I suppose he knows of it."

"Oh, yes." Phemie nodded. "Why, more often than not he comes through that way. Doesn't he, Netta?"

Netta's lips twitched. "Indeed he does. As does Mr. Lambert."

Mr. Frake frowned. "So, both of those gentlemen could have entered the house by that route."

He tapped the side of his notebook with his pencil. "At least the Underhills are in the clear on this one."

Netta looked up. "But they aren't. At least, Mr. Underhill knows of it. Whether he has spoken of it to Lady Beatrix or not, I wouldn't know."

Mr. Frake glared at her. "I thought as your cousin and Mr. Underhill didn't get on."

"He attended a house party here, before their feud became quite so heated. They used the secret door as part of a game they played. Mr. Underhill might well remember it."

Mr. Frake took himself off to find Haskins and inspect the door.

Roland remained for a moment, his gaze resting on Netta. "Take care of her, Aunt Phemie," he said, and strode out after the Runner.

Netta rose, stiff, and shook out the muslin skirts of her dressing gown.

"Do you come to bed?" Phemie asked.

"I would never sleep." She went to her wardrobe, reached for her riding habit, then realized it might not be safe for her to venture forth alone. For one terrible moment, the scratching at her door sounded loud and threatening in her memory. But where did caution leave off and cowardice begin? She pulled the velvet garment out and donned it with Phemie's help.

"You will take Roland with you?" the little woman asked, anxious.

Netta paused as she reached for her hat. To ride

with Roland. "Yes," she said, mostly to herself. At the moment, she could think of nothing she would like better. But would he agree? Probably, she realized with a pang of regret. He would undoubtedly consider it his duty to keep his Little Lady Hen safe.

She found him in the stillroom with the Runner. Nothing, it seemed, had been learned from the door. It remained on the latch; anyone could have come in or gone out.

"But that doesn't necessarily mean as someone did," Mr. Frake pointed out.

"By which he means we are still suspects," Roland explained.

Mr. Frake bestowed a pained look on him and excused himself to interview the staff.

"Well, Little Hen?" Roland's gaze rested on her. His expression clouded, and he looked away, toward the wall shelves with their myriad bottles and jars.

Her heart twisted. Did he weary of her company—or did she prove a constant reminder of her father's unfair treatment of him? Or possibly—just possibly—had he thought of her so long as his Little Hen that he had trouble now seeing her as a young woman?

That last thought gave her hope, and she gathered her courage. "Will you ride with me? If you don't, I shall go alone."

"Is that a threat?" A touch of reluctant amusement eased the lines of strain about his eyes. "Very well, then. I will change and meet you in the kitchens in twenty minutes." He headed for the door.

He'd agreed; he wouldn't try to avoid her. Her spirits lifting, she set off to raid whatever she could find for a breakfast she suddenly wanted.

With only a little rummaging, she found a cheese and a loaf of bread baked the night before. She cut slices from each, then perched on the edge of the great wooden table and ate. By the time Roland joined her, she dusted the crumbs from her fingers.

He raised his eyebrows as she handed him the share she had cut for him. "I will send to London today for your servants to return."

"I will be glad to see Cook back." She watched as he finished his slab of bread and cut another. "Why not close Tavistock House for the season?"

He straddled a slatted chair, leaning over the back. "I intend to return as soon as I have settled Desmond's affairs here. But I will hire my own staff, I will not steal yours."

She swallowed her dismay at the thought of him leaving. "You may find they might prefer to work for the earl of Tavistock."

His lip curled. "I could wish Desmond alive again, if only to spare me that onus. Come." He rose. "I feel the need for a long gallop."

She walked in silence by his side to the stable. Her head just topped his shoulder, she noted; she found his massive presence comforting — and very distracting. She could only wish he found her the same.

They waited while Roland's groom readied their mounts, then Roland cupped his hands and threw her into the saddle as if she weighed no more than a feather. He swung onto his own great chestnut stallion and led the way out of the yard and down the drive. At the lane Netta nudged her eager mare into a canter, passing Roland. The stallion's stride lengthened to match, they cleared the hedge separating them from a field neck and neck, then the stallion pulled ahead.

Netta threw herself into the race, leaning low, expending every ounce of her own energy along with the mare. Roland remained ahead—though not by much, just enough to goad her onward, to tease her with the hope of passing. They sailed over another hedge, then a rock wall, which brought them to a dirt lane that they followed until her tiring mount stumbled. Netta reined in at once and swung to the ground to check her blowing mare's legs for possible injuries.

Roland trotted back to join her. "Pick up a stone?"

"Just tired, I think." She released the last leg. "Poor girl." She stroked the animal's steaming neck, then started walking back the way they had come, leading the mare. Roland jumped down and walked at her side. "It doesn't seem right," she said at last. "Great-aunt Lavinia—" She broke off, then turned to look up at him. "She died because of me."

His brow snapped down. "Don't talk nonsense."

"You know it isn't. Someone tried to break into my room, someone who dared not risk being seen or identified." Her voice dropped. "It will seem very odd without her. She has always been a part of my life."

"Lives change." A harsh note underlay his words. "Usually just in time to shatter all your plans."

Netta slowed. "Will it really be so terrible, being Tavistock? Are there not any advantages? Both my father and Desmond seemed to enjoy it."

"I would prefer any other title. Or none at all. I was content with my lot."

She tried to read his expression, but his face remained a mask. "I am surprised you ever came near Ravenswood at all, before Desmond's affairs demanded it."

"I was curious. I had hoped—" He fell silent, not finishing his thought.

"That you could face it without 'the gall of bitterness, and in the bond of iniquity'?"

His lips twitched. "Something like that. I had thought myself more forgiving. It seems I was wrong."

They continued in silence until Netta's boot started to chafe her foot. Roland tossed her back into the saddle, then swung onto his own horse. His strain had eased, she noted. They still didn't speak, but at least she didn't feel as if he resented her presence. That was something, she assured herself.

At the stable, they handed their horses over to

the waiting grooms, then returned to the house. While Roland stopped to speak to Haskins, Netta went straight up the stairs to change her dress and remove the lingering aromas of the stable from herself. At the last landing, though, she came to an abrupt halt, not wanting to traverse the next few steps to her bedchamber.

There would be another funeral, another period of mourning.

The servants had long since carried Great-aunt Lavinia's body to her room. Now a maid knelt before Netta's door, scrubbing with a brush and bucket of water. Netta closed her eyes. Whether in her imagination or in reality, she still smelled blood and death.

Would any amount of scouring cleanse the carpet where Great-aunt Lavinia had lain? Or would her ghost now haunt Ravenswood Court? With a shiver, she realized the thought might not be all that fanciful. Would her beloved Desmond join her? No, he preferred London. His ghostly presence would remain at Tavistock House. She could only be glad that establishment belonged to Roland and not her.

She would change her gown later. She ran back down the stairs, then slowed as she came into sight of the main hall. Roland stood before the pier table by the door, glancing through the morning mail that lay on the chased salver. One letter he held as if weighing it before he broke the wafer. He scanned the contents, then lowered it. For a long moment he stared straight ahead.

"Good news?" Netta approached, uncertain.

He transferred his gaze to her. "It is from my solicitor. My offer has been accepted for Larkspur. I will leave for there as soon as the Runner permits. Have no fear, you will not be troubled by my presence much longer."

Her heart sank. "You may stay as long as you wish."

"I have already stayed longer than that," came his brutal response.

She looked down. "You will always be welcome in my home."

A short laugh escaped him. "This is one home I hope never to set eyes on again."

Stricken, she raised her gaze to his.

His mouth tightened. "Do not pretend to be surprised, my girl. I have made no secret of how I feel. I shall be only too glad to shake the dust of this place from my feet. Ravenswood—and you—" he added with determined emphasis "—represent a part of my past I am only too anxious to forget." He turned on his heel and strode off toward the quiet of the bookroom.

Chapter Fifteen

In the late afternoon, Benjamin Frake once more rode up to the stables at Ravenswood Court and turned his tired roan over to the lad who hurried out to meet him. With a last pat on the animal's sweat-dampened flank, Frake turned to the house. How, he wondered, would they take the information he brought? Much could be learned from reactions, it could. He looked forward to finding out a thing or two.

Lady Henrietta's eager voice hailed him as he crossed the gravel drive. He turned and saw her hurrying toward him, one hand holding down the wide-brimmed straw hat that perched on her fiery curls. Her other held a pair of shears, and over that arm hung a curved wicker basket filled with flowers.

"Have you learned anything more?" she demanded as she neared.

"Not as much as I should like, m'lady." He shook his head. "Still, a little is better than nothing, I dare say."

"I'll know better when you tell me." She regarded him with large, anxious eyes.

He smiled. "Where is his lordship?"

Lady Henrietta drew in a deep breath. "The devil take his lordship," she muttered on the merest breath of sound.

Oh, ho, so they were at odds were they? Pretending not to have heard, he allowed her to lead him toward the French doors into the bookroom.

Roland Galbraith, eighth earl of Tavistock, sat behind the great mahogany desk, tying up a bundle of papers. He looked up as they entered, and his brow furrowed.

"Anything of any use?" Frake nodded toward the stack Roland pushed to one side.

"Notes for the past few plantings. Made by the farm manager. I intend to send them to the estate room where they belong. Would you care to examine them?" A touch of dry irony colored his words. He rose and came around the edge of the desk.

"Thank you kindly." Frake awarded him a bland smile. "I'd be pleased to have a look."

"What have you learned?" Lady Henrietta demanded once more, interrupting him. "He is being quite exasperating," she informed Roland. "He refused to tell me anything until you were present."

"I assure you, my good man, there was no need to wait." Yet a spark of interest lit Roland's eyes. "You might as well let us have it now."

"It isn't much," Frake repeated. "Mr. Underhill and Lady Beatrix were supposed to be at a ball with that uncle of his, Sir Reginald Underhill. Only seems as if that pair left a mite early. Shortly after ten o'clock, in fact."

"It must not have been an engrossing party. I cannot say I blame them." Roland leaned back against the desk.

"Blame?" Frake rocked back on his heels. "Now I can't say as I'm laying any blame yet. It just seems an interesting fact that a person on horseback could cover the distance between Brighton and here in about twenty minutes. I know. I just tried it myself."

"So one of them could have been here by, say, a quarter to eleven?" Roland watched Frake with a growing intensity.

"Just so, m'lord. They would have had time to reach this here estate before her ladyship saw someone in the garden—and long before Lady Lavinia was murdered."

Lady Henrietta shook her head, her expression bewildered. "But the Underhills would have no reason to want me dead."

"Well, now, m'lady, I've been giving that some thought, I have. There's no reason whatsoever to assume your stalker's purpose was murder."

"Do you mean he wanted just to—to terrorize me, then? For the sport of it?"

"Now, m'lady, I don't mean any such thing. It's generally assumed, though, that you are now

257

an extremely wealthy young lady."

A short, derisive laugh escaped her. "By whom? Surely no one who knows the Galbraith affairs."

"It's the assumption as can do the damage," Frake explained. "If you was abducted and held for ransom, most folk would think it likely your cousin Miss Wrenn or the new earl would pay whatever they demanded for your safe release. A hefty sum would pay off a great many gaming debts—with a tidy bit left over."

Lady Henrietta sank onto a chair and stared at him. "Abduction," she breathed, as if the thought had never before occurred to her.

Frake watched her with care. Becoming color tinged her cheeks, as if she found the idea a relief. Well, he would, too, if he'd thought someone was out to murder him. Better abduction any day. And her reaction appeared natural, not as if she merely wanted him to believe she was relieved.

"You said it is generally assumed she is wealthy." Roland looked up from the table where he poured a measure of brandy into a glass. He handed it to Lady Henrietta, who accepted it absently and took a sip. "How do you know this?"

Frake drew his pipe from its resting place in his pocket. "Hear things, I do. Comes from knowing what questions to ask and where to ask them. Been at it a goodly number of years, I have."

"Abduction. Good God." Roland strode to the hearth and leaned one elbow on the mantel. "I suppose you shall next have every gazetted fortune hunter in town making up to you, cousin."

Lady Henrietta shivered. "Is there any way of letting people know the truth?"

Amusement flashed in Roland's eyes. "What, do you wish to take out an advertisement in the *Morning Post?*"

She cast him a pained look. "Without being vulgar about it, I mean." She turned back to Frake. "Would someone who only intended to abduct me murder my great-aunt? And with Roland's dagger? They would have to have located that."

Frake looked at Roland and raised his eyebrows. "Where had you left it, m'lord?"

"The devil if I remember. In here, I suppose. I might have used it to cut twine for other bundles of papers. Yes, I believe I did."

"The Underhills," Lady Henrietta mused, and frowned. "Do you believe they planned this together?"

"Well, now, m'lady, I can't say as I *believe* anything for certain. Just a possibility, as you might say. It could have been planned by them both, or by either one of them. Or by neither of them, for that matter. Just something else to think about."

A knock on the door interrupted them. Haskins entered, a long-suffering expression on his gaunt countenance. "Lady Beatrix and Mr. Underhill, Master—m'lord," he announced "I've put them in the Blue Salon."

Lady Henrietta choked over her brandy and went off in a coughing fit.

Roland merely raised his eyebrows. "Thank you, Haskins. We will be with them in a moment." He drew a handkerchief from his pocket and handed it to Lady Netta, taking the glass from her.

"I'm sorry," she managed at last. "It was just so—startling."

A light glinted in his lordship's eyes. "I doubt they intend a daring daylight abduction. At least, I would not begin one by having the butler announce me. Are you quite recovered?"

She rose. "Mr. Frake, do you accompany us?"

They entered the salon a few minutes later to find Josiah Underhill, his face redder than usual, leafing through the pages of a racing form. Lady Beatrix sat on a matching chair opposite him, glowering out the window. Frake followed the direction of her gaze, but found nothing at which to take exception in the charming prospect of the curving drive and shrubbery.

"Hah! There you are." Underhill rose to his feet. "Come to redeem m'wife's vowels." He thrust a draft drawn on his bank at Roland. "There. Thank you to retrieve 'em for me."

That gentleman inclined his head. "I believe our good Runner has them in his custody. But I will certainly write you a receipt and see the vowels themselves returned to you as quickly as possible."

"Burn them, for all I care." Lady Beatrix glared at him.

Frake took the draft from Roland's hands and examined it. "Would you mind telling me where you obtained the money to cover this?" He peered across at Underhill, schooling his countenance into an expression of innocent curiosity.

Underhill snorted. "No secret about that. Followed Tavistock's lead. Your cousin's," he corrected himself with a nod to Roland.

"Disreputable lead," Lady Beatrix amended.

"Which was?" Frake prodded.

"What? Oh, just unloaded some of m'cattle." Underhill fingered the form he still held.

"Would have been no need had you not let Tavistock gammon you into buying bone-setters and roarers in the first place," his wife stuck in.

Underhill's color darkened alarmingly, and his mouth worked as his fingers clenched on the paper. "At least I don't game with Captain Sharps!"

Her lip curled. "You've neither the wit nor the nerve."

Frake cast a considering glance at Underhill's fulminating expression and intervened before the man could be taken off in a fit of apoplexy. "I was wondering if you both might be able to help me."

261

"It would be the very thing if you could." Lady Henrietta leaped to his assistance. "Roland, will you not send for refreshments?"

"Eh?" Underhill blinked, his expression crestfallen, as one who had the wind taken out of his sails. "Oh. Drop of porter, if you have it, Tavistock." He looked at the rolled-up racing form he had been clenching and somewhat sheepishly smoothed it out.

Frake strolled the length of the room while Roland sent Haskins for porter and ratafia. He wouldn't mind a tankard of ale himself after the work he'd put in this day, but he had a sorry feeling he had many hours more to go. He glanced over his shoulder to where Lady Henrietta had drawn up a chair beside Lady Beatrix and engaged their visitor in a low-voiced conversation.

He didn't know what to make of that little spat between husband and wife. It could be their normal way of conversing with one another. He'd have to look into that. On the other hand, it might have been a performance with a purpose. Underhill's temper evaporated like a puff of smoke caught in a breeze. But what did they hope to accomplish — short of diverting their listeners from any further discussion on where they might have gotten the money to redeem those vowels? He'd just go and have himself a look-see as to how many horses no longer resided in the Underhill stable.

Haskins returned with not only the beverages but also a plate piled high with biscuits and slices of a rich-looking cake filled with nuts. The new earl busied himself pouring from the various decanters. Frake declined with a shake of his head, but accepted the chair his host offered.

"Now, then, Lady Beatrix," Frake began after Underhill had drained his first glass and held it out for a refill. "I know who sat at that table with you that last night you was gaming with the late earl. Supposing you tell me just what happened, and if any of them was acting peculiar like."

She hesitated, a touch of defiance in the flickering glance she directed at her husband. He paid her no heed, his entire attention apparently concentrated on the plate of cakes. "Already several people at the table when I sat down." Her square hand tightened about her crystal glass. "Suppose you're only interested in those who might have had anything to do with his death." Her brow wrinkled. "Lambert. He was there before me."

Frake drew out his Occurrence Book and jotted that down. "Go on, m'lady."

Her fingers twisted about the stem. "I played for a little over an hour and a half. Losing heavily."

"As you could see from her vowels," Underhill stuck in.

Lady Beatrix rounded on him, but Frake intervened. "If we could just be going on? Thank you. How did Mr. Lambert do?"

That seemed to give Lady Beatrix courage. She straightened her shoulders. "Cards ran steadily against him. Then Sir Archy joined us. Just before I left the table, that was."

"And why did you leave?"

"My husband came in."

Underhill snorted. "Not the sort of company I want m'wife keeping. Not a real sportsman among 'em. No sense of honor, that's their problem. No nerve. Couldn't look their grouse square in the eye and shoot it. Tavistock in particular. Always up to some havey-cavey game." He shook his head, then frowned. "Fellow was up to his tricks that night. Remember the way he smiled, Trixie?"

She shook her head, though to Frake it seemed as if she remembered very well.

"Smiled," Underhill repeated. "That villainous smile of his. Boded ill for someone, you mark my words. Said something, too, now I come to think of it. About having completed something, some evil deed, maybe. Tell you what, my good man." He waggled a finger under Frake's nose. "Should quit wasting everyone's time and find the fellow Tavistock cheated that night. Then you'll have your murderer."

"I'll bear that in mind, sir. Now, then, m'lady, can you remember who was sitting where, when you went home?"

"About two hours later, that would have been. Lambert—he was still there. Had slumped over his cards."

"Something dashed smokey about that," Underhill stuck in. "Lambert don't normally drink to excess."

"If he did this time." Beatrix turned an enigmatic smile on Mr. Frake.

Frake took his cue. "Think he was playacting, then?"

Lady Beatrix gave an expressive shrug. "Didn't myself count the number of bottles he broached. Most unlike him, though, to let himself get fuddled at a gaming table. Prides himself on keeping his wits about him—or so he says."

Interesting, that. "And Sir Archibald?"

"Still at the table, too. Had lost a great deal by all appearances. Tavistock had a considerable pile of vowels before him. Must have had his pockets bulging when he left."

Frake looked up. "Indeed? Now I distinctly remember his lordship's valet mentioning only a few vowels from Sir Archibald. That was certainly all we found."

Lady Beatrix tilted her head to one side. "Maybe Tavistock asked him to write a single one covering the total amount at some point. Wouldn't be unheard of, especially if he'd written a great many for small amounts."

"Archy's luck might have changed," Underhill suggested. "Maybe he won most of 'em back.

Never did seem like Tavistock to win more than a pittance. Far more likely to dip too deep." He jutted his head forward, peering at Frake. "Any more questions from you? No? Come along, then, Trixie. Just time for a bruising ride before Uncle misses us. Maybe stop for a bite at an inn, eh? Devilish food m'uncle serves," he explained to the others.

Netta walked the Underhills to the door, then turned back, a resolution growing within her born partly from fear, partly from frustration. Life, she decided, had become far too confusing. Murder, abduction . . . and Roland.

He considered her a constant reminder of his unhappy past. Yet while Mr. Frake had questioned the Underhills, Roland's gaze had kept straying to her; she'd been vividly aware of it. No matter what he said, what he perhaps wanted to believe, he must care at least a little for her. Somehow she had to make him admit it.

She would not give up without a fight he would long remember.

Yet how could he think of contentment—or love—when violence, distrust, and death filled his mind? The murders of Desmond and Great-aunt Lavinia haunted them, needing to be avenged. This terrible chapter of their lives had to be put behind them, she realized, before they could look toward any future.

But the investigation seemed to go nowhere, except perhaps in circles. Somehow, they needed to narrow the field of suspects, find the person — or persons — responsible. They needed a plan that would make it clear, beyond any doubt, whom they sought. They needed —

An idea crept into her mind, desperate, perhaps, but it just might work.

"And what would that gleam in your eye be meaning?" Frake's voice broke her reverie.

She looked up. He stood before her in the open expanse of the hall, his shallow-crowned beaver in one hand. A speculative smile just touched his lips. She must have been standing in that one place for several minutes.

She looked over his shoulder to where the Blue Salon stood open. "Where is my cousin?"

"If you're meaning his lordship, he's gone back to the library."

"Good. I want to talk to you." She hurried back to the apartment where they had sat just a little while ago. After closing the door behind them, she gestured for the Runner to take a seat. She perched on the edge of a chair opposite.

"Now, m'lady, let's have it with no roundaboutation." The faintest lilt of a Scots accent colored his words. "What have ye in mind?"

"To have done with this matter." She sprang to her feet and paced the perimeter of the Aubusson carpet. "I do not believe I can tolerate the uncertainty of this situation for a moment longer. And I simply will not wait around for someone to either kill or abduct me."

"Well now, m'lady, I can't say as I blame you none. Still—"

She gestured him to silence. "I intend to take matters into my own hands."

"But m'lady—"

"If you will help me, I mean to offer myself as—as bait and lure my would-be assailant into a trap."

Chapter Sixteen

Mr. Frake folded his arms across his chest and
regarded Netta through gleaming blue eyes. "And
if I was to say no to this little scheme of yours?"

A flicker of fear raced through her, only to
steady the next moment. She had his full attention, and no trace of resignation or humoring
touched his manner. Only alertness. "You
won't." She inserted even more confidence than
she actually felt into her words. "You see as
clearly as do I, this will be our best—and quick-
est-method—to catch this—person."

"Quickest, mayhap. I'll reserve a few doubts as
to this 'best' of yours."

"If we plan this with care, I should be in no
actual danger. And it does seem likely, does it
not, that the person who is after me also killed
Great-aunt Lavinia and Desmond?"

"It would seem a bit far-fetched if'n you was
both to have made different enemies all of the
same time like," he admitted.

She found little consolation in this endorsement. "I did rather like the abduction idea. It—I felt safer with that somehow. But it doesn't explain Great-aunt Lavinia's death."

"Until we get to the bottom of this, there's no way of us knowing for certain. Now when was you fixing to try?"

"Tonight?" Her voice trembled only a little.

Mr. Frake nodded. "I'll just alert my patrol. Got them waiting at an inn only a few miles from here."

"At—of course. How naive of me. I'm surprised you haven't had them housed in the servants' wing."

His eyes twinkled. "Now, m'lady, I didn't see no need to go and alert everyone as to their presence. They're near enough. I'll just have 'em slip in all quiet like once as it gets dark."

Netta gripped the back of a chair. "And whom do you think they will catch?"

"Can't say as I can answer that with any certainty." He shook his head. "That Lady Beatrix, with or without Mr. Underhill? There's a determined streak in the both of them, there is. Or Sir Archibald or Mr. Lambert? Though to hear them talk, it sounds as if they'd both rather attend your wedding as the bridegroom than your funeral as a mourner."

Netta shivered. "Please—"

"Or Miss Wrenn?" Frake pursued.

Cousin Phemie. Netta cringed inside, unable to banish the contented sound of her long-time companion's soft humming while Great-aunt Lavinia lay dead just outside the door . . .

"Or this Cousin Roland of yours, the new earl?" He frowned. "Now, why, m'lady, did you react like that when I mentioned Miss Wrenn?"

Netta hugged herself. "She'd never try to kill me."

Frake drew out his notebook, then returned it unopened into the depths of his pocket. "Maybe not, m'lady, but she might make it *seem* as if someone was wishful to see you dead. Divert suspicion from herself, don't you see? Then again, if she up and murdered Desmond, and thought you knew, she might feel it a regretful necessity to murder you as well."

"No." Netta closed her eyes, as if blocking out the sight of the Runner could blot out the misery brought by his words. She swallowed hard and felt the few remnants of her once-stable world collapsing about her.

"Well now. No use jumping ahead of ourselves, is there?" The Runner's cheerful voice commanded her attention.

Netta shook her head, not finding her voice to answer.

"Seems as if we have ourselves a few hours still. Was you wishful to go into Brighton today as you'd planned?"

"Brighton?" She stared at him, feeling as stupid as she must sound.

"Your will." He smiled at her. "You was wish-

271

ful to sign it as soon as may be, wasn't you?"

"I'll be ready in ten minutes." She started toward the door, then turned back. "The carriage—"

"I'll order it out, don't you worry none. Ten minutes," he reminded her, and followed her from the salon.

Netta didn't bother to change her gown. Her black bombazine would do just as well for a late afternoon call upon a solicitor as it did at home. She straightened her hair, then donned a black shawl and a bonnet suitable for even a funeral, and hurried back down. As she joined Mr. Frake in the hall, the crunching of hooves and wheels on the gravel drive announced the arrival of the ancient landau. With uncertain feelings, Netta set forth with the Runner.

Her dominant emotion just over an hour later, as she sat in the solicitor's office, was dismay. The will, the apologetic man of law informed her, would not be ready for her signature for yet another day. Polite phrases about the changes necessitated by Lady Lavinia's death and recopying the document passed his lips, accompanied by deprecatory gestures.

Her mind strayed from his words. She could still make changes, if she wished. She could remove all mention of Cousin Phemie from the document. But Phemie would never try to kill her for any inheritance! Phemie *couldn't* wish to kill her for any reason. She murmured her good-

272

byes to the solicitor and turned to the door.

As she joined Mr. Frake in the small room without, a man's deep tones penetrated from the other office. Mr. Kenneth Lambert, she realized. For a moment she hesitated, and another man — the junior partner in the solicitor's firm — raised his own voice, speaking over Lambert's.

"You are haunting my office. I will thank you to restrain yourself and confine your visits to only when I send for you or you have something new to report."

"I will not be so spoken to." A sneer sounded in Lambert's haughty words.

Conciliatory sounds followed, but Netta couldn't catch the exact phrases.

"I'll damned well do as I please," Lambert retorted. "You will sell me out of the funds."

Another response followed, this one more curt.

"What the devil do you mean? Of course I have more capital."

"Mr. Lambert." The solicitor sounded harried, driven to the point of distraction. "You have run through the majority of your inheritance. I would not be doing my duty, either to yourself or to your late father, if I did not warn you most sincerely of the precarious nature of the position in which you are placing yourself. If you do not exercise the most stringent economies, I fear you will shortly be rolled up."

Silence followed this pronouncement for a full

273

thirty seconds, then Lambert's hollow laugh sounded. "My good man, have we not been over this before? I assure you, I have curtailed my expenses as far as possible. If you have not any helpful suggestions to make—"

The door opened a crack, and Netta jumped as a hand gripped her arm. Frake gestured for her silence as he drew her back, away from any appearance of listening.

"There is but one course left for you to follow." The solicitor's voice lowered in volume, but his earnest tones carried. "You have so little left. Can I not suggest—that is, have you not considered the—the domestic tranquillity and state of general well-being at which you might arrive through the arrangement of an advantageous marriage?"

Something perilously close to a snort emitted from behind that door. "Fortune hunting, you mean." Bitterness colored Lambert's words. "Do you honestly think I have not thought of that? I have put considerable effort into the wooing of one heiress and have been turned down for my pains."

Netta stiffened, angry both with Lambert and herself. She had actually been flattered by his attentions, and all the while he had thought her mistress of a considerable fortune. She wished she had rejected his offer with less consideration for his feelings. She turned and stalked from the offices.

At the street, the Runner caught up with her. "Are you feeling all right, m'lady?"

"Mortified." Her natural humor won out, and a rueful smile twitched at her lips. "Never again will I believe a gentleman when he threatens to write odes to my eyes."

"Now, m'lady." Frake smiled. "Has it occurred to you that if the gentleman is that hard up, he might not take kindly to losing to his late lordship—especially if he found out the game wasn't quite honest?"

Which made Mr. Kenneth Lambert a very viable suspect. But would he wish to murder her, as well as Desmond, when he had hoped to marry her supposed fortune? Perhaps if he doubted his ability to win her by fair means, he might try foul. If he abducted her, he had his choice of either compromising her or staging a daring rescue to make himself a hero in her eyes.

The drive back to Ravenswood they accomplished in silence. Netta stared out over the countryside, sunk in depression, not really aware of the pastures, fields, and forests spreading away from the road. What she would like most of all would be to turn to Roland for comfort, yet she could think of no one more unwilling to offer her the shelter of his arms.

Roland. No wonder he wanted nothing to do with her. He had only those unhappy memories of her home, of everything concerning her. And if someone killed her before she signed her will,

275

he would have that hated estate thrust upon him. That actually brought a smile to her lips. Poor Roland, she really couldn't allow that to happen.

Especially with what everyone would think. Her humor evaporated. Already the whole of the Polite World must gossip about him, speculate upon his guilt in Desmond's death. He had gained the most—the title, the townhouse, the consequence of an earldom. If she died, and the estate went to him as well, it would not matter to the ton that he didn't want it, that he would dispose of it at once. It would be seen only that again he profited—and he would be judged and condemned in the eyes of society.

She knew her world too well to doubt the consequences. Whether or not Mr. Frake proved him innocent would not matter after that. Roland would be rejected, possibly driven from his home and country once more. That thought distressed her.

She wanted him to be happy. His hazel eyes, etched by grim lines, filled her thoughts. Mentally, she smoothed a dark lock of hair back from his forehead, touched the angle of his cheek bone, willed the rigid set of his mouth to ease—the mouth that had found hers with such devastating results to her peace of mind.

She closed her eyes as the certainty of her love washed over her. Her childish adoration had deepened, survived the lies and years of separation, and matured into something all-encompass-ing. Yes, she would give anything to assure his happiness, even disappear from his life if the memories she aroused caused him too much pain. But she would much rather help him to create new and very wonderful memories.

And with luck, they would find their murderer tonight and clear Roland once and for all. Her resolve firmed to go through with her dangerous plan. For Roland she would risk anything.

They drove to the inn where Mr. Frake rejoined the patrol that awaited him. He stepped down from the landau with a cheery wave and a wink, and extracted from her a promise not to begin her little undertaking without first speaking with him that night. With this she willingly agreed, though she watched him disappear into the dark interior of the tavern with a sinking heart. Fighting back the sensation that she was on her own, she ordered the driver to take her home.

She reached the house with barely enough time to change for dinner. Wembly helped her scramble into her other black gown, and she made her way downstairs to the salon where Roland and Cousin Phemie awaited her.

Roland, dear beloved Roland . . .

He looked up, his gaze rested on her, and his brow snapped down in an irritated line. He refilled his glass and swallowed most of the contents in one gulp. He erected a rather efficient

277

barrier between them. Breaching that defense would not be easy.

He poured negus into another glass and handed it to her, his features now schooled into a mask of indifference. Almost she could believe he disliked her. Almost, but not quite. She took a seat where she could watch him without being obvious.

"My love." Phemie fluttered to her side and possessed herself of Netta's free hand. "My poor child, how strained you look. Now, if you are not feeling quite the thing, you must go at once to your chamber. I will bring you your dinner on a tray and a hot brick for your bed. Oh, and Lady Carncross was telling me only the other day about the most delightful posset for inducing sleep. I vow, this will be the perfect time to try it. It is no wonder you look so pale and drawn, with these dreadful goings-on."

With considerable difficulty, Netta freed herself. "I am quite all right, Cousin Phemie. In fact, I believe some fresh air would be far more beneficial to me than sleep. Is not dinner ready yet?" She cast an anxious glance toward the door. She wanted this over, finished. Her nerves stretched taut, tying in complicated knots in her stomach.

The danger would be worth it, she told herself. Roland had suffered enough because of his family. They had to finish the past before they could look to a future. And how many other

278

trite phrases could she think of to buoy her terrified spirits?

Several minutes dragged by before Haskins announced the meal. Netta swallowed her bites whole, too upset to chew, too anxious for the meal to end. She wanted to get on with springing her trap, yet she dreaded her appointment in the rose garden with the Runner—and possibly her would-be murderer. She choked over her next bite and found she no longer had any appetite at all.

She had to stay calm, not raise anyone's suspicions. They would try to stop her if they guessed. She had to act in as natural a manner as she could. She looked up to see both Roland and Cousin Phemie watching her, and her heart sank.

Finally, Phemie finished the syllabub with which she had been toying, and Netta rose, both glad and loath to escape Roland's watchful gaze. She led the way to the music room, where she seated herself at the pianoforte and concentrated on the mournful melody of a ballad while Phemie picked up her knitting. At last, the hands on the mantel clock crept toward eleven. Surely Mr. Frake and his patrol must be in place by now. She rose and headed for the door.

Phemie looked up from her yarn at once. "Do you go to bed, my love? I believe I shall go as well. I vow, I can scarce keep my eyes open."

"I could not close mine if I tried." Netta

paused. "I think I shall pace the halls for a bit."

Phemie smothered a yawn. "I shall bear you company."

"You shall do no such thing. Take yourself off to your bed." Netta bent and kissed her elderly cousin's cheek. No, she couldn't—wouldn't!—believe harm of her.

"You will stay within the house?" Phemie's worried gaze rested on Netta as the little woman followed her from the room.

"I will be very careful, I promise you." Now that was a neat evasion, she congratulated herself as she watched her concerned relative mount the stairs. She would wait a few minutes more, then go to the door where Mr. Frake would meet her.

At first, she couldn't see him. She ventured a step onto the terrace, then hesitated as a soft hiss reached her.

"In the shrubs, m'lady," Frake's unmistakable voice sounded. "You just walk about and make yourself obvious."

She pulled her shawl more closely about her shoulders and strolled with studied aimlessness along the side of the house. No one could hurt her. If anyone approached, Mr. Frake and his men would be upon him—or her. She had nothing to fear—except the revelation of the murderer's identity.

Now, with the possibility of catching the person, she realized she didn't want it to be anyone she knew, certainly not someone for whom she cared. It would be easier, in a way, had it been someone else who had been the victim and Desmond the murderer.

A twig in the shrubs snapped and she froze, then forced herself to relax. Mr. Frake's patrol—how many of them were there? she wondered. She should have asked, found out where he had positioned them. She didn't want to stray too far from help.

She continued along the length of the terrace, running her fingers along the low balustrade, then descended the steps to the level below. Was this safe? Mr. Frake hadn't stopped her. That gave her courage. Why, though, had he taken up a position near the house? Just to let her know he was present? Or did he expect her attacker to come from there?

What pleasant thoughts to take on a walk through a dark garden. It took every ounce of determination she could muster to put one foot ahead of the other, to leave the comparative safety of the tiled area and set off through the rose bushes. How long should she wait? Perhaps any would-be attackers had watched the Runner and his patrol arrive and beaten a strategic retreat. Only someone inside the house—like Cousin Phemie—might not be aware of the trap.

Phemie. She had to find the solution to this matter before the worry and fear drove her to the very doors of Bedlam.

A rustle sounded to her right and she stiffened. Branches being pushed aside? A footstep crunched on the gravel of the path from the same direction. Someone moved to intercept her.

Mustering her resolution, she kept herself from screaming. She took a step backward, then another, luring the person toward the waiting patrol. She couldn't run, not until they sprang the trap, not if she ever wanted to see the end of this.

The crunching quickened, as did the rustling of someone pushing his—or her—way through shrubs. A dark shape emerged just in front of her, and in anguish she stared up into the contorted features of Roland's face.

Chapter Seventeen

Netta faltered backward another step. "No." The word escaped on the merest breath.

Roland strode forward, towering over her, the moonlight glittering in his eyes, lending him a demonic appearance. "What the devil are you doing out here?" His voice, raw with emotion, rasped in his throat. "Are you *asking* someone to murder you?" He gripped her arm, his fingers digging through her shawl into her flesh. "You have no business being out here without someone watching over you."

"You—you appear to be," she managed.

His grip tightened. "It was the merest chance I saw you pass by the library window. What if I hadn't? What if you were out here alone? Good God," he shook her, "have you forgotten what occurred only last night?"

Hysterical relief surged through her. For one dreadful moment, she had actually feared Roland . . .

She forced her weakened knees not to desert her

altogether, to keep her upright. Still, she swayed against his solid chest, welcoming the sensation of having found a safe haven, sharing the strength that was his. She wanted nothing more than to remain like this for the rest of her life.

He set her aside. For a moment his hands lingered on her upper arms in a featherlight caress, then they dropped away. When he spoke, a vast weariness sounded in his voice. "Strive to show a little sense, Little Hen. I won't always be here to protect you."

"Not if you run away." She braced herself. She hadn't prepared for this battle, not at this moment, at least; but her heartbeat pounded in her ears, and the unbearable tension of the last few hours welled within her, demanding release.

"I am not running *from* anything, but *to* something." He glowered at her. "There is a great difference."

"You are fooling yourself. If you really wanted a new start, you would have bought any estate except Larkspur."

"Of all the absurd notions—"

"Oh, stop arguing for a moment and *think*. What really brought you back here?"

"I told you—"

She tried to meet his gaze, but he stared fixedly over her shoulder. "You came to Ravenswood before going up to London, even though you knew we would not be here. Why? Even if you didn't admit it to yourself, some part of you must have known you had to."

"This is ridiculous. I—"

"You say you want nothing to do with your past," she rushed on, "but it haunts you, doesn't it? You've spent seventeen years trying to escape, and you've failed miserably. What makes you think you can succeed now? You've got to face it, instead."

"You mean face you." Exasperation tinged his words. "Very well." One arm grasped her about the waist, the other about her shoulders. No trace of his earlier gentleness remained; he drew her against himself in a crushing embrace. His mouth clamped down on hers, forcing her head back.

She pulled her arm free from where it was trapped between them and caught his shoulder, clinging to him as overwhelming sensations swept through her. The pressure of his lips softened, and for a moment he held her with a tenderness that left her aching.

Slowly, almost with reluctance, he released her. "And what do you think I have gained by that?"

"Only you can tell me."

He stared at her in silence, then turned on his heel. "Do you come in, or do you intend to wait out here to be murdered?"

That brought memory flooding back of the trap she had planned—and their undoubted audience. Her cheeks flamed, and she averted her face as she hurried past him along a shorter route back to the house, cursing herself for an idiot every step of the way.

Yet she had to make Roland understand and

forgive, or the past would loom like a wedge which his every memory would drive ever deeper between them. So little time might remain to her; once he left for Larkspur, she might never see him again.

As they entered the library, Phemie hurried forward. "Thank heaven you were with her!" She beamed on Roland. "I could not rest until I knew her safe in her chamber, then I thought I heard voices outside. Such a shock as it gave me."

Roland didn't look at Netta. "See her well and safely locked in," he said, and marched from the room.

Phemie patted Netta's cold hand. "There, my love, I'm sure a nice walk was just what you needed, and you will fall right asleep now. Come, let me just take you up to your chamber. Your woman is waiting with a warming pan and hot bricks, and if you should like it, I shall send to the kitchens for a nice cup of steaming milk. You'll like that, won't you, my love?"

Netta started to deny it with vehemence but saw the expression of doting anxiety on her companion's face. It would do Netta no harm—except to her already strained nerves—to comply with the cosseting, and it would do Phemie a world of good. Just this once she would allow her cousin her way. Except . . .

"No milk, please." Nothing into which someone could slip a dose of poison. She felt a fool—and worse, a traitor. Yet Mr. Frake considered Phemie a possibility. Netta did not dare take any chances.

She kept her abigail with her until her cousin, with adjurations for her not to fail to send for her during the night had she need, sought her own couch. Then Netta locked her door behind the departing maid and contemplated moving a heavy piece of furniture to block the entry as well. While she considered the rival merits of budging the bulky dresser or simply forgetting the whole thing, the gentlest of taps sounded on the door.

She stared at it as if the oak panel itself would leap forward and bite her. She should peer through the keyhole, she told herself, disgusted at the fact she couldn't make her feet move. She should see who waited without.

"M'lady?"

Frake's hushed tones reached her, and a shattering sigh of relief left her weak. Only the Runner. She inserted the key with a trembling hand and swung the door wide.

He nodded. "Glad to see you have it locked." He kept his voice to a whisper. "Now, then, you was willing enough a little while ago to use yourself as bait. Are you still?"

"Sleeping bait?" She matched his lowered tones. "I think I prefer being awake."

"It won't matter, as long as you *appear* to be asleep. You remember that secret door down in the stillroom? I've left it on the latch, like, so as anyone who wants can just march right in."

She regarded him in indignation. "How excessively thoughtful of you. Did you also think to leave a map to my room, in case my murderer

287

might have forgotten his way? Or perhaps you could form a trail by setting out what's left of the family jewels?"

He grinned. "Glad to see you taking this so sporting like."

"I am?"

"Now, m'lady, with your permission, I'll just conceal myself somewheres here in your chamber. Behind that there chair, if I move the fire screen just a mite. There, that looks a safe place."

"You really believe someone will try again to-night?"

Mr. Frake looked up from the arrangement of his make-shift hiding place. "Well now, there's two ways of looking at it. Either our murderer will think we'll be in here a-waiting—him," he hesitated over the pronoun, "or else he'll figure we'd never expect him two nights in a row, which would make it safe for him. So let's just say I'm being cautious like."

And let's just say she was being nervous like, Netta reflected. She offered what creature comforts she could muster to the resolute Runner. The pillow he accepted, but declined the comforter, urging her to wrap up in it herself. Not in the least reconciled to the whole idea, Netta at last lay down on top of her bed with the quilt about her and kept her gaze fixed on the door.

She must have at last fallen asleep, for when she opened her eyes, light streamed into her room from a gap in the curtains. She sat up, alert, registering both the fact that she was alive and that

Mr. Frake no longer lurked in any corners. He had departed—leaving her door unlocked, she noted.

And what did that mean? Had he apprehended her would-be assailant in the dark hours of the night, alone and in silence? Or had some sound lured him out into the corridor? She rose to her knees, clutching the comforter about her, but could see no signs of anything unusual about her room. After a thoughtful moment, she rang for her abigail and set about getting dressed.

She entered the breakfast parlor to the sound of Roland's deep voice. The words washed over her, and the pleasant, resonant tones tugged at her heart. She had to break through the barriers he had erected against his past, or her own future would seem very bleak.

"Do you intend to come in, or do you find that spot fascinating?" Roland's words interrupted her wistful reflections.

She pulled herself together and managed a smile. "It is quite a delightful spot." She crossed the threshold, only to come to a stop once more.

Mr. Frake, heavy-eyed from his sleepless night, sat at the table opposite Roland, with the remnants of a large beefsteak before him. Smoke drifted from the briarwood pipe he held in one hand. In the other he nursed a tankard of dark ale.

He winked at her and pushed his chair back. "That was a mighty pleasant breakfast, m'lord, and I thank you kindly. Mighty interesting chat, too. Seems as I don't often find folks as is interested in such things."

Netta eyed him with suspicion. "What were you talking about? Exotic poisons?"

"Actually, Alexander Pope, which led to a discussion of Aristophanes." Roland frowned. "Do you remember how exactly?"

Mr. Frake gave a deprecating cough. "I believe something you said about Mr. Pope's translation of the *Iliad,* m'lord. It reminded me of something from *The Frogs.*"

"That's right." Roland nodded, satisfied.

Netta looked from one to the other of them, astounded. "How you can make any such comparison—" she began, then gave up. If she weren't careful, they might try to explain the convoluted twistings of their discussion which led to that seemingly incomprehensible association. At any other time, she'd find it entertaining. Under the circumstances, it would stretch her patience beyond endurance.

She went to the sideboard and filled a plate at random, her mind turning to other problems. Such as what Mr. Frake planned. Both men seemed set on being amiable this morning. Did the Runner try to catch Roland off his guard or trap him into an unwary comment?

Yet the rapport between them appeared genuine. A pang shot through her, which she recognized a moment later as jealousy. Roland steadfastly refused to acknowledge the kindred spirit that she *knew* existed between them.

As she seated herself at the table, Cousin Phemie bustled in, her bright, beaming smile greeting everyone. Why should she not be happy? Netta reflected. For a great many years, two people had made Phemie's life miserable, and now those two were both dead. Netta filled her mouth with dry toast to prevent herself from demanding outright if the dear little woman had taken to murder as a solution to her problems.

Phemie carried her tea and toast to a seat beside Roland and engaged him in conversation. Netta leaned back in her chair, watching them.

The touch of a hand on her shoulder made her jump. She turned to see Mr. Frake standing beside her, a frown in his pale blue eyes.

"If I might have a word with you, m'lady?"

Netta pushed aside her unwanted breakfast. "In the library?" Without waiting for his answer, she led the way toward that masculine retreat. It would be hers soon, she reflected, once Roland withdrew to Larkspur. She could wish it his a little longer.

"Now then," the Runner began as he closed the door behind them. "What was you frowning so about over your tea just now?"

A pent-up sigh escaped her. "Was I that obvious?"

"Not so as his lordship nor your cousin noticed anything. Trained to observe things, I am." His tone invited her to share this comment as a joke.

She managed a perfunctory smile. "I was just thinking how happy my cousin is."

"Miss Wrenn? Aye, and it can't be wondered at. Quite a relief it must be to her, what with those two gone and her favorite nephew home at last."

Netta walked to the French doors. "He'll take care of her, no matter what happens to me."

"And you was thinking maybe she'd rather be living with him than continuing the onerous role of playing chaperon to you? After all, once a person's gone and done their first murder, I hear tell doing the second one gets easier, and the third easier still, until it seems a positive shame not to keep on ridding the world of inconvenient people."

Netta clenched her hands. "Is that what you believe?"

"I was just trying to figure out like what was troubling you."

She rounded on him, glaring. "She *couldn't!*"

He said nothing. He just stood there, watching her, until she looked down, no longer able to meet his gently inquisitive gaze.

Phemie. He really believed it was Phemie. Netta forced her mind from that thought, not able to face it, and groped for another topic. She found it close at hand. "My will. Mr. Wickstone promised to have it copied out and ready to sign this morning. I believe I will go into Brighton at once."

He considered a moment. "An excellent suggestion. I will escort you there. And I believe we will call upon a few people on our way back."

If it had been his intention to divert her from her worries with that bit of information, it worked. While the identities of the people whom they would visit seemed obvious to Netta, she found herself speculating upon the possible reasons.

This time, no unpleasant surprises awaited her at the solicitor's office. She read through the neatly prepared will, signed it, and the Runner and Mr. Wickstone's clerk served as witnesses. As she handed back the legal document to the smiling solicitor, relief washed over her. Roland would no longer benefit — materially, at least — from her death. Surely that must clear him of suspicion in the event something happened to her now. And Phemie — she blocked that thought from her mind. She only left her companion a competence. Roland's presence in England would offer Phemie more security than the promises of that document.

She forced her attention to the matter of what the Runner hoped to accomplish at their next destination. They climbed into the landau, and Frake gave the driver an unfamiliar direction on the Marine Parade. Netta tried to compose her soul in patience. The few Fashionables who populated the seaside resort could not long hold her attention, and instead, she tried to interest herself in the gardens and rows of houses undergoing restoration.

The squawking of gulls reached her, along with the salty tang of the air. She breathed deeply, welcoming the freshness. She had spent far too much time indoors of late. Once this business was over, she would go away for awhile. If only it could be to the Lake District, to Larkspur.

The sea, glittering with the noontide sun, greeted her as they neared the end of the Steyne. To the accompanying cries of the sea birds, they turned onto the Marine Parade. Here tall houses rose along one side, and on the other, a few bathing machines already were scattered along the shore, although the weather could not yet be thought hot enough to lure more than the hardiest into the water.

The house before which they shortly drew up appeared wholly unfamiliar to Netta. Mr. Frake alighted, and she climbed out after him at once. "Whom are we seeing?" she asked, her curiosity overcoming her.

"This is the home of Sir Reginald Underhill."

The Underhills! Had they not gone through their stories fully only the day before? Perplexed, Netta allowed the Runner to usher her up the few steps to the front porch, where he applied the knocker with vigor.

A portly butler with receding hairline and austere aspect admitted them into the hallway, then ushered them into a front salon to await Mr. Josiah Underhill. Netta strolled to the bow window and watched the rolling waves.

Almost at once, the door behind them slammed open and Underhill stomped in, his brow dark. "What the devil do you mean by—oh, you here, Lady Henrietta? Beg your pardon. But by Jove, this is the outside of enough, that dratted Runner fellow of yours hounding us like this. We redeemed m'wife's vowels. What more do you want?"

"Only your cooperation." Mr. Frake stepped forward, his calm manner and bland smile diffusing the tension in the room.

Underhill melted under it. "What are you wanting, then?"

"Only for you and Lady Beatrix to come to Ravenswood tomorrow in the late afternoon. About six, perhaps?"

They next called at Mr. Lambert's lodgings, and while Netta waited in seething impatience in the landau, Frake left a similar message with Lambert's man.

"What are you planning?" Netta demanded as he climbed once more into the carriage.

"A little gathering, m'lady. I intend to summon Sir Archibald, as well."

"Why?" With an effort, she kept from screaming the question at him.

"Well, m'lady, there's two very strong possibilities for this here case, but before I can pursue one, I've got to eliminate the other, like. So I'll be off to London as soon as we gets back to Ravenswood."

"Then you think you know who—" She couldn't complete her sentence.

"Oh, aye, m'lady, I've got my guesses, now. If I hears what I thinks I'll hear in London, I'll make my arrest tomorrow evening."

Chapter Eighteen

At four o'clock the following afternoon, Netta stationed herself in the Ladies' Sitting Room, which had as its advantage, aside from sufficient sunlight for setting a delicate stitch for the better part of the day, an uninterrupted view of the gravel drive. Her embroidery lay in a crumpled heap on the table at her side; she had no thought for anything except what the Runner would reveal.

She perched on the edge of the window seat, willing the minutes to fly past. It was still too soon for their invited guests to arrive, but why did not Mr. Frake himself return? Had his investigations not gone as planned in London? She'd received the impression he'd made the journey to answer one simple question. Surely he must have had time and more for that.

Unless the answer was not the one he anticipated. Could he have been wrong in his reasonings? Would he make it back in time, or leave her alone with a houseful of suspected murderers?

For a moment, her irreverent sense of the ridiculous got the better of her, and she envisioned a roomful of dagger-fingering, horse pistol-wielding, masked brigands.

And under each mask lurked the face of someone she knew, some she even loved. The thought left her ill. No, the matter would be far more straightforward. Mr. Frake had gone to London to settle the question of the gaming debts, once and for all. He would then receive final corroboration from his former suspects and proceed with his arrest of Cousin Phemie.

Netta closed her eyes against the sting of threatening tears. She still couldn't believe it possible—she didn't *want* to believe it possible. She loved Phemie far too much. Dear vague, whimsical Cousin Phemie. No, she had to be wrong.

The clock in the hall below chimed the quarter-hour before six as a half-dozen horsemen finally approached up the drive. Netta sat forward, peering out the window, and identified the lead rider as Mr. Frake. With his Patrol.

Netta rose to her feet as if in slow motion, then made her way downstairs. Why did she feel as if she went to her own execution? Sudden, violent anger surged through her, that someone she knew could have subjected them all to this uncertainty and fear. For one furious moment, that crime loomed larger and more unforgivable in her mind than the murders of Desmond and Great-aunt Lavinia.

When she reached the hall, Haskins stood by

the door, taking the Runner's hat.

"Where are the others?" She rushed forward.

"Now don't you worry none. They won't make theirselves seen nor heard 'til I'm ready for them." He glanced at the clock, his expression grim. "Looks as if we didn't leave ourselves a minute to spare. Let's get that library arranged just the way we want it." He raised questioning eyebrows toward the aged valet. "Send in Jeremy, will you? I'll want a table and several chairs rearranged."

"What are you trying to do?" Netta hurried after him down the hall.

He paused at the door. "Now, m'lady, if you'll let me be for a bit? Perhaps you can go find Miss Wrenn and bear her company? She's promised to remain in her chamber until I send for her."

Frake disappeared within the library and a moment later she heard his voice, answered by Roland's deep tones. If only Roland would welcome her being with him, she could use his comfort. A moment later, the unmistakable sounds of furniture being dragged across a carpet reached her.

With a heavy heart, she went to seek out Phemie. Yet did she go as a companion or a jailer? She started toward the north wing of the house, but as she crossed the hall, a peremptory rap of the knocker brought her up short. Haskins was nowhere to be seen, and it lacked but a few minutes until six. The first of their expected visitors, it seemed.

Netta opened the door and found herself facing

Lady Beatrix and Mr. Josiah Underhill. Both stared at her in astonishment.

"I'll be damned," Underhill muttered.

Netta resisted the impulse to bob a curtsy, but in spite of her better intentions, a trace of a lower class Sussex accent crept into her words of greeting. "If you'll step this way, please? Mr. Frake is expecting you."

"So he should, after ordering us to come." Underhill marched inside.

Lady Beatrix cast her an appealing look. Still no Haskins. With a mental shrug, Netta took Mr. Underhill's cloak and hat, and Beatrix's shawl, then escorted them to the Blue Salon to await the Runner's pleasure.

Underhill frowned. "Where the devil—begging your pardon, but where are your servants?"

"Let us find out." She tugged on the bellpull, then seated herself, gesturing for her guests to follow suit.

"Be devilish glad to get this business settled." Underhill disposed of himself on the comfortable sofa. "If that Runner fellow of yours wants us for anything else, he'll be out of luck. We're leaving for home—Kent, y'know—first thing in the morning." He sighed. "Nothing like the country. Had all of m'uncle I can stomach, and vice versa, I'll wager. He—" He broke off. Roland appeared in the doorway, and Underhill regarded him with a jaundiced eye. "You ain't the butler, either."

"Mr. Frake is ready." He avoided Netta's eye.

He led the way to the bookroom, where the furniture had now been arranged to represent a gaming table.

Netta could see no sign of the Runner. Haskins, though, arranged on a table several tankards, glasses, and an assortment of decanters.

Underhill inspected the former. "Home-brewed? I'll just have one of those, if you please." He took a long swallow, closed his eyes, and nodded. "Tolerable, very tolerable." With the air of one prepared to wait in comfort, he took a chair and waggled the tankard at Roland. "Just telling your cousin we're off for home in the morning. Might go on to Scotland, you never know. Ever fished for salmon? There's a real life for you."

Netta stared at him in disbelief. He acted as if he hadn't a care in the world. Did he put on an act to impress everyone with his innocence, or did he truly not have a thought in his head except for the sport he hoped soon to enjoy?

Netta felt a touch on her sleeve and turned to see Lady Beatrix, her expression troubled. The woman withdrew into the hall and Netta, curious, followed.

"Can't have Underhill overhearing this." Beatrix closed the door behind them and drew Netta down the hall. "Can we return to the salon? Won't be but a moment." Without waiting for Netta's response, she retraced their steps of a few minutes before.

Once inside with the door safely closed, Beatrix hesitated, as if not knowing how to begin. She

300

paced to the window, then turned around. "Where did you find my vowels?"

"In Desmond's room." There seemed to be no point in wrapping it up in clean linen with someone as blunt as Beatrix.

That lady swore. "The devil. Beastly man. I suppose you know what he intended?"

Warm color suffused Netta's cheeks.

Beatrix snorted. "No wonder you ain't mourning him. You're well rid of him, make no mistake about that."

Netta kept silent. It was hardly fitting for her to agree, no matter how much she might.

Beatrix fixed her unwavering regard on Netta. "No need to tell Underhill about it, is there?"

Netta frowned. "But—"

"Oh, he knows I gamed with him, all right. But no use letting him know the insult Desmond intended. Not that he'd have gotten away with it, of course." She snorted again. "Had my carriage pistol in my reticule. Intended to make him accept my diamond studs in exchange, then take my vowels and leave."

"I should think your husband would only approve of that."

Beatrix directed a scornful look at her. "Wouldn't believe me. Convinced I ain't got an ounce of gumption, just because I wouldn't take a green hunter over a regular rasper. The colt didn't have the heart, but Underhill swore it was me." She shrugged. "Men. They'd rather believe in their horses and dogs than in their wives. Have I your

301

promise?"

"Unless it is absolutely essential to bring it out. Though to tell the truth, I cannot see how it could be."

Beatrix nodded. "Thought you'd be reasonable. Well, let's get on with it then." She led the way from the salon.

Netta followed, numbed, aware of how empty most marriages must be. Hers with Desmond would have been just as bad. And what would be the lot of Roland's wife? Very different — and very wonderful, she realized. She closed her eyes as a pang of longing shot through her.

By the time they returned to the library, Archy had arrived. He stood near the window, elegant in buff pantaloons and a new coat of green superfine. He edged around to Netta's side. "What has this Runner fellow in mind?"

Netta shook her head. "He is being very mysterious. I collect he has said nothing yet. Perhaps he is waiting for Mr. Lambert, so that everyone will be here."

"Then it seems we won't have long to wait."

Netta, too, heard the masculine voice in the corridor, and Haskins ushered in the last arrival. Lambert looked over the assembled company and a sneer settled on his classically handsome features. With studied nonchalance, he carried Netta's fingers to his lips. His smoldering gaze met hers.

She returned it with coolness. After a moment his lip curled and he stepped back, awarding her a

302

bow which held nothing but mockery. It hit her that he let her know—intentionally—that he never cared one whit for her, only her supposed fortune.

Well, that should have put her in her place, she reflected as he strolled to the table and helped himself to one of the remaining tankards. She found herself smiling. Really, he ought to have taken lessons from Desmond in the art of delivering set-downs. She could think, off-hand, of at least half a dozen little tricks that might have made his attempt more effective.

"We are all here?" Frake entered through the French doors and looked around. "Very good. Haskins? If you will just run and fetch Miss Wrenn? And the rest of you, will you be seated where you were that last night? I will take the late earl's position, and the rest of you please take your own. We'll just leave empty chairs to mark the positions of those who aren't here."

Netta withdrew to a settee a little removed from the table arrangement. Roland leaned against the jamb of the open French door. His gaze strayed to her, then returned to the others. A gentle breeze drifted in, bringing with it the scent of the roses from beyond the lower terrace. Too beautiful an evening, Netta reflected, on which to catch a murderer—or murderess.

Phemie bustled in, the shawl she currently embroidered gathered in one hand. She beamed on the assembled company and accepted with a smile the chair into which Mr. Frake directed her. Her doting gaze rested on Roland, then shifted to

Netta in a calculating manner. It sent a chill up Netta's spine. Humming to herself, the little woman arranged her needlework, selected a new color of silk, and set to work. It seemed as if she had no idea of the seriousness of what occurred.

Netta dragged her own gaze away from her companion and instead stared blindly across the terrace. She felt the most wretched traitoress, hating herself for suspecting the woman who had taken such care of her. It simply could not be possible; she could never seriously believe her beloved cousin a murderess. Yet whether it was true or not, it seemed very likely Mr. Frake intended to arrest her.

If only she could determine which of these people in this room had really killed Desmond and Lavinia! She could not rid herself of the conviction she failed Phemie, for only the revelation of the real criminal would turn the Runner from his apparent purpose of taking poor Cousin Phemie into custody.

A shudder shook her shoulders. Desmond and Great-aunt Lavinia lay dead, the Runner would take Cousin Phemie up for murder . . . and Roland, rejecting even the thought of her, would so soon leave for his own estate. Her life had disintegrated about her. No, surely Mr. Frake could not believe dear, sweet Cousin Phemie guilty.

She dragged her attention back as Sir Archy declared in a surprised tone, "By Jove, I'll bet I was cheated! Well, if that don't beat the Dutch."

"You all were," Underhill chimed in. "Trixie,

told you dozens of times the fellow was an outsider. Fuzzing the cards, by gad!"

Lambert's lip curled. "His own friends, at that."

As if cheating strangers were any better. The oddities of gentlemen, Netta reflected.

Frake, however, merely nodded. "That probably explains how his lordship won so much money from you, Sir Archibald. By the bye, what happened to that single, large vowel you wrote?"

"The what?" Archy looked up, his countenance registering surprise. "Didn't need to write one, you know. My luck changed. Won most of it back."

Beatrix blinked. "With Desmond playing with notched cards? That hardly seems likely."

Archy hunched a peevish shoulder. "If you are any of you worrying, I intend to pay up in the near future."

A short laugh escaped Lambert. "Lucky for you Tavistock is dead, if you're under the hatches again. He intended to collect immediately, as I recall."

Frake shot him a piercing glance from beneath bunched eyebrows. "What's that?"

Lambert lounged back in his chair. "I heard Tavistock say something about calling at the Dower House right after the engagement ball to collect what was his. He rambled on for awhile after you left, Carncross, but not much made any sense at the time. He was pretty badly fuddled by then."

"So were you," Underhill shot at him.

Lambert ignored the interruption. "Seemed pretty set up about it all."

Mr. Frake took a deep breath and nodded. "So, Sir Archibald, I take it you gamed away the Dower House, just as your grandfather had done with Ravenswood Court."

"What a pack of moonshine!" Archy straightened in his chair. "It's what Tavistock was after, all right and tight, but he caught cold when I began winning again. You remember that, don't you?" He appealed to Lady Beatrix and Mr. Underhill for corroboration.

Lady Beatrix shook her head. "I wasn't at the table then."

Mr. Underhill stared at the Runner. "That's what Tavistock meant when he said he completed the deed!" he exclaimed. "Thought he meant some vile act. Well, just the sort of thing he would mean. Only this time it really was a *deed*."

"Which you, Sir Archibald," Frake fixed him with a penetrating eye, "destroyed the night you ransacked the bookroom at Tavistock House."

"By Jove," Lambert breathed, staring at Archy with what appeared to be dawning respect.

Archy, pale, shook his head in vehement denial. "This is outrageous! There—there is no proof!"

"Well, now, sir, that's not likely, is it? His late lordship didn't strike me as the sort of gentleman who could keep quiet about such a coup. He would have told someone."

"You can bet on that," Lambert chimed in. "Even if he promised he wouldn't. Just like him to

306

gloat."

"M'lord." Frake looked to Roland, who joined him. "Can you tell me if this is your cousin's fist?"

"What is it?" Unable to keep away, Netta went to peer over the Runner's shoulder.

"Notes on the worth of the Dower House and its contents," Roland told her. "Yes, it looks very like Desmond's fist—at least what I've seen of it in his papers over the last few days."

"He wouldn't have that if he hadn't been after the house." Lambert studied it and emitted a soundless whistle. "That's a pretty penny to wager."

"Not proof, though." Underhill shook his head. "The boy's right about that."

Frake inclined his head. "It will take time, but somewhere, someone will remember. Never you doubt I'll find that person."

Lady Beatrix stared from one to the other of them. "Are you actually accusing that—that *fop* of killing Desmond?"

Frake beamed. "That's the ticket."

"But—*how?* How could he have done it? What does he know of poisons? I certainly wouldn't have known enough."

"Well, now, he's spent a great deal of time helping Lady Henrietta and Miss Wrenn in their herb garden. I'd wager he knows his fair share."

"Not the sort of thing a man carries about in his pocket, though. That's doing it too brown." Underhill shook his head, though with regret.

Frake drew out his briarwood pipe. "Where do you suppose he spent the day of the ball?"

Lambert toyed with his tankard. "At his club, I should think. That's where he spends most of his time."

"Well, this day he didn't. Everyone I spoke to remembered seeing him at an unusually early hour of the morning. Quite surprised to see him up and about, they was. You see, I spent last night and this morning making inquiries into the movements of all of you, on the principle that the murder was only planned after the gaming, and not to prevent the marriage, after all. I was able to account for everyone's actions except Sir Archibald's. But the time he was missing was just about what it would take him to ride from London to Ravenswood and back. So it is my duty, Sir Archibald, to arrest you for—where is he?" Stunned, the Runner looked about.

Netta gasped. Sir Archy was no longer in the room.

Lambert lunged to his feet. "Where the devil—?"

"Really, Kenneth." Cousin Phemie, who had sat humming softly to herself during the entire discussion, broke off and clucked her tongue. "Your language, dear boy. Archy must have stepped out to the terrace. He probably wanted a breath of fresh air. It has become uncomfortably warm in here, has it not?" She returned to her embroidery.

As one, they rushed to the door, with Frake swearing fluently under his breath. Roland burst out first onto the terrace, followed by the Runner and Lambert. The Underhills emerged next, with Netta bringing up the rear.

"Spread out and head for the stable," Frake ordered. He pulled a whistle from his pocket and blew a shrill blast. "Block off the Dower House," he shouted as his men appeared almost at once from around the corner of the building.

"Didn't you have them deployed to prevent his escape?" Roland demanded.

"Thought I did." Frake shook his head and muttered a word that didn't reach Netta. "They were only just out of sight. How could he have avoided them? Haven't done anything this foolish in the whole of my career."

And how could they have let him just walk out of the house like that? Netta wondered. They had become so preoccupied with *how* the crime had been committed that they completely ignored their villain!

Only they didn't think of him as a villain. He was just Archy, the would-be Tulip they all knew, whom most regarded with a measure of sneering contempt. And so he had outwitted them.

Or had he? She knew Archy—and his tricks—better than the others. This time, too, she would not underestimate him—or his desperation. But she would need help. Frake already disappeared along the path leading to the river, and the others vanished toward the stable or the Dower House. Only Roland lingered, as if guarding her.

She caught his arm and pointed after the retreating figures. Out of the corner of her eye, she could just see a massive shrub on the edge of the terrace nearest the house. "Don't look, but Archy used to hide in that bush over there, when we played as children." She kept her voice low so it wouldn't carry.

"Did he? I wonder if he still does." Louder, he added: "I want to make sure Cousin Phemie is all right." He strode toward the library, then swung about and parted the full, leafy branches.

Netta, some twenty feet behind him and to the side, caught the glint of the sun on the barrel of Archy's pistol. She drew back, out of his line of sight.

Archy emerged, pale and trembling, and gestured Roland back with the weapon—one of Desmond's Mantons, Netta noted. She pressed against the shrubbery, and spiky needles pricked through her dress. Archy already had killed twice and tried to kill her on several occasions—*why?* She thrust the bewildered thought from her. Right now, he would kill Roland unless she did something to help.

Desperate, she sought anything to use for a weapon. Not a single broken branch met her frantic gaze. She looked farther afield and caught sight of a small clay pot filled with geraniums resting on the corner of the balustrade. If Archy would just keep moving, he'd have his back to it and she could reach it.

She made shooing gestures at Roland from out of Archy's sight and hoped her cousin would correctly interpret them. Apparently he did, for he continued to back up, luring Archy on. Archy's stance relaxed, as if he believed his current victim too afraid to challenge him.

Just a foot farther. . . . He wouldn't see her now. She waved to Roland again, then inched her way along the Italian tiles toward the brilliant pink flowers. Thank heaven for her soft-soled slippers, which made only the merest whisper of sound. But if Archy heard it—It didn't bear thinking about.

Roland stopped. "Tell me something, Carncross. I can understand your killing Desmond. Even Lavinia, if she got in your way. But why Netta?"

"Quiet." Archy advanced another step.

So much for Roland's attempt to divert him, she reflected. In another moment, though, she'd reach that pot. Her fingers closed about the rim, and she raised it, took careful aim, and heaved it as hard as she could.

It slammed against Archy's shoulder, and the pistol went off. The ball shattered a tile, tore through the thigh of Roland's breeches, and nicked the edge of the low balustrade. Archy staggered into Roland, who clutched his bleeding leg, and the two went down.

For a moment they rolled, then Roland swung—connecting only with his opponent's arm. Archy ducked and sprang to his feet. Roland dragged himself after him, the blood dripping down his leg. He staggered, and Archy proved the worth of his brags of having spent time in Gentle-man Jackson's Salon by landing Roland an unexpected facer. With strength born of terror, he forced Roland's back against the low terrace balustrade.

Fifteen feet below them lay another paved terrace. Netta, frantic, grasped the geranium's mate, but before she could hit Archy with it, Roland threw him off and landed him a leveler. Archy staggered, tripped over the railing, and fell to the pavement below.

Roland, breathing heavily, dragged Netta into his arms, preventing her from seeing the results.

"What—?" she managed to gasp against his shoulder.

"He landed on his head."

Frake emerged from the shrubs, pounding toward them. He stopped on the lower level and shook his head, then peered up at them. "Shooting him would have been neater," he called.

"Perhaps. But he had the gun, not I."

Netta heard the shouts of the others, their rapid footsteps. She buried her face deeper into the soft wool of Roland's coat and fought back her tears.

"Don't mourn him." Roland's voice sounded harsh. "Remember, he's been trying to kill you."

"But why?" She pulled back to look up into his face. The pain she read there shocked her. Her gaze lowered to his breeches, now soaked in blood. "You were hit! Come inside, we've got to take care of it."

Phemie stood in the doorway, watching. Netta

sent her for Mrs. Haskins and pressed Roland into a chair. If she concentrated very hard on his wound, she could keep from thinking about what went on outside.

He tore off his neckcloth, formed it into a pad, and pressed it against the wound. "Only a scratch," he assured her.

Still, Netta could not be easy until it had been washed, dusted with basilicum powder, and bandaged. At last, Roland leaned back against the cushions with the glass of brandy she pressed into his hand and took a sip.

"Now." She knelt at his side and ignored the commotion that still went on outside. "Why did Archy want to kill me?"

He took a long swallow of his drink. "Apparently he killed Desmond out of desperation to keep the Dower House. Which reminds me, I shall have to cancel all those debts and repay the Underhills since Desmond cheated. Anyway, when Archy succeeded in getting away with that, I think he must have set his sights on Ravenswood, as well. The first time he followed you, he might have been hoping only to scare you into selling. Or he might have intended to kill you even then. I'd already told him I wanted none of this place."

"So he only had to kill me and let you inherit in the certain knowledge you would turn around and sell him the estate for a song." Netta shuddered. "Do you know, I never thought to tell him about my new will, leaving this place as a home for orphans."

He touched her cheek, his expression grave. "Then his mother put the thought of marrying you for the estate into his mind."

A shaky laugh escaped her. "So he had a choice of killing me or marrying me. How delightful to think either would satisfy him. I wonder if he really cared which he did?"

He brushed from her cheek one of the flame-colored curls that had pulled free of her collapsing chignon. "I doubt you would have lived long after your wedding."

"Pleasant thought. I'm beginning to understand how you feel about this place. I believe I will sell it to Lady Carncross after all. Richmond — he will be Sir Richmond now, won't he? — will be down from Cambridge next year. I am sure his mama will be only too glad to teach him estate management." She studied the hands she clasped in her lap. "I suppose you will be leaving to take up residence at Larkspur at once?"

"I'd go tomorrow if it were possible. I suppose by the end of the week, at the latest. I — "

"How pleasant that will be." Cousin Phemie beamed at them from the doorway. She bustled in and picked up her abandoned embroidery. "I visited Larkspur once, on a public day, you know. Such a lovely place, with a brook just stuffed with trout and the most extensive gardens. We will all three of us be very happy there, I make no doubt."

"Cousin Phemie." Roland's sharp tone cut her off.

314

"Now, don't be bashful, dear." Phemie patted him on the shoulder. "You know perfectly well it is what you both want. Now I must go and sit with Lady Carncross. Poor thing, she will be quite shocked. Though to be sure, she will have the move to Ravenswood to look forward to. That will quite lift her spirits, I make no doubt." Humming to herself, she hurried off.

Roland, his expression harsh, started to rise.

Netta caught his arm, preventing him. Gathering her courage, she said: "She is quite right, you know."

"I do *not* know." He surged to his feet, catching the arm of the chair for balance as he put his weight on his injured leg.

A painful heaviness expanded in her chest, making it difficult for her to breathe. "You are blaming me for the sins of the family. Has it not occurred to you that I suffered at their hands also?"

"Little Hen." He bent forward to touch her cheek, then shook his head. "I am not blaming you, but you would be a constant reminder of all I want to forget. Do you not realize that fact has tormented me ever since I first saw you again? My beautiful, delightful Little Hen. I couldn't bear it if I came to hate you."

He did want her with him. Hope surged through her, and with it, inspiration. "Then you intend to renounce the title and change your name? After all, it will never do for you to spend the rest of your life wincing every time someone

315

addresses you."

"Good God." He stared at her, his expression arrested, as if the fullness of his predicament had not yet occurred to him.

"See?" She could barely disguise her triumph. "You carry your nightmare with you. You cannot escape. Your only choice is to forgive."

He shook his head. "That is asking a great deal."

"Is it? You have thought of us collectively, have you not? As 'the family'? But have you truly something for which to blame *each* of us? Or only one?"

"Your father—" he began, only to stop short. His brow clouded, as if he ran each of his relatives under review.

"It was only Great-aunt Lavinia, wasn't it? You've been willing to forgive her present eccentricities. Can you not do the same for those of the past?"

He drew a deep breath. "Eccentricities. Lord, she has manipulated us all with them, has she not?"

"Only imagine how much she would enjoy the knowledge she can continue to do so, even after her death."

His brow snapped down. "The devil—"

So near . . . "Are you going to grant her complete victory by letting her continue to influence your life?" she asked.

His mouth thinned. For a long minute he said nothing, as one powerful emotion chased another

316

across his countenance. "After seventeen years," he declared at last, "it is not easy to forgive, to change my way of thinking."

"You do not want to hate me, do you?" She rose and went to him. "Is there no way I can help?"

He touched her cheek with one finger, and his frowning gaze rested on her face. Slowly — as if with reluctance — the harshness eased from his expression. "And what would you do, Little Hen?"

She said nothing. She merely gazed at him with all the love she possessed.

Fire ignited in the depths of his hazel eyes. *"Not my Little Hen, it seems. My little love?"* He said the words slowly, testing them. "Do you think you could help me grow accustomed to that?" He cupped her face between his hands. "My little love," he repeated.

Gathering her courage, she wrapped her arms about his waist. With a low groan that sent a shiver up her spine and her heart soaring, he dragged her against himself, burying his face in her tumbled hair. She clung to him, for the first time sure of his love.

At last, she whispered: "Is this helping?"

His lips brushed her throat, and he pulled her even closer, to the imminent peril of two of her ribs. "It's a beginning — and becoming easier every moment." Satisfaction sounded in his voice. This time his mouth found the sensitive spot behind her ear. "Everything I didn't dare let myself want," he murmured.

She freed one arm, only to catch him about the neck and drag his head to hers for a long, desperate kiss. When she could speak again, she asked: "Do you think there is hope for us, then?"

"Oh, my beloved." A soft chuckle set his shoulders shaking. "That is the safest bet a Galbraith ever made."